The Always Place

Suzanne M. Hurley

The Always Place

"Are you okay?"

Her eyes popped open and Chrissy/Chris was staring at her. Yep, him, for sure. She recognized that concerned look.

"You're not going to faint or anything?" He reached out as if to grab her.

She backed away. "I'm okay."

Heat burned her cheeks as she caught herself staring at his lips.

Yes, he had even kissed her. Her first kiss from a boy. Mind you, on the cheek, but still her first. In truth, she wasn't even sure he meant it intentionally. She'd fallen off her bike and he had helped her up, worried as anything, and somehow his lips had touched her face. Might have been purely accidental, but even though at ten she'd thought boys were still icky, she really hadn't minded.

She started to say something, to tell him who she was, to see if he remembered, then stopped. She was being anonymous these days. No way was she going to break that for anyone. And besides, he wouldn't recognize her with short black curls. That is, if he could see anything under her hat. Back then her hair was florescent red and she had braided it much like Emma did, to keep it out of her face. She also went by the name Alex. She just wished he'd stop staring at her. And why was he squinting?

"Do I know you?" He took a step back, eyeing her up and down.

The Always Place

Suzanne M. Hurley

A Wings ePress, Inc.
Women's Fiction Novel

Wings ePress, Inc.

Edited by: Jeanne Smith
Copy Edited by: Bev Haynes
Executive Editor: Jeanne Smith
Cover Artist: Trisha FitzGerald-Jung
Images Century

All rights reserved

Wings ePress Books
www.wingsepress.com

Copyright © 2025 by: Suzanne M. Hurley
ISBN 979-8-89197-978-9

Published In the United States Of America

Wings ePress, Inc.
3000 N. Rock Road
Newton, KS 67114

Dedication

A big hearty thank you goes out to three special ladies in my life. To my sister Maureen, whose loyalty, laughter, and love spur me on.   To Sheila Mazza, who reads all my books the minute they're released and 'gets me.' And to Sheila Rogers for all our lunches at the river which never fail to inspire me. Thanks also go out to Marja McGraw for reading, commenting and helping with my rough attempts. To Mary Lou, for her continual guidance.

To my family, in thanksgiving, for all of their support.

To Jeanne Smith – the best editor ever, who helps give my words wings.

To Trisha Fitzgerald for her lovely covers and the entire Wings' staff for their dedication and hard work.

Thank you.

Prologue

"Quick." Wendy's fast, high-pitched words flew out of her phone. "Flip on your TV. Channel six."

"What's going on?" Alexandra jumped up from her desk. Usually Wendy, her best friend in the whole world, was calm. One time a fire had broken out at their university dorm and while everyone freaked, her friend moved door to door, making sure every student got out safely. Nothing rattled her. Was there a world disaster happening? Someone died? A tragedy? An event that finally shook stoic Wendy?

She ran to the couch, searched for the remote, found it under a throw pillow, hit the button for the TV, and another for channel six. She recognized the talk show host sitting behind a desk. "Sheena? Are you kidding? You want me to listen to Sheena?"

"Shhhh … keep watching."

Holding the phone to her ear, Alexandra plopped down on the couch. Talk shows weren't her thing. She didn't enjoy watching a bunch of people spout off, but she knew that Sheena was a renowned psychologist garnering high ratings. Who didn't know that? Her picture was plastered on buses and billboards. Tackling controversial subjects, confronting people with secrets to hide, and juicy gossip were her specialties.

"Good morning, everyone." Sheena's hair was bright blonde, slicked back. Her toothy grin stretched across her face. Bright red lipstick, heavy eye makeup, and big gold hoops completed her ensemble, along with what looked to be a blue sparkly onesie. "And welcome back. Today we are talking about best-selling author Alexandra Ayers, her quick rise to the top, and just as quick fall to the bottom. Splat."

Really? Sheena was talking about her? Groan. The visual made her ill. Or guess it could be the bag of gummy bears she'd inhaled, struggling to come up with a viable ending to her new book, her current work in progress. Why couldn't they leave her alone? Enough, already.

"I'm not watching this, Wendy." She grabbed the remote.

"Trust me. You're going to want to see it."

"Well, all right. I'll give it a few more minutes."

Alexandra dropped the remote and grabbed her favorite knit throw, tossing it over her, burrowing under it. Might as well be comfy. She kept her phone to her ear.

The camera switched to her guest.

Her eyes widened and her mouth dropped.

Jake—her Jake—was perched on the chair beside the host's desk. Sitting straight up, her heart galloped. Tousled brown hair, black suit, red tie, black suede boots. All so familiar. All so loved.

"Did you know he was going to be on?" Wendy asked.

"No, of course not. I would have told you. Had you over. He never breathed a word."

Then again, she hadn't spent much time with him lately. He was going through a busy patch at work and texting was all they were doing. He was supposed to be at a real estate conference at the moment. How did he end up on Sheena's talk show?

"Is he trying to surprise you or something?" Wendy's voice grew softer. "Is this some kind of grand romantic gesture?"

"Maybe. I guess. Could be why he's been so unreachable lately, bordering on secretive."

But if he was planning something big, wouldn't he want her there? In person? Or at least tell her to watch? She glanced down at her phone to see if she had any unread messages. Nope, none.

Squinting, she zeroed in on his face. He didn't look so great. His complexion was as pale as his white shirt, even under what was sure to be TV makeup, and he was clenching the sides of the chair. Nervous? About being on TV? He shouldn't be. He loved attention. Craved it, even.

"What is Alexandra Ayers really like?" Sheena leaned closer, eyes widening, looking like she was salivating at possible dirt being thrown around.

Dirt? No way. If that was what she wanted, the interview was a waste. They were in love and Jake would tell her nothing unless positive and upbeat. The whole truth.

"We want to figure out the author behind the flop," Sheena continued, raising her voice. "We tried to get her on the show, but her agent declined, and since you're her fiancé, you know her best."

They had tried to get her on the show? No way. Her agent would have shot that down stat.

Alexandra pulled the blanket tightly around her, feeling all warm and toasty hearing the word fiancé, waiting for Jake to say nice things about her, about their love, how he proposed at one of her book signings, and that they were getting married in a few months. She glanced over at her wedding dress, wrapped in plastic, hanging on a hook in the wall by her closet. She'd just tried it on that morning, loving the feel of it swirling around her ankles, and was sure Jake's eyes would tear up when he saw her in it.

"Maybe he's planned your honeymoon and wants to surprise you on TV?" Wendy, again.

"Huh?' Alexandra had forgotten they were still on the phone together. "Oh, never thought of that. What a great idea."

Really? Was it? She was hoping for private time, away from reporters and news outlets, not wanting their destination announced on national TV.

Wait.

Jake's eyes rolled upward. His signature move when annoyed. Maybe Sheena's question bugged him. But why was his face scrunching up as if he'd just chomped on a sour lemon and the biggest scowl she'd ever seen appeared.

"What is she like?" His voice grew louder. "I'll tell you what she's like. Alexandra Ayers is lazy, mean, horrible, and selfish. In short, a narcissist."

"What?" Alexandra and Wendy screamed, echoing each other.

Nausea struck again. So much for a romantic gesture.

"Really?" Sheena clapped with glee, her face erupting in pure joy, enjoying this, probably planned for this, knowing her ratings would soar. "Oh, tell me more. I thought she was another American sweetheart, writing books about love with happy endings. That is, until lately."

Jake shook his head. "She's a fake. Did you read her latest?" He held up *Fairy Tale Crushed*. "What a mess this is."

As far as Alex knew, he had never read it, or any of her books. Just couldn't be bothered.

"Are you still there?" Wendy's voice sounded panicky.

"Yes." Alexandra couldn't bring herself to stop watching, mesmerized, as Sheena's eyebrows shot up.

"It sure is. That book bombed. Jake, can you shed some insight as to why she wrote that horrid ending to her novel, tanking it, angering her readers, resulting in horrible reviews?"

"No, I can't." Jake dropped the book on the floor, creating a loud bang, throwing his hands up in the air. "I told her not to write that garbage. I told her readers would be upset. But would she listen? No."

Alexandra shrieked, louder than ever, threw off her blanket and stood.

Liar.

She wished she had a brick. She'd have tossed it at the TV and smashed it to bits.

"Are you still engaged to her, Jake?" Sheena moved even closer. Any more and she'd topple over the desk onto his lap.

Alexandra squatted in front of her TV, shoving her face as near as she could, taking in every inch of his face. His eyes flickered up and down again.

"Of course not. I dumped her."

Confusion, hurt, pain rippled through Alexandra's body like a series of stinging stab wounds.

"You heard it here first." Sheena stood, dancing like she'd scored the biggest scoop of her career. Maybe she had. "We break now for a commercial. More about Alexandra when we return."

"I'm on my way." Wendy hung up.

Alexandra couldn't move.

She felt encased in cement, heavy, solid, stiff. Ripples of shock shooting through her. She looked down at her engagement ring. A green emerald framed with tiny diamonds. He'd had it engraved. 'All my love forever, Jake.' Right now, it felt like a burning band of fire.

"Get it off me. Get it off me."

Yanking it from her finger, she finally moved one leg, then the other, made it to her feet, and marched to the balcony door. Sliding it open, she hurried out to the edge of her balcony and hurled the ring off into space.

"Take that, Jake." Was that her laugh? She sounded maniacal. "You good for nothing rat."

Should she have done that? Not sure, but it sure felt good to do something. Anything.

Tears flowed.

Here came the pain. The humiliation. The sadness. The hurt. Blowing through her like a racing car at full speed.

She slumped down on the synthetic grass rug.

Reality hit.

Her latest book had indeed bombed. She hid her head in her hands. And as if that weren't enough, her fiancé, the man she loved, had just dumped her in front of millions.

If she wasn't so devastated, it'd be a great plot for her next book.

She hoped Wendy would get there soon.

One

Eight Months later

"Let's get down to business, Lexy."

"Business?" Her eyes narrowed.

What kind of business do you discuss on a first date? In a pub?

Shuffling her feet, she took a sip of coffee, choking on it as she witnessed how fast he chugged his beer, banging his mug down. Planting his elbows on the table, he leaned forward.

Whoa! She jerked her head back. Their table was so small, their noses almost touched. A wave of minty mouthwash colliding with some kind of spicy cologne washed over her. The combination was tart, unpleasant, distasteful, actually. He was way too close. What was happening? And what was his name? Oh, right, Albert. And she was going by Lexy Errol these days, not Alexandra Ayers. She mustn't forget the fact she was using an alias and blow her own cover.

"I'm looking for a cook and housekeeper." He grinned, or leered, was a more accurate description. "All wrapped up in one. Someone who will take care of me and also help me with my work."

"Another beer?" A server appeared out of nowhere, reaching for the empty glass.

Good. He moved back.

"Yes, certainly." His head jerked up and down.

"No, thanks. None for me." Lexy needed to stay alert. Something was off about this guy.

"One beer coming right up." The server left, heading toward the next table.

"What do you think? Are you interested?" He shoved a strand of long hair behind his ear.

Interesting that in his profile photo, his hair was short. Not that Lexy disapproved of long hair, but he looked completely different. Cute, though.

Clasping his hands on the table, he turned his head, shooting her the side eye.

Side eye? What was that about?

Lexy pushed her chair back; in case he did the whole leaning in thing again.

"Soooo you're looking to hire someone?" she asked. "This is actually a job interview, not a date?"

"No, silly, I want a wife."

Silly? He made a preposterous proposal and had the nerve to call her silly? He was joking, right?

Hmm ... maybe she was being punked?

Twisting her neck, she searched for cameras. None were obvious. Were they hidden?

"You're not answering."

She whipped her head back. What happened to the sweet accountant she'd gotten to know in their daily emails and texts? The one who loved to chat about good books and movies? Of course, it'd only been a week. How ridiculous to assume this date would be exciting, based on their interesting conversations. How could she possibly know someone after only a few emails? They'd never even talked on the phone. What was she doing here?

You're an idiot.

"You're kidding, right?" She downed the rest of her coffee fast, apologizing to her tongue for the burn. "I know nothing about accounting." Checking out the exit door, she wondered if she should make a run for it.

Wendy's voice popped in her head. "Give him a chance. Maybe you misunderstood."

Best friends could be such a pain.

Deep breath in. Deep breath out.

"Accounting?" His widened. "What are you talking about? I'm into pigs. I'm a pig farmer."

"What?" The words pig farmer were so loud, she felt a burning sensation rise in the back of her neck, twisting, turning, centering on her cheeks. A quick glance let her know everyone in the pub was staring.

Uncomfortable, she drummed her fingers on the table. Really, she had nothing against pigs. Why she adored baby piglets and how they stumbled around looking all sweet. But his dating profile stated he was an accountant. No pigs were mentioned.

"I need someone to help me feed them," he added.

"Here's your beer." The server placed the mug on the table. "Holler if you want another."

"Will do." He finished half the glass in two seconds. "Oh, and besides the pigs. I need someone to feed me, too," he roared, ending it with a snort, much how a pig sounded. "See? I'm funny, too."

Please, stop, she felt like yelling, but didn't want to garner even more attention.

"So, you lied about your work."

"Figured you'd walk away if you knew I was a farmer."

Nah, she wouldn't. She grew up helping her grandpa milk jersey cows every spring break and had great respect for the hard work it took to keep a farm running smoothly.

"You do realize I'm a writer? I put it on my profile." She was glad she hadn't used her full name as an attempt to disguise who she really was. Not that she assumed he'd recognize it, but just in case. Guess she'd lied, too. "I'm not looking for another job. I have my own work."

"Work?" He shrugged. "I don't consider writing a real job. You can squeeze your stuff in between chores. You're not famous or anything."

Not real? My stuff? Squeeze it in?

Like that was going to happen.

Verdict in.

She was outta there.

Grabbing her purse, she stood. "Gotta go. Thanks for the coffee." Throwing a few bucks on the table, she sprinted out the door.

"Hey, where are you going?"

She didn't look back.

Stupid, stupid, stupid.

Why had she bothered coming? She was such a bad judge of character.

Pulling a hat out of her bag, she tugged it on, adding her sunglasses. Halfway down the block, her phone rang.

Turning fast, making sure Albert wasn't chasing her, she ducked into an alley. Stopping, she grabbed her phone out of her purse, noting the name across the screen. Wendy, checking in.

"Hi," she answered.

"How's it going?"

Giggles in the background had her smiling. Baby Jacob. Such a joyful little guy.

"I can hear squealing. What's he doing?"

"He's playing with the stuffed duck you gave him. So? How's the date?"

"Not good."

"You didn't walk out again, did you?"

"Guilty."

Lexy explained what happened.

"Well, gotta give him some credit." Wendy chuckled. "At least he's a man who knows what he wants."

"Sure does. And can you visualize what life with him would be like? All about his wants and needs."

Silence.

Lexy could hear the quacking of the toy duck. "Wendy, are you there?"

"Yes, yes. Sorry. Jacob dropped the toy and I picked it up for him. So, the date's over? Already? Is this a record?"

"Unfortunately it is, ten minutes exactly."

"And your last one was twelve. I think you should call Guinness."

"Well, I used to be kind and stay, not wanting to hurt my date's feelings, but found out I was the one who ended up a mess. I didn't even have the energy to do the whole 'it's not you, it's me' talk. I had to get out of there fast."

"Sure, I get it. I saw it happen too, through your descriptions."

A teen walked toward her holding a carton of French fries. Big fat ones. The kind she liked best. Her stomach automatically rumbled. Lexy scurried to the end of the alley where he'd come from. Aw...bliss. Wafts of onions, grease, burgers flew out of a chip wagon, bathing her in deliciousness.

"Just a second." Lexy stepped up to the window, and a young man appeared.

"May I help you?" He pointed to a board off to the right. "We have a burger and fry special on right now."

"I'll take it."

"You're getting food, right?" Wendy asked. "I heard the word fry."

"Yup. Haven't made it through a dinner date yet. But keep talking, I've got time."

"It'd be nice if you could find someone." Her friend's voice got lower. "Jacob, eat your banana. Although I have to admit your fascinating date stories are what I live for."

"Glad to entertain, but remember, I'm not trying to find a real match. I'm doing this for research only." Sure, she had secretly hoped she'd find someone nice and they'd hit it off. So far, not a chance.

"I know. But remember, Elaine met someone online who she eventually married. When's your next one?"

"Elaine was lucky. But I don't believe in my own happy ever after, and online dating hookups are exhausting. That makes three horrid ones in a row. Too bad I didn't have a boyfriend in high school who had ditched me. Isn't that what all those romantic movies are about? You somehow end up back in your hometown and reconnect with an old love." Her food appeared on the counter. Shoving her phone between her cheek and shoulder, she pulled her wallet out of her purse, grabbed some cash and handed it to the guy. "Thank you. Keep the change." Picking up the bag, she walked to a nearby bench and sat.

"You're eating, I'll let you go. Call you tonight. Jacob, stay in your highchair."

Picturing the little guy making a run for it, Lexy giggled as she hung up and put her phone away. Opening the carton, she picked up a greasy golden fry, blew on it, and shoved it in her mouth. Closing her eyes, she savored the salty crunch and the soft texture on the inside. Ahhh ... her eyes popped open as she pulled the paper off the burger. Pickles, mustard, ketchup and mayonnaise oozed from under the bun. Who needed a man when you had food like this to savor? She downed it in minutes, taking note of the chip wagon's name. *Len's Food.* Short, to the point, and easy to remember. She'd have to come back. Sure, she was eating too much since her break-up, but it got her through many lonely days. Many? Correction—all of them.

Loud clicking sounds rang out, as if someone was pounding on the pavement. She twisted around to look. Oh, no, Farmer Albert had entered the alley.

Instant paranoia set in. Had he figured out who she was? Did someone at the bar tell him?

No time to run, she dropped her head and kept it down, glad she had a hat on. Her red hair was hard to miss.

Don't move.

Two

Clickety clack. Cowboy boots walked right on by.

Whew.

Hats rock.

But how sad that Lexy had become fearful of everyone. What did she think cowboy Albert would have done, even if he had seen her?

A flash of movement caught her eye.

Wait!

More paranoia.

Was that a paparazzi behind that bush? Nah. She'd picked a pub in another town to escape them. But had one been in the bar, recognizing her when the pig farmer yelled and followed her? Saw her put on a hat?

Nooooo...

Her publicist assured her things had died down and she was no longer newsworthy. Maybe. First the uproar over her book, then being dumped on air, had ignited a whole other level of interest. Now, it'd run its course, and she hadn't seen anyone going after her in ages. But she couldn't stop the terrifying feeling of being followed. The fear of someone stalking her every move, making her days miserable. Lovely, even compassionate articles were not what they were after; they wanted horrid gossip. Anything, true or not, to get readers clicking on their stories. More clicks equaled more sponsors equaled more money.

Shoving her trash in the bag, she stood, about to make a run for it when a man popped out with his dog, holding a poop bag.

Good grief. No paparazzi. Thank goodness.

Tossing the remains of her feast in a garbage container, Lexy circled around to her car. Looking back and forth to make sure no one noticed her, she got in fast, started the car, and pulled out from the curb. She wondered if she'd ever stop being suspicious.

Shoving in a CD, she waited.

"I will survive," she screamed when the chorus hit.

Her mantra these days.

Playing the song over and over, she neared her building, detoured into the drive-thru at *Phil's Treats*, picked up a coffee and a chocolate donut, then drove straight home. She pulled into her parking spot, enjoying the feeling of finally having arrived at a place of peace. The fact she loved her condo was at least one good point in her favor. Grabbing her purse, donut, coffee, she hurried out of her car and into the front foyer.

"Hi, Fred. Gottcha something." His face lit up as she placed the coffee and donut on his desk.

"Well, thank you, Ms. Ayers." He rolled his chair closer and opened the bag. "My favorite, too."

"Anything exciting going on tonight?" One day she'd have to write a story about the life of a doorman. He had told her some fascinating tales over the years.

"Well..." his voice trailed off.

"Ooooh, good. Something juicy, I hope?"

She watched him pull a small box out of a desk drawer.

"Someone found this." He hesitated, then held it out to her. "I put it in a box. I believe this is yours."

Dropping her purse, she tugged off the cover. "Noooo … couldn't be." The ring. Jake's ring. Back to haunt her. She should have tossed it in a lake.

"I recognized it, remembering you showing it to me the night your gentleman proposed."

"Yeah." Slamming the cover back on, she shoved it into her purse. Pain hit, tears formed, head down, she picked up her purse and hurried over to press the elevator button. "Gotta go. Have a good evening."

"You, too. And Alex?"

She glanced at him, wiping her eyes.

"Remember. I'm here if you ever need me."

"Thanks."

The elevator doors opened and she got in, pressing floor number six.

Too bad Fred wasn't single. He was the best security guy ever. Kind, compassionate, and had shielded her many times from prying reporters. He was a lot like her grandpa. More tears. She missed her grandpa a lot.

Finally making it to her condo, she unlocked the door and rushed in, shutting it behind her. Safe at last, she tossed her hat and coat on the couch, plopping down on her favorite chair, not caring her hands were still greasy. Stains come out. Well, maybe not on white fabric, but big deal.

Jake.

Stop thinking about him. Hard not to when his ring just surfaced. Plus there had been no closure. None at all. After his horrid appearance on TV, he'd refused all her phone calls. She'd even shown up at his apartment and if he was home, he had refused to answer the door. At work, his office secretary repeatedly told her he was out. The only message she got was a scribbled note she'd received in the mail one day, saying he wanted his ring back. Yeah, right.

Leaning over, she pulled the box out of her purse, opened it again and took hold of the ring. Staring at the glittering stones on the gold band, she remembered how excited she was when he had gotten down on one knee and proposed in front of a crowd of readers. She thought she had it all. A writer whose books were a success, a fiancé she loved with all her heart, and a ring that was not really her style, but at least he tried.

All fake.

Should she toss it again? Nah. Somehow it'd boomerang, coming back to haunt her.

Jumping up, she rifled through a kitchen drawer, found an envelope and stamp, threw the ring in it and addressed it to Jake's office. She had no idea if he had moved but at least his business would know where he was. There. She'd toss it in the mail tomorrow. Closure, finally.

After splashing her face with cold water, she sat back on the couch. Her ex wasn't all she was upset about.

Another disastrous date.

So much for *Hearts Forever* dating app.

So much for researching the subject of love.

Her laptop rang out, signaling she had mail. Big deal! Looking over at it sitting on her desk, all she could see was the screen with the blank page. Shiny. Glowing, actually. Irritating her. Stressing her defeat.

Where were her words?

After months of trying, she should have a ton of them by now and a well-developed chapter. Or at least an outline. After all, she had a deadline to meet. By contract.

Sure hard to write a love story when you have none in your life.

Hence, the dates.

She could barely remember what it felt like to share meals over candlelight, late night walks, snuggles before a fire. Lexy had hoped dating would rev her up, get her creative juices flowing, make her believe in love again. Or at least experience someone's eyes lighting up when they saw her.

Nope, all those blind dates were a bust. Lots of people just looking for a one-night hookup. She was not interested.

A loud groan filled the air. Was that from her? Had to be, since no one else was there. She wished she could pick up the phone and call her mom.

She sat straight up.

Time to figure this out.

Her fiancé had dumped her eight months ago. She still had that darn wedding dress she'd taken ages to find. Her writing career was a mess. No one cared that she'd had three bestsellers readers raved about and a possible movie in the works. One bad book and she was slammed. She'd been stalked and terrified by reporters jumping out at her, wanting comments about her book bomb, always asking what had happened to her. She was afraid of everyone. She'd stopped looking at social media and the trolls out to get her by trash talking. Online dating was horrid. Sure seemed as if everyone lied in their bios, as well as retouched and photoshopped their pictures so much they were unrecognizable when she met them. Okay, she lied too. A little bit.

Her heart picked up speed as she flicked her eyes back and forth. Jumping up, she screamed, "Enough."

Nothing was going well.

She had to make a change.

She had to get out of there.

This apartment, this city, this life.

Walls were closing in and she was fed up with confusion.

You're a loser. You'll never amount to anything.

She had always made fun of people who tried to 'find themselves.' A cliché for sure, but it seemed to apply to her now, since her life was in such chaos. She needed to do something. Anything. To fix it.

Yes, she had to find herself.

She was that desperate.

Grabbing her phone, she tapped in the number before she could change her mind.

"White and Merrill law office. This is Linda. May I help you?"

"Alexandra Ayers. Is Jim White in?"

"Sure is, Ms. Ayers. I'll put you through."

"Are you finally ready?" Jim's voice was equally loud and soothing.

"Yes, I'll do it."

"The keys are on the way."

Three

Swallowtail Lake.

She'd made it.

Flipping off her sandals, Lexy dropped on the sand, burrowing her feet in its warmth. Who cared if her white sundress got dirty. No one would see it and no more dresses after today. She planned on living in shorts and tees all summer. Completely relaxed.

The five-hour drive had been exhausting. She'd had little sleep and except for a couple of gas station stops, she'd kept on going, just wanting to get away fast.

Lucky her.

This was a private stretch of beach not open to trespassers. Yes, a nearby cottage existed, but Jim said it'd been boarded up for years. Besides, she couldn't see it anyway due to a large clump of trees existing between both buildings. She was all alone. Just what she wanted. And maybe, just maybe, a change of venue would be exactly what she needed.

Wait a second.

Familiar panic set in.

Had anyone followed her?

Sneaky paparazzi?

Perusing the area, she saw nothing. Not even a flicker of wind. Good.

Big breath in. Big breath out.

Would she ever get over this fear? She was still indescribably lost in it. Hoped so, but for now she continued checking everywhere she went. Just for reassurance.

She reached up to make sure her hair was tucked under her hat and pulled off her big round sunglasses to see everything clearer. The sky was blue, the lake calm, and big fat marshmallow clouds floated by. Tipping her head up towards the sun, she closed her eyes, savoring its heat wrapping around her, as beads of sweat formed on her forehead. They felt good. Cleansing. She sniffed, loving the whiffs of nearby blossoms that hung in the air.

Peace descended.

You shouldn't have written that book. Everything you do is a failure.

A ripple of pain sliced through her belly.

Typical. Right in the middle of feeling good, something bad had to happen.

Bending over, she sucked in deep breaths and the cramps finally eased. Medical tests had revealed nothing, but they kept happening. Stress, probably.

Fairy Tale Crushed.

Her big flop.

Sure it made money. Oddly enough, more money than her three bestsellers. Go figure. Everyone rushed to read the book labelled a mess, then raced to pound out bad reviews, relishing taking someone down. Of course, she knew reviews were a part of a writer's life, but she'd never had so many horrific ones before.

And the gossip. Oh, the gossip.

Reporters even created a theme, "What in the world happened to author Alexandra Ayers." Whacko stories were written about how she'd deliberately created an awful book, drawing attention to herself, knowing reviewers would slaughter her and she'd get more press, and ultimately make more money. Or how someone else had written her earlier bestsellers and this one was her own and a total dud. Then her all-time favorite, she'd been abducted by aliens and forced to write that book. Photoshop had even created a picture of her bent over her computer, surrounded by stereotypical little green beings.

So sad.

People loved to see others fail.

In this case, she couldn't blame them, though. She was the author, it was her work, and she had veered away from her regular style. Her real truth was idiotic, and a secret. One she couldn't bear to acknowledge, even to herself.

"Love is in the air..." Ugh. She'd have to get rid of that smarmy ringtone.

Lexy eased her phone out of her pocket, glancing at it to make sure Wendy wasn't calling – nope, not her, just an alarm. She hit the mute button. The ringing was probably some dumb alert about another bad review, and she was sick of them. And besides, she'd sworn to stay off it, keeping it close only in case of emergencies. No way did she want to talk to anyone except her best friend or agent. Considering tossing it in the lake, loving the image of the piece of metal sinking to the bottom, she decided against it. Wendy would kill her or hire the FBI to hunt her down. Besides, she needed the contact numbers she'd saved over the years.

Pushing it back in her pocket, her fingertips touched the paper she'd shoved in there. Oh, right. She'd forgotten about it. Pulling it out, she unfolded it, a newspaper clipping Fred had handed to her as she left. Glancing at the headline, a surge of nausea rose.

'Alexandra Loses It.'

No way was she reading this. Then again, he wouldn't have given it to her if he didn't feel she needed to see it. Better take a look.

The first two words in the article were the name Maggie Everson.

What?

Maggie, a kid she hadn't seen in over twenty years, gave an interview about how they'd been best friends until Alex had turned into a drama queen, narcissist, and a meany in every way. Narcissist? Meany? Had she been in touch with Jake? And 'in every way' – she'd actually said that. She glanced at the date. Two days ago. So she wasn't totally non-news, stories were still being written. And the photos Everson sold of the two of them on a school bus trip showed Lexy frowning in every one of them. Pulling the paper closer, she could tell her frowns were photoshopped. Not even a good job of it, either. And Maggie? With the long dark hair? Nope, she wouldn't recognize her if she ran into her. She barely remembered her, but judging by the comments below, people ate it up.

She knew why Fred had given it to her. He always felt she was too trusting, and he wanted her to be more careful. He was right.

Crumpling up the paper, she screamed, "Leave me alone." Her echo flew back across the water, haunting her.

Jumping up, she walked, kicking sand as she went. Her angry strides made her feel better. She wondered what made that woman believe she had the right to comment on her? They'd never been best friends. Barely even acquaintances.

Oh, who was she trying to kid?

Reporters, of course, often offered big bucks for stories. Or at times threatened people. Or lured them by saying their names would be in the paper, as well as online, and they'd be famous, which could lead to endorsements or job offers. An honest one was hard to find, since the goal was to get people to read their articles, anyway you could. The more interest, the better. Once again it hit her how often readers didn't care about the truth. Many reporters didn't either. Negativity sold and if reputations were destroyed? Oh, well.

Had it always been like this?

Enough.

Ripping the crumpled paper into tiny pieces, she shoved it back in her pocket.

Forget about Everson.

Picking up a smooth flat stone, she pivoted sideways, bent her knees the way her grandpa taught her, aimed, and threw. Skimming the lake's bright shiny surface, it bounced three times.

Splat. Sunk.

She related.

Sighing, she realized a lot of inner work was going to have to happen to pull herself out of her blahs. Blahs – her word for feeling down, depressed, sad. Trudging back, she slipped her sandals back on, grabbed her glasses and headed to the cottage. She hadn't even been in it yet. She'd just rolled in, parked, and run to the beach, just like she had as a kid.

Drawing closer, it registered that this was now her cottage. Shockingly, she owned it. She knew her grandpa had sold everything to help pay for her grandma's care, so she was surprised to discover he'd held on to it, left it to her mother, who then left it to her.

Now in full view, she stopped in her tracks. Her breath caught in her throat.

Four

An abandoned shack rose before her.

Jim had told her the building was dilapidated, but she had never expected it to be this bad.

What happened to the sweet little cottage of her youth? Heartbreaking, since her grandparents, who had inherited it from their parents, worked hard to keep it looking good. Then again, the rundown state was all her own fault. She couldn't bear to come here after her grandparents passed. It hurt too much. Her mom had even asked for her help, but she had just made up busywork to keep away. She should have been out here making sure everything was as beautiful as it used to be to honor her grandparents and her mother. They'd be appalled to see it like this. Shame on her.

Faded cherry red paint peeled off the walls in strips. The two window boxes, normally showcasing her grandmother's prized flowers, were hanging sideways off rusty nails. The once grey door had faded into a dull ash color and the whole building tilted, as if about to collapse. It reminded her of comedies where you booked a vacation sight unseen and arrived to a nightmare.

And the front yard...

Lexy almost turned and left.

The grass was knee high and weeds she couldn't even identify tangled together, looking like a scene from a horror movie.

Or a jungle.

She half expected monkeys to appear. Or a rhinoceros. A lion?

Now she understood Jim's email telling her that as a housewarming gift, he had sent her a lawnmower, which was apparently tucked away in the shed in the backyard.

Go on. Go inside.

Hopping over weeds on the path to the porch, a loud creak sounded out. Monkeys? Nope. A loose sign, clinging desperately to a rotted post almost hidden behind an overgrown bush, swung back and forth. Considering there was no breeze, the noise freaked her out. The letters were faded, but she could still make out Writer's Bliss. Right. She'd forgotten her grandpa, who she'd always credited as her chief nurturer for her love for words, had given the cottage a name.

Grandpa.

He loved to write.

She had fond memories of him carrying around a notepad in his back pocket, pulling it out to write down his thoughts about his fishing trips, the garden, or anything that struck him. He often submitted articles printed in *Farmer's Daily*, an old newsletter circulated among his farming crowd. She remembered asking him if she could add her opinions as well and he gladly let her do it, surprising her one day with her own notebook sporting a picture of a little redheaded kid on the cover. She looks just like you, he had said. She still had that tiny book along with many others that had joined it.

How apt that she was here to finish her novel at Writer's Bliss.

Maybe.

First, she'd have to see if the cottage was livable.

Walking up the steps, at least they seemed okay, sturdy enough, she pulled an envelope out of her purse, opened it up and took out the keys. She stared at the door. Jim had been wanting her to check out the building for ages. Use it or lose it, he kept saying. He constantly made her aware that she could sell it for a small fortune, since the land it sat on was incredibly gorgeous and sought after, but it held too many memories for Lexy to even consider such an offer. Memories she was now having a hard time facing. Memories that were bittersweet.

Did she really want to go in?

Maybe she should stay at a hotel tonight.

Oh, go in. Don't be such a scaredy cat. Do it.

Deep breath in, deep breath out, she inserted the main key, pulled hard on the doorknob and with a loud groan, the door swung open. She stepped in. A rank, musty smell smacked her in the face, setting off a sneezing fit.

Ugh. She left the door open.

Eyeing the greyish sheets strewn over furniture, probably white at some point, coughing attacks continued as dust flew around her. Rubbing her eyes, taking a few more steps into the living room, sweet nostalgia sliced through her as she realized it had been left exactly the way her grandparents had it, minus the cloths. Her eyes were drawn to the two paintings hanging on the walls, also covered.

Tears slid down.

Even though her mother had a busy law practice, she painted sunrises for relaxation. Morning was her favorite time of day, and she had a real fascination with all the colors accompanying the sun as it rose in all its splendor. Lexy knew she'd find two of her originals under those cloths. She couldn't bear to look at them yet. Sure, it'd been over a year since her mother's passing, but it still hurt. A lot. She missed her so much.

She searched for the seashells off in the corner, and yep, they were still there. She snapped her fingers. That's right. A nautical theme ran throughout. She'd forgotten that, too. The living room was the seashell room.

A noise. A scurrying sound. Probably mice. Double ugh.

Her breath caught in her throat as she glanced at the entrance to the kitchen. She half expected her granny to appear, a glass of milk in one hand, home-baked cookies in the other. She jerked her head toward a big green oversized chair where her grandpa used to sit, always wanting to read her a book. She'd snuggle up beside him and listen to his deep voice pull her into exciting escapades of whatever characters he became.

Love is in the air ... Get rid of that sound.

Pulling her phone out, she took a glance. Wendy. She hit answer.

"You made it. Thank goodness." Her best friend let out a long groan of relief. "I know driving's not your forte. In fact, you hate going long distances."

"I told you I would."

"Somehow, I didn't believe you. Or hoped you'd stay here. How is it?"

"Dusty. But the beach is gorgeous."

"I bet. I can't wait until we visit."

"I'll have it cleaned up by then."

"Don't work too hard. I can help."

"You might have to. The whole exterior needs to be repainted."

"I'm in. Love to paint. Gotta go. Jacob's looking for his Play-Doh. If I don't catch him quick, it'll be all over the floor, in his mouth, or both. Love you."

"Love you too."

She admired how Wendy had no problem with emotion. Back in college, she'd been embarrassed when her roommate said 'love you' every time they parted, but now she liked it. It made her feel secure. And cared for.

Shoving her phone back in her pocket, she walked up the stairs to her bedroom. The door was shut.

Could she handle going in?

Do it.

Yanking it open, she was greeted by a mural of sweet dolphins dancing across one wall. She remembered helping her mom and granny paint it – best fun ever. And the fact they managed to get paint all over themselves. She turned her head to check out her desk.

Was it still there?

Yes. Her favorite treasure as a kid. Her grandpa's typewriter stared back at her. One summer she had proclaimed she wanted to be a writer and woke up the next day to her grandpa presenting her with this typewriter during breakfast, announcing, "I wrote many articles on this old antique and now I want you to have it. A symbol of how much I believe in you."

She walked over, leaned down and blew the dust off the keys. Pulling a piece of paper from a stack beside it, she inserted it, turning the roller so it fit nicely. Hitting a few keys, amazed the cartridge still held ink, she wondered if the 'M' key still stuck. Yep, it did. She had meant to come and get it all those years, but never got around to it, once again avoiding painful memories. He sure would be sad if he knew she had become an author who was now the butt of reporters' jokes. Swiping at her wet face, tears still flowing, she decided to sleep in the living room that night. She couldn't face staying in her old room quite yet.

Next, the kitchen. She couldn't bear to check out her mom's room nor her grandparents'.

Practically running from her room, she hurried downstairs and walked into the green room, also known as the kitchen. A faint whiff of vanilla greeted her and she closed her eyes, remembering afternoons baking cookies and devouring them. "Don't eat the raw dough," her grandma used to constantly say. Opening her eyes, she saw the same minty color on the walls, slightly faded, and the room still held the big, long oak table where they shared many a meal. This was the lobster room, and she was sure once she pulled down some of the cloths, she'd find photos of the red creatures she'd once been fascinated with, as long as no one cooked them. There was even an old lobster trap off in the corner.

Whew. So many remembrances of the past. More bittersweet than anything, since all her favorite people were gone now.

Why had she come here?

Enough. She'd made her decision and wasn't going to haggle over it. She was here and cleaning needed to be done. Pronto.

Holding her nose to prevent another sneezing fit, she pulled off the sheets hanging over the furniture, leaving them in a pile on the floor, and ran out to get the cleaning supplies she'd brought.

Wait. What was that?

Stopping, she stood still.

Whimpers?

Little high-pitched cries?

They were coming from a bush.

Rushing over, she pushed aside the branches.

No way.

Five

Chris leaned back in his chair, glass in hand, taking a sip, reveling at how good it tasted. His mother still made the best lemonade, executing the perfect blend of tart and sweet. He chuckled at his six-year-old niece scurrying around on the beach, putting the finishing touches to the sandcastle they'd built. Once again, he was reminded how independent she was when she'd announced, "Let me finish. You go sit." She sounded just like her mother.

Elizabeth.

Pangs of sorrow swept through him like an army of red ants that had attacked him once as a kid. Stinging, hurting.

He missed her.

She was a terrific big sister, always looking out for him. He still recalled her taking him by the hand and leading him into school on his very first day. He was scared, and she had whispered, "I'll always have your back." And she did. Always. Like a second mother, when his father passed away a few years later.

He downed the rest of his lemonade and set the glass on the ground, lost in memories. He had been so excited when she had given birth to Emma. He'd been out jogging when he got the call that she was in labor and if he'd been running a marathon, he would have won at the speed he summoned up to get to the hospital fast. The first time he'd held tiny Emma, he'd fallen in love and embraced the role of uncle or unca, as his niece called him. He'd stepped up when Elizabeth's husband decided kids weren't on his radar and left, so Chris had been a part of every one of the little girl's triumphs. First time she rolled over, the time she took her first step, and the day she declared him her unca. She still called him that, even though she knew the correct pronunciation. He found it an endearing nickname.

He'd never built a sandcastle with her, and watching Emma today, he realized not only did she sound like her mother, she acted like her as well. Elizabeth was a talented, in high demand, interior designer and it amazed him seeing Emma distribute leaves, twigs, and rocks to create carpets and walkways, couches and beds. She even pulled the fuzzy pink barrette out of her hair and attached it to a stick, mimicking a tree, which she placed near the front entrance. Standing back, she clapped her little hands, obviously thrilled with her handiwork, then walked around the castle, stopping to rearrange several items, getting it just right. He quickly pulled his phone out of his pocket and snapped a photo of her. She even mimicked Elizabeth's strut when she was proud of her work. Kind of a half hop, half dance move.

More important, she kept on smiling as she played.

Closing in on her face, he snapped another photo.

He often feared he'd never see that toothy grin again. Chris related because he also had a tough time being cheerful and positive for Emma, after the horror. The horror was what he called it, for horrific circumstances had changed their lives forever.

His thoughts had taken a turn for the worse.

Again.

They often did lately.

Struggling to escape them, he looked around, taking stock of the sparkling sun holding court in a bright blue sky, waves rippling through the water, and trees swaying gently. Hard to believe that twenty years ago, he had been on this very same beach. It had only been for two weeks, but it left its mark, for his memories were of rollicking fun that he never wanted to end. Something he'd had little of lately, but surprisingly since they'd arrived, he already felt peace settling in. Tension rolled off, and he was thrilled Emma loved it there too. Not to mention his mother, Meredith. Of course, she was the one who brought him there years earlier, leaving him with his grandpa. He looked back at Emma's blonde pigtails swinging in the wind, when suddenly a vivid memory shot through him.

Startled, he sat up.

He was ten years old, entered a sandcastle competition, almost exactly where his niece played. His partner was his buddy, also ten, with bright red hair – clown hair she called it – twisted into pigtails like Emma's that swayed back and forth when she talked. They'd felt they were too old and too cool to play with sand but wanted to win the prize, ten free ride tickets at the local carnival. The mini roller coaster was their goal.

Squinting, lost in memories, he recalled their excitement as they created a fort equipped with a rampart, moat, and a drawbridge fashioned out of popsicle sticks. They'd won and he'd even held her hair back when she'd thrown up after ride number five. Of course, eating four bunches of candy floss before riding the coaster was probably what did it.

He hadn't thought of her in years.

She was such a sassy, outspoken whirlwind, definitely his best friend back then, and he had really missed her when vacation time ended and they'd parted. They had meant to keep in touch but never got around to exchanging phone numbers and addresses. Once in a while, he had considered looking through social media for her, but since he never knew her last name, it would have been pointless. As the days and years marched on, she was pushed to a corner of his mind, dusty, and rarely looked at. In fact, he'd forgotten her.

Until today.

"Unca Chris. Unca Chris. Why are you laughing? Is my sandcastle funny?"

He shook his head, pulling out of the past. "Oh, no, honey. You have built the most beautiful castle I've ever seen."

"Yayyyyy. Now I'm hungry. Can we get something to eat?"

"Yes, of course. Nana mentioned picking up your favorite pizza in town."

"With pepperoni and mushrooms?"

"Of course."

She clapped in excitement.

"But let me get a few more photos of your castle first."

"Yeah. Let's do that."

He snapped away, zeroing in on several with Emma posing in front, grinning ear to ear. He was definitely framing those.

"Now come on." He slid his phone into his pocket. "Let's go get Nana."

"Yeah, let's."

She threaded her fingers through his and they walked back to the cottage. For probably the one hundredth time, he hoped she would be okay. He was all she had now. Well, him and his mother, and he wanted to give her the life she deserved. The life his sister had wanted for her.

His mind flicked back again to that little redheaded girl he once knew so many years ago. He could really do with a dose of her *joie de vivre* right about now.

He wondered what had happened to her.

Six

The sun hit hard, blinding her.

Kneeling, Lexy rubbed her eyes and held out a hand to block the glare. Something fuzzy was there. Some kind of furry scarf? A hat? Had she imagined whimpers?

Suddenly the scarf/hat moved, and two little eyes peeked up at her.

Another whimper.

Awwww...

She melted.

A puppy.

"Oh, sweetie." Pushing away branches, she saw the little guy shaking. His crying grew louder. Darn. She'd scared him.

"Hey, buddy, I'm just trying to help."

Eyeing him, not touching, hoping to minimize his fear, she could see no visible signs of cuts or bumps, but they could be internal. She noticed his whimpering and trembling abated when she spoke. Maybe it soothed him?

"Are you feeling better?" she cooed, heart pounding.

The pup leaned forward and licked her hand.

"Oh, little one. Thank you. Now, I need to touch you. Just to see if you're okay."

A tear rolled down as she kept up a steady stream of talk while running her fingers over him, feeling how skinny he was. His trusting eyes never left hers as she discovered several mats in his hair, but was glad not to feel or see any cuts or bumps.

"I know you're scared, but I'm going to take you to see an animal doctor. You might need some help and we have to find out who you belong to."

Thank goodness a veterinarian clinic existed in the nearby town of Willow. She remembered there had always been one and on the way to the cottage had noticed it was still there. She calculated a ten-minute drive to get there. Glancing at her watch, she figured if she hurried, she'd make it before closing.

"Hey, sweetie. You can trust me."

Picking him up ever so gently, she held him in her arms as she opened the trunk of her car. Dumping a box holding her shoes, she pulled a T-shirt out of her bag, placing it over the bottom. Nice and cozy.

"There you go." She slowly lowered him onto the shirt. "This should keep you snug and safe in the car. Oh, you're shaking again. You're okay. Everything will be alright." She placed another T-shirt over him.

Opening the passenger door, she put the box on the floor so he wouldn't slide off. Settling in the driver's seat, she took off slowly so as not to startle the pup, picking up speed as they went.

Now where was that office.

Driving down the main street, she turned her head back and forth, finally spotting the sign: *Miller's Veterinarian Clinic.* Pulling to a stop, grateful an empty one was right in front, she jumped out and opened the passenger side.

"Hi cutie," she crooned. Picking up the box, she hurried in, eyeing a young woman at the front desk. She speed-walked over.

"I need some help," she said softly, not wanting to alarm the pup.

"What do you have there?" The woman stood and leaned over the desk.

Lexy checked her nameplate, Helen. Her pixie cut highlighted the softness in her eyes. Lexy trusted her immediately.

"I found this little guy on the beach, and I don't know how long he's been there."

"I'll get the vet right away." Helen directed her to a room off to the side. "And your name?"

"Lexy Errol."

"Be right back."

Sitting the box on the examination table, Lexy petted the pup gently. "You'll be okay, little one." She was afraid to handle him too much in case she might cause some kind of damage.

Almost immediately, an elderly man arrived. Grey hair, kind eyes, and a smile on his face.

"My name's Doctor Dan." His eyes flickered to the box. "Who did you bring?"

Lexy explained, while he ran his fingers over the pup.

"Since he's frightened and used to you, how about you take him out and hold him on the examination table."

Lexy loved that he was thinking solely of the pup's comfort.

"I'm here, sweetie." She repeated this over and over while she held him firmly on the table. The vet checked his ears, eyes, and mouth.

"He is a boy and looks like a pup from an abandoned Havanese litter someone found earlier today on the beach. This one must have gotten away. He would be about three months old. Roughly. I need to run a series of tests. Thanks for bringing him in."

"Can I stay to see his results?"

"Of course. As a matter of fact, you can continue to hold him while I draw blood." She held the pup tightly while the vet poked him with a needle. "Now, I'll just take him back for an x-ray and check for heartworm. I'll have Helen assist to make it go faster. It'll just take a few minutes."

Sitting, head in hands, Lexy whispered a prayer, something she hadn't done in years. She couldn't get the pup's eyes out of her mind. The way he looked at her, vulnerable, so scared, and she wanted more than anything for him to be okay. Hearing footsteps, she glanced at the door. In walked the doctor holding the dog with Helen trailing behind, a bowl of water in one hand, food in the other. Doctor Dan looked happy. Whew.

"So far, everything checks out just fine."

Lexy sighed in relief, reaching out for the little guy. Doctor Dan placed him in her arms.

"He's dehydrated and hungry and has no chip, just like the others. We'll see if he'll take any food and water." Helen put the bowls down and Lexy eased him onto the floor, squatting down beside him, poking her finger in the water and holding it towards his mouth. The pup hesitated at first, slowly licked it off, then lowered his head in the bowl to lap up more. He next attacked the food, eating every bit of it.

"What will happen to him now?" she asked, as Helen hurried out to answer a ringing phone.

"The other ones are at the animal shelter right next door. They'll bathe him and comb him out. As you can see, he has several mats in his hair. This little guy will join them until he's adopted."

"Oh." To her surprise, the little pup looked around and came prancing towards her, tail wagging.

"Looks like he's thanking you," Doctor Dan said. "He sure likes you."

Lexy had never had a pet and was touched when he reached his paws up to lick her face. Staring into his eyes, she saw warmth and trust with a touch of confusion, similar to her own these days. Her breath caught as a warm glow spread, something she hadn't felt in ages. Love, perhaps? Joy?

"Er, can I have him?"

You can't take care of a puppy. You can barely take care of yourself.

Doctor Dan stepped back, eyeing her.

"Have you had a dog before?"

"No. But I will take good care of him. Promise."

"Well, you already have, getting him here pronto. You both seem in sync, judging how he's taken to you. How about you foster him for a while, and we'll see how it goes?"

"I would love that."

"Okay, I'll get Helen to assemble the paperwork. You're Lexy Errol, right?"

Paperwork? Oh, oh. Should she give him her real name? Be totally honest?

"Um, I'm actually Alexandra Ayers."

Yes, she had to. Anything to keep this pup safe and she couldn't put a fake name on legitimate forms. If found out, she'd be labeled a liar, untrustworthy, possibly sued, and she'd lose this little guy for sure.

"Really?" His eyebrows rose. "Any relation to George Ayers?"

"Yes, he was my grandfather."

"George and I used to be golf buddies." His head tilted. "Wait a second. You're the famous author, right? Alexandra Ayers. Of course. George was always going on about his granddaughter the writer."

Her heart thudded.

"Yes, but I'm keeping it quiet these days. I'm going by Lexy Errol now. Just needing time to myself without a lot of press on my case."

Had she ruined it all? Would he think she was crazy going by a different name? Would he keep her secret? Call a reporter? Try to make a buck? She sucked in a breath, exhaled slowly. More important, would he still let her have the little pup? She crossed her fingers, suddenly feeling nauseated.

"Please," she added. "I really will take good care of him."

Doctor Dan squinted, as if still sizing her up. Lexy felt like grabbing the pup and making a run for it but knew that would get her nowhere and only add dog kidnapping to her list of crimes.

"Okay, fine by me." He smiled. "Any relation of George is a plus on my side. Also, I seem to recall a problem with your last book. Or at least that was what my wife said. So Lexy Errol it is. Your secret's safe with me. Besides, I see how much you already love this little guy."

"Oh, thank you."

"No, thank you. Finding good homes is what I aim for. I'll do the paperwork myself so when you sign your real name, no one will know but me." He winked. "George was a good friend of mine, and I know he adored you. So, anything for his granddaughter."

"I appreciate this."

"How about you and Helen bathe him, brush out the mats, and I'll get the forms ready."

"Great."

"Be back in a minute."

He hurried out and Lexy raised her eyes to the heavens. "Thanks, Grandpa. You always look out for me."

Seconds later, Helen came in, leading them to a sink in the back.

Lexy watched intently, one hand on the pup the whole time to reassure him, observing how Helen handled him. He didn't like the water so much, but calmed down when she spoke to him soothingly.

"You have the magic voice," Helen said. "He sure trusts you."

"I'm thrilled about that." Lexy helped brush out the mats, which was easier with the detangling soap working its magic.

"There he is, nice and clean." Helen stood back looking him over. "I won't use the blow-dryer on him. I think he's had enough to scare him for the day."

After towel drying him, Lexy got a good look. His coat was a shiny golden color with patches of black popping up around his face, ears and tail. He was absolutely gorgeous.

Helen led them back to the room.

"Here you go." Doctor Dan came in, handing over a sheaf of papers. "Looks like you're anxious to get him home. How about you drop them off when you come back for a check-up in a week. Here's a crate you can use, and I've tucked some food inside."

"You are so kind."

"Well, I think you're the kind one, taking him home."

"And I won't let you or him down."

"I know you won't."

She listened intently as he went over a few basics about dog care, handed her a book on it, then helped her load everything in her car. This time she put the crate right on the seat, secured it with a seatbelt, got in the driver's side, and waved goodbye.

Seven

"Yahoooo," Lexy screamed as she pulled away from the curb. Eyes misty, her emotions exploded. "Hey sweetie, you're with me for now. And if I'm lucky, forever. Hope you don't mind me calling you sweetie until I figure out your name." She glanced over quickly, once again moved by the trust in his little eyes.

A flashing OPEN sign grabbed her attention.

"Hey, guess what's over there. A pet store." Helen had told her about it, but she didn't realize she'd be lucky enough to find it still open.

She pulled to a stop. "I think we need a few toys and some treats."

Carrying the little guy in, she grabbed a cart, placed him in it and walked up and down the aisles looking for supplies. More food and water bowls, towels, treats. She loved watching the pup, nose up in the air, sniffing like crazy. "This must be heaven to you."

"Hey lady, can I pet your dog?"

What? Lexy looked around.

A small girl, maybe five or six, had appeared out of nowhere. She had long blonde braids and looked adorable. Angelic, even.

"Well, he's a little scared right now. How about you just look at him." Lexy picked him up, holding him in her arms, and squatted down.

"Okay." The little girl got down on her knees. "What's his name?"

"Well, he doesn't have one yet. I just met him today."

"Did you buy him?"

"No, I found him."

Her eyes grew wide. "You did? Where?"

"In some bushes."

"Oh. Is he okay?"

She looked worried and, oh my goodness, teary-eyed.

"Yes, yes, he sure is. I got him checked out by a doctor."

"Oh, goody."

A grey-haired lady hurried over. "My goodness, Emma. Don't go hiding on me."

"I'm visiting the pup, Nana. The lady said he's scared." Emma pulled something out of her pocket. A tiny doggy cookie. "Can he have a treat?"

The older lady stood back and nodded, giving it the thumbs up. A silent and lovely way to let her know they were safe.

Lexy grinned. "You can try."

Emma slowly put it close to him and after a bit, the little pup moved to sniff it.

"Look, look. He's wagging his tail," Emma said excitedly. "He's taking it."

"Sure is." Lexy chuckled. Emma's excitement was contagious. "He likes you. Thanks for being so gentle."

"Can I pet him now?" Emma asked.

"How about just one little pat."

Emma gently touched the pup.

"Now, c'mon Emma, we need to get going. We're going to pick up pizza, remember?"

"We have to go too," Lexy said, standing, noticing Emma was reluctant to leave. "I think this little guy will be ready for bed soon."

"All right. Bye puppy. Bye nice lady. Hope to see you again."

"Me, too," Lexy said, surprised she meant it. Emma seemed sweet and obviously genuinely loved dogs.

"Thanks for being so kind to her," the elderly lady said.

"No problem." She watched them walk away. They reminded her of all the times she had shopped with her own grandmother, red braids swinging, and so much excitement. Her pup gave a little squeak. "Don't worry. I haven't forgotten you." She placed him back in the cart.

Lexy gathered up a few more things, checked them out at the counter, which was surprisingly busy, and headed toward the door.

"Hey, lady."

Was someone calling her? Again? Did they recognize her?

Turning her head, heart thumping, she saw the same little girl running toward her, Nana right behind. She skidded to a stop. "I bought a toy for your pup. A lamb. Can I give it to him?"

The older lady's eyes twinkled.

"How kind. Yes, you sure can."

Lexy picked up the pup and leaned him down so the girl could reach him.

"Here, this is for you." She placed the little lamb close to him.

Lexy was surprised to see him try to take it in his mouth, tail wagging. She held on to it so it wouldn't fall.

"He really likes it." Lexy gave her a high five. "Thank you."

"Goody. Now he won't be lonely. Bye." The girl skipped away.

Interesting comment. The little girl didn't want the pup to be lonely. Was she identifying with the dog? Lexy hoped she was okay, but judging by her attentive grandmother, she sure seemed loved.

She continued pushing the cart to the car. So far being in Willow had been an adventure. An exciting one, too. People were friendly and now she even had a furry little roommate. She tucked the pup in his crate, unloaded the supplies, and took the cart back to the store.

Driving home, another sign caught her eye. A for sale sign swaying in the wind, was perched in front of the Matthew Willow community center. The town had several large willow trees gracing the main street, and most people figured that was how the town got its name. Not true. She'd forgotten it had been named after the Willows, long-term residents, who had contributed much to the wellbeing of this community.

They had also built this center.

She slowed down. All the windows in the large red brick building were boarded up, and the grassy area in front was obviously neglected. Uncut and weedy.

Memories shot through her of packing a lunch and biking there as a kid where she'd play games all day long. Oh, and arts and crafts. She remembered how glue and glitter became her friends one summer. One time she worked all afternoon on a get-well card for her mother. She struggled for hours trying to draw her mom's favorite animal, a horse, and this nice little blond boy had seen her frustration, as well as how it resembled a cat, and offered to draw it for her.

Ouch. She had to stop thinking about her mom, for a while anyway. It still hurt so much.

Think about that sweet little boy who helped her, instead.

She hadn't thought of him in ages. He showed up that summer for a few weeks, stayed at the cottage next door, and they used to hang out together. She wondered whatever happened to him.

But how sad to see the center closed.

She glanced over, glad to see the pup was fast asleep, tiny paws holding the lamb.

"Sleep well. I'll take good care of you."

Will you?

It felt so good to be caring for something other than herself for a change.

So darn good.

Especially this scrap of a dog who had captured her heart already.

Eight

What was that?

Lexy pulled her blanket up over her face.

Something woke her.

Foggy with sleep, she willed herself to stay still.

Listen.

Was that scratching?

At the door?

Her heart pounded so fast she thought it'd explode.

Was there a wild animal trying to get in?

Mice? Racoons?

A human?

Was it already in the house?

Struggling to fully wake up, she eased her blanket down. She couldn't hide away forever and she needed to run for help. Or at least call.

Was that whimpering?

Wait a second. Didn't she come home with a pup?

Sitting up fast, she groaned.

Idiot.

She'd forgotten she'd fallen asleep on the floor. Every muscle ached.

More whining. More scratching. She looked over at the crate.

"Oh, honey, so that's the sound I heard." She shuffled closer. "You're crying." She reached for the latch. Wait. Remember the words in the book Dr. Dan gave her. Never let a dog out when whimpering or barking or he'll keep on doing it to command attention. Leave him there until he's quiet.

"I'm here. You don't have to worry." Soothed by her voice, he stopped in seconds, and she quickly undid the latch. Thank goodness.

"Come on out."

The noise of the door being released scared him and he cowered at the back, but soon made his way to her, the little lamb in his mouth.

Lexy patted his head, gentle as anything, not wanting to be pushy or rough in case she spooked him again. Slowly getting up, she led him to the back door for a potty break, grateful he followed her. He looked so tiny, she was tempted to carry him, but knew not to treat him like a baby. She needed to build his confidence, and he seemed fine when she opened the door. He dropped the lamb on her foot, so she picked it up, watching him tilt his head back to sniff. Fortunately, the back yard was fenced in, courtesy of her grandparents, but was unruly and probably looked like a jungle to the little guy. Mowing was on her list for the day,

"Take your time." She'd have to name him soon. Honey, sweetie, and cutie were getting old.

He sniffed around, getting lost a few times amid the many green obstacles, did his business while she cheered him on, then ran back to her. Putting his paws up on her leg, he let out a bark, or at least she assumed his high-pitched squeak was a bark. Not sure what he wanted, but she handed him his lamb, and he immediately wagged his tail. Aha, she'd guessed correctly. So the little girl was right. The toy was a comfort to him.

"Breakfast time." She opened the door and he trotted in behind her and sat watching her get her coffee started and prepare his food.

Once again, his tail flew back and forth every time she talked, so she kept up a stream of chatting away, figuring he liked it. If he continued to enjoy her voice, he was going to make the best sounding board ever. One where she could bounce story ideas off of. Maybe he could help her finally write an ending to her current work.

She placed bowls of food and water on the floor, sitting as well, watching him approach, sniff, put the lamb down on the floor, then start to eat.

Good. A nice, healthy sign.

Taking a deep breath in and letting it out, she had to admit it felt wonderful just hanging there watching her pup instead of immersing herself in turmoil, stressed out over her book and the fact she couldn't seem to finish it.

Unfortunately, turmoil was the way she usually started every day.

She recalled the excitement when her first novel had been published. She had danced around her apartment, overcome with happiness and awe. What an honor and what a whirlwind. After hours, months, and days of holing up in her apartment writing, she was thrust into book signings, interviews, tours. She adored her readers, treasured their support, still tried to answer all of their letters and was over the moon when a fan club was created.

Things changed. Fast.

Her once pure, write from the heart passion, became a mass of problems.

Writing was no longer fun.

You were never good at it. Just lucky.

"Hey."

She'd been so immersed in her thoughts; she hadn't noticed her pup so close. He had put his little paws up on her leg and when she leaned toward him, he licked her face. Her heart melted. Was he saying thank you?

"Hi there." She cuddled him in her arms. "Did you have a nice breakfast?" He raised a paw to touch her chin, and she giggled. "You really are a sweetie." Waiting ten minutes, she led him out again, since the book stated that taking pups out after eating was a good habit to get into. She was surprised he grabbed the lamb again to take with him. Definitely and for sure, his little security blanket.

"Good boy." Bingo. It worked.

Now, coffee.

They came back in and she poured herself a cup.

"Awwww ... bliss." Nothing like caffeine first thing in the morning. "Hey, let's go for a walk along the beach, little one."

She looked down. Where was he? He had been right beside her. Racing around, she spotted him curled up on the mop, head resting on the lamb.

Whew.

Poor little guy.

She bet he hadn't slept much in days. Picking him up, she put him in his crate, or his little home as she liked to call it, keeping him safe, noticing he never opened an eye. He was that out of it. She placed the little lamb beside him, so he'd see it when he woke up.

Sipping her coffee, watching him sleep, a plan formed. She had once figured she'd stay at the cottage, rarely leaving except for walks, but with a dog she'd be in and out of town to see Doctor Dan and the pet store.

Time for plan B.

A haircut.

Necessary to make sure no one recognized her. Even though reporters were supposedly leaving her alone, she could never know what would set them off again. It also made more sense since she'd be grocery shopping as well and fire engine red hair was hard to hide. She was sure gossip would ignite again if they felt she was in hiding.

Taking a deep breath in and blowing it out slowly, her effort to remain calm, she fished scissors out of a box she'd marked 'kitchen' and marched to the washroom, wiping down the bathroom mirror so she could see clearly.

Drum roll, please.

She picked up the scissors along with a handful of red curls.

She had never cut hair before.

Don't do it.

Do it.

Don't.

Do it.

Yes.

Go for it.

Snip, snip, snip.

Grimacing, she watched long red strands fall to the floor. Ouch. They shone like rubies on the black carpet.

Not done yet. One more step to go.

Running back to the living room, noting the pup was still asleep, she rummaged through her bags. Got it. Black dye. Back in the bathroom, she mixed the liquids, smeared it on, and set her phone timer for twenty minutes. Great. It gave her time to figure out her puppy's name. Pulling open her laptop cover, she sat at the kitchen table and started Googling. Reading down all names beginning with the letter A, one grabbed her. Asher. It meant happy and blessed. The name was perfect because she sure felt blessed having this little one enter her world. All settled. She was definitely calling him Asher.

Her phone vibrated. Time to wash the dye out. After jumping in the shower, Lexy noticed her hands shaking as she watched the stream of black dye circle and disappear down the drain. What had she done? She was nuts to do this. Certifiable.

Toweling off, she dressed and stood in front of the mirror. Eyes closed.

One ... two ... three...

They popped open.

Yikes.

Nine

She looked like a poodle with a bad haircut she'd once seen on a funny poster.

No offense to poodles.

Lexy barely recognized herself.

The inky blackness made her face paler than usual, and her freckles beamed like beacons. Fortunately, she had natural curls which covered the uneven parts and even looked mildly planned. Fluffing it up, she grimaced. Now it looked like she'd stuck her finger in a light circuit with wavy pretzel hair taking over. Oh, well, it would have to do, and besides, few would see her like this. She also had an assortment of hats she'd be wearing anyway.

On with the day.

Bounding into the living room she saw her pup was still sleeping, so she tackled the kitchen. Dust, dirt, begone. She made great headway until a sound drew her back to check on her new roommate. How cute. He was sitting in his crate, tail thumping, not the least concerned she looked different.

"Hi there. Guess what? I named you Asher."

Did he really wag his tail harder? Or was that wishful thinking? She was going with the former.

"Glad you like it." She let him out. "Or at least I'm taking that as a like."

She tossed on her biggest floppy hat, unfortunately bright orange, which could probably be seen from Mars. Note to self – buy hats with more muted colors. She fetched her sunglasses, fastened Asher's harness on his wiggly little body, and clipped on a leash.

"Yeah, I know, a leash is a lot to get used to. But you'll figure it out." She was surprised when he led her over to his little home so he could get his lamb. "Sure, you can bring your buddy."

She opened the door, stopping for a moment, allowing the sun to embrace her. Its warmth felt good. She noticed her steps had more oomph in them, almost dance-like, and watched with amazement her pup slowed down every few seconds to sniff something.

"Guess we'll call our walks sniffs until you understand the concept. But go ahead. Everything is all so new to you and I'm loving your excitement."

"Hey there, nice lady. Remember me?"

Lexy whipped around.

She couldn't believe it. The same sweet girl she'd met in the pet store was standing there. She had hoped to see her again, but never thought she really would. And honestly, she had to stop reacting to every person speaking to her. Her heart couldn't take it.

"Hi. Emma, right?"

"Yeah, you remember."

"Sure, I do."

Interesting, the girl had no problem identifying her with black hair. Of course, the hat covered most of it anyway and the pup holding the gift she had given him, was a dead giveaway. This time she got a good look at Emma standing there, rubbing a braid between her fingers, while her other hand pulled down a top that had ridden up. She was a tad on the plump side, and it looked like she was trying to cover herself. Lexy could relate as she pulled down her own tee. She'd put on some chocolate and pasta pounds during this last year of stress, but she felt sad that this adorable little girl seemed self-conscious at such a young age.

"Emma, please don't run off like that."

The same elderly lady hurried towards them. Her grey hair was twisted into a long braid that flew behind her. In the bright sunshine, Lexy got a clearer look and registered that she had the most beautiful face with twinkly eyes and glowing skin. Lexy guessed she was in her sixties.

"Sorry, Nana. Look. The puppy has the toy I gave him." Emma dropped in the sand and Asher approached slowly.

"Hello," Lexy said. "We met yesterday."

The lady's eyebrows rose for a second. "Oh, you changed your hair."

Lexy giggled. Guess it must be pretty bizarre to see someone with bright red hair one day, and black the next. "I did. I'm Lexy, by the way."

"And I am Meredith. We're staying in that cottage." She pointed to a bunch of trees. "Of course you can't see it from here."

"Oh, I didn't realize anyone lived there."

"Yes. Just recently."

"Did you give him a name yet?" Emma asked.

"I just named him Asher."

"Cool. Never heard it before."

"It means happy and blessed."

Emma patted his head. "I like it. Hi, Asher."

As if performing for a crowd, the little pup started jumping around and chasing his tail. Round and round he went until he stopped, staggering a little, while everyone clapped.

"Would you like to come back for some lemonade?" Meredith asked. "We were just going to have some."

"And cookies too," Emma added. "We baked them. Chocolate chip."

"Well, okay."

She really didn't want company of the human kind, but didn't want to stomp on their hospitality. Maybe having some people contact would be good for her. And homemade chocolate chip cookies sounded pretty great too.

"You sure now?" Meredith asked, raising her eyebrows.

"I'm sure."

Meredith led them down the beach to an opening that Lexy knew led up to the cottage. She wondered if the building was still called Yellow Rose, for it had yellow everywhere, walls, window framings, flower boxes. Except the door, which was painted green. She still couldn't see the building, but several yellow chairs faced the lake beside a yellow table with a large wicker box on it. Looked like the yellow theme prevailed.

"Take a seat. I'll be right back." Meredith walked toward the path leading to the cottage.

"Do you need some help?" Lexy asked.

"No, no. I'm fine."

"Pssssst."

Lexy looked over at Emma, who had her finger pressed against her lips.

"Can I show you something?" she whispered.

"Sure."

"Follow me."

Emma led her around a tree off to the right of the picnic table. "See that pretty bush there?"

"The one with the purple flowers? The lilac bush?"

"Yes. Lilac. I forgot the name." She squatted. "Look."

Lexy picked up Asher so he wouldn't topple over anything and glanced where the girl was pointing, bending down to get a better look.

"A cocoon. A cocoon," Emma said softly, bouncing up and down.

Lexy moved closer and sure enough, under a leaf hung a cocoon.

"Guess what?" Emma said.

"What?"

"A butterfly is going to come out of that, and Mommy loved butterflies."

Emma's eyes were wide and filled with excitement. Lexy also registered the fact the little girl was sharing something very important with her.

"I love butterflies too. They are so beautiful. Thanks, Emma, for letting me see this."

"Well, I saw the butterfly on your shirt, so I thought you'd like this."

"You're right. I do."

Lexy'd forgotten her shirt had a tiny butterfly on the sleeve, a symbol of the designer. This girl was very observant. She'd even found a cocoon where most people wouldn't have even noticed.

As Emma continued to watch the cocoon with great intensity, Lexy wanted to ask about her mom, but didn't want to break the moment.

"Emma, where are you?"

"Oops, Nana likes to see me at all times. I throw my ball here during the day so I can run over and check it out fast with no one knowing."

Smart girl. But why not share it with her Nana? Hmm ... interesting.

They hurried back around the tree.

Meredith was holding a pitcher of lemonade, and a plate heaped with cookies sat on the table.

"Oh, good, you're here." She opened the wicker box with the other hand and pulled out glasses.

After she poured, they all sat.

"I brought down a dog cookie." Meredith pulled it out of her pocket and handed it to Emma. "But you must ask permission to give it to him."

"Can I, can I?"

"Of course you can." Lexy enjoyed her excitement.

The pup had come alive again and was doing his thing, wandering around sniffing, checking out his surroundings.

"Here, Asher." Emma squatted down beside him. He gobbled it in ten seconds and followed her back, probably hoping for more.

"See, we made these," the little girl said, passing her a cookie. "I added lots of chocolate chips."

Lexy took a bite. "Yum … they're good."

"Look it."

Lexy swung her head to the side.

"A white butterfly. How beautiful."

Emma watched it until it flew away. The girl definitely had a thing for butterflies. In a way, Lexy did as well, loving the whole hiding away and emerging even more beautiful cycle. Maybe that would happen to her after this time of quiet. She choked back a laugh. Okay, with a pup and now a little girl next door, maybe not so quiet. But guess she could pretend she was just living in a bigger cocoon, sharing it with others.

"Can I play with Asher again?" Emma jumped up.

"Sure."

Lexy leaned back, stretched out her legs, feeling at peace for a change, as she watched the little girl and pup play. Asher had really warmed up to her.

"She's enjoying the dog," Meredith said. "Thanks for indulging her."

"She's gentle with him and Dr. Dan said Asher needs to socialize."

Silence.

Lexy closed her eyes, feeling the warmth of the sun, a gentle breeze brushing across her face and loving not hearing traffic and horns.

"You seem sad."

Opening her eyes and sitting up, Lexy looked over at Meredith. She thought she'd been holding in her turmoil and panic well. Hiding under a pretense of peace.

"Just a lot on my mind." She squirmed around on her chair.

"Sorry to interrupt. I didn't mean to interfere. Guess my concern overruled my common sense."

"No problem." But no way was she going to talk and possibly leak who she was.

Meredith remained quiet again, which Lexy liked. She also didn't delve into the older woman's life as to why they were out here alone and where was the girl's mom. They sat in silence, a rare thing.

Oh, no.

First one tear, then another.

Lexy jerked her head to the side, as more tears fell.

What was happening?

You're a big crybaby.

Seemed as if Meredith's gentle, concerned presence had somehow lulled her into safety where she let loose.

"Go for it, dear. Let yourself feel," whispered Meredith. "Every tear you shed is releasing your reservoir of pain."

Really? Reservoir of pain? This woman was super observant, probably where Emma got it, but Lexy felt silly, yet a bit relieved.

Emma walked back toward them, so she wiped her face fast, glad the girl hadn't noticed.

Time to go. She got up and grabbed Asher's leash.

"Thank you for the lemonade and cookies."

"Thanks for letting me play with Asher."

"He certainly loves you."

"And I love him." Emma leaned in to kiss the pup.

"I'm here if you ever need someone to talk to," Meredith said softly.

"Thank you."

To her surprise, Lexy actually felt better. Guess Meredith was right. Somehow, her reservoir of pain seemed a little less. And it felt good.

Ten

"Do you have to go?"

Emma's sad, quivering voice pierced his heart. Chris looked over to see his niece running toward him, wrapping her arms around his legs, peering up at him, tears rolling down her cheeks. Kneeling, he pulled her into a hug.

"I do, honey. But you and Nana will have fun until I'm back in a few days and then I'll be here for good."

"I miss you when you go away."

He pulled back, wiping her tears with his fingers. "I miss you too. But hey, how about you walk me to the door, then I hear that you and Nana are going swimming."

"Okay."

She clutched hard as they walked hand in hand to the kitchen. He was so glad his mother was a terrific grandmother, because it sure made leaving Emma a little easier.

"Here's a bag of goodies for the road and beyond." Meredith handed him a large shopping bag. She grinned. "The brownies are on top."

"Thanks. You definitely spoil me."

"I figure you'll be busy packing and won't have time to cook."

"You're right. Thanks again."

Kissing her on the cheek, he hugged Emma again, got in his car and sped off.

Was he doing the right thing? Moving here? For good?

Reaching in the bag, he grabbed a brownie and took a bite. Just couldn't resist.

When tragedy struck, Emma had been so sad it broke his heart, a heart already cracked with pain. Understandingly so, but the depth of her feelings had crossed the line when it got to the point she didn't want to eat, go to school, or leave her bedroom. The only thing she still did was go to the community pool to swim once a week. She was like a little fish, irresistibly drawn to water, probably because her mom was on the swim team at college and arriving at the pool for workouts was something they did regularly.

Other than that, she was a mess. His mother, a skilled psychotherapist, had tried to help, yet neither of them could coax her out of her gloom. Even a little bit. Everyone grieved differently, and at their own pace, but he had been worried she'd never smile again.

And then Yellow Rose cottage came up for sale.

It had been a fluke that he had seen the advertisement. He'd been sitting in Starbucks drinking coffee waiting for his mother and Emma to arrive, when he had flicked through a newspaper lying there. A picture of the cottage jumped out at him and with it, a flood of happy memories which he hadn't thought about in years. He had been grinning widely when they'd arrived and he had noticed Emma's eyes squinting when he showed her the picture, telling her how he had stayed there briefly as a kid and had the time of his life. He would never forget what happened next and the conversation that ensued.

Emma had grabbed his hand. "Is that a butterfly painted on the door?"

"Yes. Yellow Rose is on Swallowtail Lake, named after the tiger swallowtail butterfly which is yellow and black. It looks like the one on the door."

He watched her eyes light up, as if an inner glow had been ignited.

"Did you see one?" She grabbed his hand.

"Yes. Many times. They hang around there so much, the lake was named for them."

"And did you swim every day?

"Yes. Every single day."

"Really? Like you can spend the whole day swimming if you want?"

"Yes."

Was that a smile?

His mother had looked over at him, eyebrows raised.

"Would you like to go see Yellow Rose?" he had asked, figuring she'd say no, her standard answer those days.

"Yes, please."

Capturing the moment, building on her excitement, the next day they'd driven there to check it out. Arriving, Emma, who had been quiet on the way there, had immediately asked, "Where's Swallowtail Lake?"

Chris had led her down the short trail through the woods and the moment Emma saw water, she ran to the edge of the lake, arms stretched out, head lifted toward the sun. Catching up, he was shocked to see her smiling the biggest smile he'd seen in ages. Immediately he wondered if this was just what she needed – a fresh start, a new town, a lake where she could swim all day if she wished. At least in the warmer months.

Next, they had taken a tour through the cottage and when he had shown her a bedroom on the top floor with a window seat that looked out on the water, she ran over and promptly curled up on it. He had left her there and hurried back down the stairs to chat with his mother. They had made a quick decision and she had joined him back in the bedroom with Emma.

While his mother observed, he had asked, "Would you like to live here, Emma?"

He had wondered what she'd say. Her usual 'no'?

To his surprise, Emma clapped her hands screaming 'yes' at the top of her lungs. She jumped up and threw her arms around first him, then Meredith.

So here they were, living in Yellow Rose cottage on the outskirts of the town of Willow.

He popped in the last bit of brownie.

He hoped it would all work out. He had been given advice about not making any huge changes after a loved one's death for at least a year, and it hadn't been quite that, but Emma's reaction was always the deciding vote. And she seemed to love it there.

But no more time to think. He had arrived at his destination. Pulling into the parking lot, he found a spot and stopped. Marnville school stretched before him, his home for five years teaching eighth-grade students. He had enjoyed every minute and was going to miss it.

Time to go in. Today he'd pack up his office. Tomorrow he'd grab the last couple of boxes from his apartment and he'd be back at Yellow Rose for good.

Chris grabbed his briefcase, the shopping bag, exited the car, and as he walked to the front door, a car pulled up and a familiar person got out on the passenger side.

Oh, no.

Jenny, his ex-girlfriend.

She hadn't seen him yet, and he sure didn't want to talk to her. He was just about to turn around, pretending he'd forgotten something, when a man leaned out of the driver's side and yelled, "See you tonight, honey. I'll miss you." He blew her a kiss.

Honey? Stunned, he stopped in his tracks.

They had only officially broken up three months ago, and she already had someone new? Someone who dropped her off first thing in the morning, called her honey, and said he'd miss her?

Shocked, he couldn't pull his eyes away as he watched her blow the guy a kiss right on back as the car drove off. And then she saw him too.

"Oh, hi, Chris." She looked at him, then down at her shoes.

"Hi. So you found someone new this fast?" He had no right to say that, nor judge her. They weren't together, and it was none of his business. His mind knew that, but his heart sure didn't. He needed to get a grip.

"Um, sort of. Heard you're moving away."

"Yes."

"Well, hope it works out for you."

"Thanks."

Her head rose, she glanced at him briefly, turned and walked away.

Noticing she headed to the front door, he hurried to the back of the school and entered through the gym.

Reality hit.

Seeing her still hurt.

They had worked together with students on the school newspaper, which had led to late nights and grabbing takeout. Eventually they'd started hanging out after hours, just the two of them, dating ensued, drawing them together as a couple. He enjoyed her company a lot, but was never quite sure their relationship would have lasted. Cracks developed, even before his niece came to live with him. But he had still been willing to give it a go. To see where it led. Then his life changed drastically and eventually she walked away. Ran, was more like it. What really got him was her reason for ending things. And doing it when he would have really appreciated the support and help.

He had to get over it.

Relationships were a thing of the past.

He had Emma to think of, more sandcastles to build, and another dream to pursue. He reached into the shopping bag.

And brownies to eat.

At least that got him smiling again.

Eleven

How should I end this book?

Lexy stared at her laptop, willing words to appear.

Nothing.

Flexing her fingers, preparing to type, she waited for inspiration to take over.

Nada.

The whole manuscript had been edited and ready to go – except for the ending. And she couldn't seem to finish it, no matter how hard she tried.

What made sense? What would tie the whole story together?

She had a few ideas, but were they the right ones? Forget about the fact this book could destroy her career forever if critics hated it. Another flop would do her in. What was in her heart? What did she want to say? And why was it so hard?

Forcing herself, she typed—two words—Sarah walked. That was it. She didn't even know where Sarah was going.

Maybe she was just tired from all the work she'd done the day before. Mowing the lawn, cleaning the cottage, finally tackling the bedrooms. Emotionally and physically draining, but so necessary.

Excuses, excuses. She was running out of them.

Getting up, she crept over to make sure Asher was still asleep. And he was, looking all cute and cuddly. She wished she could crawl in beside him and curl up for a nap too, but doubted she could fit inside the crate. Besides, she had no time to sleep; she had work to do. Yeah, right. No inspiration equals no writing.

Quietly opening the front door, she sneaked out, slowly shutting it behind her so it wouldn't bang. She curled up on her granny's rocking chair, which she'd found tucked away in a closet. Yesterday, she'd dragged it out, dusted it off, placing it exactly where it'd always been, where Granny used to sit, watching her swim and play in the sand.

The sun rising, seemingly out of the water, soothed her. The sky, with its orange, purple, pink, violet coloring, welcomed the day.

She sure wished she could feel the same.

Why couldn't she write?

Because you're a lousy writer.

Her deadline loomed before her, drawing nearer each day.

She leaned back staring at the water. Oh, how she used to love it here all those years ago. Memories popped up, trotting across her mind as if on stage, begging for attention. On the last day of school, she'd race home, her mom would have the car all packed and they'd drive to Writer's Bliss for most of the summer. Her grandparents would take a break from the farm and join them for a while, then full time when they retired and sold the farm. They were the best of times, living in their bathing suits, swimming for hours, taking the old rowboat out, fishing with Grandpa, baking with Grandma, chatting all the time with her mom, building sandcastles, chasing each other, having picnics. She could still taste those peanut butter and jelly sandwiches. And yes, she used to stuff them with pickles, too. Weird, but oh so good.

She often sat on this very beach in the evening, curled up with Teddy, her well-worn stuffed bear with the one ear, dreaming of her future. She pictured herself traveling around the world, but most of all becoming a writer. Yes, writing was definitely her passion. Words were in her blood, and every night as a kid, she had faithfully written in the notebook her grandpa had given her, describing what she did during the day. Exhausted, she'd fall asleep at night and wake up excited, raring to start all over.

Where had that kid gone?

The same question twirled round and round. Where had her joy of writing gone?

Somehow it had dwindled away during the writing of *Fairy Tale Crushed*. That book had sucked every bit of delight out of her. No wonder her readers didn't like it and critics slashed it.

She didn't like it, either.

And now she was all alone.

Her grandparents had passed. Her mother died over a year ago. No boyfriend either.

More pain.

Stop thinking about that.

The last time she was here was when she was ten, the summer her mom got sick.

Don't think about that, either.

She should write about all the things she didn't want to think about. It would fill at least two books.

She needed to get back to her writing. She couldn't let Ingrid down. Again. Her agent had stuck with her through all the down times and she owed her. Big time.

She needed to get some words down and form a chapter.

Now.

Standing, a wave of dizziness hit, and she fell back on the chair with a bang, feeling like she'd been hit on the head.

Whoosh!

Was it physical pain? Emotional?

Definitely the latter.

Bad reviews haunted her, crashing out of nowhere, sneaking up on her without warning.

"Worst book ever. How did this ever get published? Waste of time and money. I'm sending it back."

In the past, she'd gotten several awful reviews on her bestsellers too. They'd hurt because sharing her heart through words laid her bare to the world where unkind reviews sliced to her very soul. Her agent kept telling her to get used to it because there would always be readers who didn't like her books. True. But she didn't have to like it.

What really bothered her was that—admit it—in this case her readers were right. She had really let them down.

Her ex-fiancé's words rippled through her thoughts.

"Your books are too lovey-dovey. Too syrupy." Jake had crossed his arms, his stance widening. "You always have happy endings. They're silly. Stupid. Sappy. Life isn't like that. Have a relationship end for a change instead of shmaltzy books with too many kisses and promises of forever. A lot of your readers feel the same as me."

"Have you read any of my books?" Lexy had been surprised. She had always dreamed of having a fiancé who supported her by taking an interest in her work, but Jake never did.

"Of course not. But your bad reviews go on about how ridiculously mushy they are."

Mushy?

"But they're bestsellers."

"A fluke. Just a fluke. You need to write a realistic book with a not-so-fairytale ending."

And so she did. Exactly what Jake wanted. She scrapped her own ending and substituted his.

And critics went wild.

His version failed. Drastically.

Hard to believe she'd achieved her dream of becoming a bestselling writer, only to have it collapse around her.

Deep breath in, deep breath out.

Enough pain.

Somehow, she had to fix this.

Getting up slowly and carefully, tossing off any bouts of dizziness, she walked into a wagging Asher.

"C'mon sweetie, let's go out."

Unlatching the crate, they headed outdoors so Asher could do his business and explore, checking out any smells that might have appeared overnight.

Coming back in, they got breakfast and while her pup played with his favorite toy—the stuffed lamb, of course—she sat in front of her computer again, willing words to appear.

Wait a second.

An idea formed.

She knew what she needed to do.

Jumping up, she raced to the kitchen where she had left her briefcase. Opening it, she pulled out *Fairy Tale Crushed* and curled up on the couch in the living room. Asher put his little paws on her knees, wanting to join her but not being able to jump that far. She scooped him up and he curled beside her, tired already from his burst of energy.

Her mom often said when life was a mess, retract, and start all over at the beginning. The beginning for her was this book. She needed to re-read it again—supposedly being called part one—and then look at what she'd written in part two so far. Hopefully, studying this book, in a place of peace, would lead to a conclusion. Finally.

She had to keep reading. Keep searching. And somehow understand her hesitation about adding an ending.

Immersing herself in the love story of Sarah and Nick, she reached the part where they declared their love for one another. Reading this slowly, deep in reflection ... bang!

She looked up.

Bang!

What was that?

Twelve

Oh, no.

A knock at the door?

Fear grabbed on and Lexy's heart raced so fast she wished she'd invested in a defibrillator.

Jumping up fast, she almost tripped over one of the couch legs. Great. So much for being quiet. Tiptoeing to the window, she knelt and peeked out.

A man, bent over, so she only saw the top of his head.

Blond hair.

A reporter? Was there a camera? She couldn't see. Not going to chance it.

Stepping back, she picked up Asher, threw on a hat and sunglasses, and rushed to the back door.

Another knock.

"Lexy, Asher. You there? Can I visit you?"

Wait! She stopped. She knew that voice.

Rushing back, she opened the door, leaving her hat and glasses on, still in disguise mode. Emma stood there, grinning widely, holding up a bag.

"Hi there." Her pigtails swung around her as she reached up to pat Asher.

"Well, hello." Lexy glanced over at the man standing beside her, figuring he was her dad.

"Sorry to bother you." He looked a bit sheepish.

"Yeah, I made him come," Emma said. "I have a present for Asher."

"Oh, well come on in." Lexy stepped to the side, putting her pup on the floor. Emma immediately plopped down and pulled a stuffed bunny out of her bag. "Can I give this to him?"

"Yes, of course." Lexy pointed at his tail. "Look at how excited he is."

Emma held the toy out to the wiggling pup. Asher grasped it, shook it, and ran around the living room, Emma behind him chuckling.

"Sorry, again, for arriving unannounced." The man's voice was deep and apologetic.

Lexy raised her head, pulling off her sunglasses, this time taking a good look. He was certainly tall. He turned to look at her and...

Falling into someone's eyes was an expression Lexy had never understood – until now.

He had the most stunning pair of big blue ones. The kind that were bright, clear, and direct and made you want to confess something. Actually, that would be something Wendy would say to get a rise out of someone. She maintained some people had such honest eyes she felt that every time she saw them, she should tell them something she'd normally hide. Confess a flaw. He reached out his hand for a shake.

"Chris Leverton."

She shook. "Lexy." She had a hard time pulling her hand away. His felt warm and strong and safe. Really? She sensed that after one shake?

"I have cool treats for Asher too." Emma reached again into the bag. "See?" She held up a sack of what looked like dog cookies.

Lexy was glad of the interruption.

"They're safe," Chris whispered.

"Can I give him one?" Emma asked.

Lexy saw the bag had the name of the local pet store on it and knew they'd be okay. Not to mention they had her dad's approval.

"Sure, go ahead. He'll love one."

She opened the bag, dug one out, and held it up. Asher dropped the toy and ran over.

"Emma insisted we buy some goodies and the toy and bring them over." Chris shook his head. "I couldn't get her mind off the pup. Hope we're not bothering you too much."

"Aww ... sweet. You're not bothering me at all."

"She loves that dog. Asher is all she talks about."

"They certainly are cute together."

For the second time, Lexy had to pull her eyes away from him to stop from staring. And for some odd reason, she wanted to reach up and touch his hair.

His hair? Strange. She'd never even wanted to touch her ex-fiancé's coif, which was always full of some kind of greasy product.

What was with this guy? She'd seen tall blond men before. But not those eyes. And how strange that she felt that bizarre pull towards him. As if somehow she knew him.

Watching him hunker down to pet her pup and noticing how gentle he was—smack—it hit her. Like a slap on the face.

She did know him.

She stepped back shaking, as a kaleidoscope of dripping ice cream cones, cotton candy, running on the beach, shooting hoops at the center, tripped across her mind.

Closing her eyes, she pictured a young blond boy, full of life, mischievous and fun. She remembered his hair was long and always falling in his face and it drove her nuts. She used to pull it back so he could see, or so she could at least witness his expressions. She'd even held his hair off his face when he drew the most beautiful horse she'd ever seen for her mom's card. And here he was standing beside her. The kid who'd helped her. Twenty years ago.

What was his name?

Oh, right.

Chrissy. She knew he went by Chris, but she'd tease him by calling him Chrissy to get a blush out of him.

He was her buddy back then, and they'd been inseparable. She couldn't believe that standing before her was the same guy she'd been thinking about a few days ago when she saw the center was being sold. You'd think the fact he'd introduced himself as Chris would have been her first clue. She had once adored him.

"Are you okay?"

Her eyes popped open and Chrissy/Chris was staring at her. Yep, him for sure. She recognized that concerned look.

"You're not going to faint or anything?" He reached out as if to grab her.

She backed away. "I'm okay."

Heat burned her cheeks as she caught herself staring at his lips.

Yes, he had even kissed her. Her first kiss from a boy. Mind you, on the cheek, but still her first. In truth, she wasn't even sure he meant it intentionally. She'd fallen off her bike and he had helped her up, worried as anything, and somehow his lips had touched her face. Might have been purely accidental, but even though at ten she'd thought boys were still icky, she really hadn't minded.

She started to say something, to tell him who she was, to see if he remembered, then stopped. She was being anonymous these days. No way was she going to break that for anyone. And besides, he wouldn't recognize her with short black curls. That is, if he could see anything under her hat. Back then, her hair was florescent red and she had braided it much like Emma did, to keep it out of her face. She also went by the name Alex. She just wished he'd stop staring at her. And why was he squinting?

"Do I know you?" He took a step back, eyeing her up and down.

Oh, no. Divert, divert.

"Is this a pickup line?" Oh, what a stupid thing to say. Of course, he wasn't flirting. No vibes going on there, for sure.

He stepped back fast. "No, no. Sorry to make you think that. I just felt that I had met you before."

Was he blushing?

"Nope. We've never met." What a liar she'd become, but at least he let it go and turned away to watch Emma and Asher. He was probably insulted at her stupid accusation.

She was still surprised to feel such a powerful pull toward him after twenty years. After all, she'd only known him for two weeks. Of course, that mop of blond hair was fashionably cut and he was definitely more filled out than when a kid. Quite muscular, as a matter of fact. Not that she'd really noticed or anything. Darn. Was she blushing now?

He also had a daughter and obviously a wife.

She needed to stay away from him. Not to mention, it also might be hard to keep lying to him. Distractions were definitely not on her agenda, and oddly, her urge to touch his hair was way too strong and over the top.

This time, not because it bugged her.

Forget him.

Fast.

Thirteen

He found his redheaded girl.

Chris' heart raced as he followed Emma back to Yellow Rose. Halfway back, she started skipping and he joined in, feeling lighthearted for a change, pretending to be a kid again, just making sure he didn't trip.

"You're being silly, Unca." Emma shrieked, pointing at his twisted feet.

Yeah, he wasn't too good at the whole skipping thing.

"Hey, I think I'm amazing at this." Hamming it up, he pretended to stagger, and Emma shrieked even more.

"I'll show you." She gave him a mini tutorial and they continued to skip, this time more in sync. He felt he could fly if he tried, still in shock, but good shock.

He just couldn't believe it.

His long-ago buddy was back. The impish, mischievous kid he'd had a crush on. Just a little one, though. At ten, he hadn't been too fond of girls.

The black curly hair threw him off, plus the huge hat and sunglasses, but he would never forget her smile, her laughter, her spunk. And he had even kissed her once. On the cheek, of course. He had been so worried when she had fallen off her bike that he gave her a little peck on the cheek when he helped her up. More in relief that she was okay. Of course, he came from a long line of cheek kissers, especially his granny, so not much to it. Besides, back then he thought her lips were funny looking, always curled up in a smile, even at rest. He used to tease her about that.

She was definitely Alex, even though she identified herself as Lexy.

And to think she'd been on his mind just a few days ago.

Had he conjured her up? Fabricated her? Dreamed the whole scenario?

He had almost blurted out her name, but she didn't show any signs she knew who he was, so he kept quiet. And when he suggested they knew each other, she'd flat out denied it.

Odd.

She'd changed her name and obviously dyed her hair, so something was up. But maybe she genuinely didn't remember him. Maybe those two weeks had meant nothing to her.

Had he changed that much?

Could be.

His hair had been longer as a kid, unruly, just plain messy. It drove Lexy crazy because she could never see his eyes and one time she even brought an elastic and tied it back.

But Lexy was Alex. Definitely. No doubt whatsoever.

"Unca Chris. Unca Chris. Let's run. Race you to the water."

"I'm coming. You better get going."

Emma picked up speed and hightailed it to the edge of the lake, getting there first.

"I beat you. I beat you." She jumped up and down, flapping her arms.

"You sure did." He faked panting hard. "How about a swim?"

"You don't have your bathing suit on."

"My shorts will do."

She pulled her shirt off. "Look it. I got my strawberry suit on."

"Your favorite one." She looked so cute with eyes aglow with excitement. He wanted to remember her like this forever.

"Let's go." She took off into the water.

He ran after her, splashing around, enjoying watching her swim. She was good at it and the other day had asked for more lessons, so he had enrolled her in classes that would start up soon. Swimming was definitely her safe place.

"Yoo-hoo. Lunch is ready."

Chris looked back to see his mother on the shore. He waved. "We'll be right there." He swam over to Emma, floating on her back. "Are you hungry?"

"Yep. Race you back to Nana."

She was really into racing these days.

"This time I'll beat you." He chased her, once again pretending to fall, never tired of hearing her giggles as she helped him up.

"Guess I'll have to teach you to run, too." She was very patient with him, as she pulled him to shore. Meredith looked ecstatic, probably as thrilled as he was that Emma was a much happier little girl these days.

As they walked up to the cottage, Chris trailed behind, as once again thoughts of Alex/Lexy swarmed him.

He couldn't get over finding her after all these years and right back where they'd met. He had always thought she was cute with those flaming red pigtails flopping around her face, but she was now breathtakingly beautiful. She still had that radiant glow about her, shiny eyes, and a smile that always made him want to smile right on back. And those lips. They weren't funny-looking anymore. No way. She was much taller than he would have imagined. He could no longer call her squirt like he used to. Also, the little girl he knew always had a huge reservoir of kindness that encompassed everyone she met, and rescuing a puppy was so like her. And of course, she'd have all the compassion and patience in the world to allow Emma to play with him.

He noted an element of sadness about her, particularly in her hunched shoulders, and if he looked at her when she wasn't aware, her eyes looked teary. He wondered what that was about.

Maybe if he saw her again, he could jog her memory. He'd like that. A lot. He'd love a friend right about now, especially one he'd had such fun with in the past and had once thought they were kindred spirits.

But she was hiding out for some reason. Changing her name and appearance seemed pretty serious. Drastic, even.

Was she in some kind of trouble? Needing a break from something or someone? Running away?

He hoped to discover what was up. Not in a nosy way. He just wanted to help someone who had meant a lot to him once and, obviously by his glad reaction to seeing her again, still did. Of course, she might not need help, but he'd love to be there for her. Only if she wanted that, of course. Time would tell.

Fourteen

"C'mon, Asher. Off to the vet we go. You can bring a stuffed toy."

Lexy watched as he ran over to his toy box filled with gifts she'd given him. Ignoring them, eyes sparkling, he grabbed the lamb, then the bunny, going back and forth until the lamb won out. Looked like he enjoyed Emma's choices way more than hers, which created a sweet bond between them. Fine by her. Hopefully, he'd be able to see his pal when Chris wasn't around. Especially since she planned to avoid him.

Chris. Nope. Not going to think about him.

Doctor Dan had called to see how the pup was doing and wanted them to drop in so he could take a look. She stuffed all her hair under her hat, not wanting the doctor to think she was crazy at the change of color. Attaching his harness, hooking on his leash, it hit her that she smiled more these days, laughed easily, and woke up excited to see her pup and greet the day. Asher was like a tiny little angel saving her life. He truly lived up to his name—a blessing.

"Let's try out your puppy car seat." She was amazed at the fact they had such a thing and was impressed at how it clasped to the seat and even had a strap to tether the pup to it.

"Here you go." She lifted him up and into it. Asher looked quite proud of himself sitting as if he were a celebrity waiting for a photo op.

They took off to the veterinarian's office. Once again, Lexy loved driving traffic free without continual noise, honking horns, and crowded roads.

"Aha. We lucked out with a good parking spot." She pulled in, parked, unhooked Asher, snapped on his leash and he trotted in the door beside her.

"Well, well." Helen looked up from her computer. "Doesn't even look like the same dog."

She came out from behind her desk and Asher rushed to greet her, wagging away. She ushered him to the scale. "He looks so much better and he's put on a pound. Good work, Lexy."

"I'm just so thrilled to have him with me." She felt like a proud mama, almost tempted to pull out her phone and show photos of him.

"Nothing like a pet for company." Helen led them to one of the examination rooms. "The vet will be right in."

Lexy loved how inquisitive Asher was, sniffing around, checking out his surroundings. He was definitely not as nervous as the last time.

"Good morning," Doctor Dan said, walking in the door. "How is Asher today?"

"He seems fine. Oh, and I left the completed paperwork over there on the counter."

"Thank you." He checked him out and gave him a required vaccine. "He's doing great. And how are you enjoying him?"

"I love him. He's such a joy to have around." She tried not to gush, but knew she was doing so anyway. "Here's some photos I took." She couldn't resist.

"He's looking good and having fun." He leaned back, crossing his arms. "And so are you. How about we declare him officially yours."

"Really?"

"Really."

"I'd love that." She threw her arms around him. Pushing back, embarrassed, she said, "Sorry. I'm just so excited."

"Glad to see it. I was also wondering if you would be interested in taking obedience classes. A really good dog trainer lives not far from you. And since you've never had a dog, it might help."

"Great idea."

He pulled a card out of his pocket. "Here's her number."

"I'll be sure to call." She stuffed it in her back pocket. "And thank you so much."

She led Asher out, waving goodbye to Helen, who was on the phone.

Joy bubbled. A joy she'd never felt, coursing through her veins, bursting through her heart. Lexy picked her pup up and hugged him. "You're all mine now and we're going to have so many adventures together." He licked her face. "I take it that you're content too? Well, you're going to get more so. Next stop, the pet store. Might as well leave the car here and walk."

She put him back down and Asher reveled in all the new sniffs. The five-minute walk took twenty, but Lexy didn't care. Everything was new to him, and he needed time to explore. Finally reaching the store, she walked in with Asher running back and forth, just beside himself with all the smells. Lexy picked up a few more treats, toys of course, and even found a small plaque that said, 'Our first home together.'

Perfect.

"You're new here, right," the elderly clerk said, as she filled two bags with more treats and toys.

"Yes. Guess I bought too much."

"Well, you sure love your pup. My name is Chelsea. I'm the owner here. Janet, who waited on you the other day, said the store was so busy she didn't have time to give you this." She reached down and pulled up a bag. "I have a special doggy care package for you that we give to new pet owners."

"How kind. How much?"

"All free. It even has a tick remover in it. You might need that."

"Thank you."

"Just let me know if you need anything and if we don't have it, I can always order it in."

"Wonderful. Thanks, again."

Asher let out a bark. "Guess he agrees," Chelsea said.

On the way out, Lexy noticed a café across the street with outdoor tables. A lot of new businesses had sprung up since she'd last visited, and this was one she was thrilled about. Guess she had been too involved with her pup to see it before. She loved the name painted on the window in big green letter's – *Hope's Bakery.* A dose of hope was something she needed right about now, especially when it came to her writing. Missing her daily vanilla latte back in the city, she crossed the street, hoping they might have it. She was glad to see a *Pets are Welcomed* sign on the patio. Picking up Asher, she walked in to heavenly smells. Closing her eyes, she savored sweet wafts of bread, vanilla, coffee, cinnamon. Heaven on earth.

"So who do we have here?"

Lexy opened her eyes to a pleasant-looking lady behind the counter. A sign behind her advertised lattes. Thank goodness.

"This is Asher. I hope you don't mind that I brought him in while I get a coffee. I'll keep him in my arms the whole time until we sit out on your patio."

"Not at all. By the way, my name is Hope. What would you like?"

"I'm Lexy. So, you're the owner?"

"Sure am."

"Great place. Well, I'd love a vanilla latte and a chocolate chip muffin, please."

"Would you like some water for the pup and I believe I have dog biscuits?"

"Why sure. That's very kind of you."

"Not a problem. Go on out. Pick a seat and I'll bring it to you."

"Okay." Lexy pulled out her wallet.

"Nope. First one's on the house."

"Why thank you. Oh, and by the way, I love your name and the name of the cafe."

"Well, we all need a little hope in our lives." She grinned. "Or a baked good, or two."

"Sure do."

The town of Willow she remembered had been full of kind people. Looked like it still was.

Walking back through the bakery she noted how cozy everything looked. Red tablecloths, vases of assorted flowers on every table, and photos of the town covered the walls. A gift section was off in one corner. Such a warm, friendly place.

She pushed open the door, picked a table and sat. Minutes later, Hope brought out the food, coffee, and water.

"If you want seconds, let me know." Three customers walked in, so Hope waved and followed them.

Asher lapped up the water. She'd have to remember to bring some, and a bowl, everywhere she went. She took a sip of her coffee. Aww ... bliss.

"Hello there."

Fifteen

Instinctively planting her feet, half off the seat, ready to take off if the voice belonged to someone she didn't want to see, Lexy relaxed.

Chris stood there. Or ... she giggled. Chrissy. She felt like a little schoolgirl facing her first crush. Imagine giggling around a boy at her age.

"Mind if I join you?" he asked. Interesting how he still cocked his head to one side when waiting for an answer. He also looked good in a black tee and jeans.

"Go ahead." She couldn't very well say no. So much for avoiding him, but rudeness was not her thing. And who was she trying to kid, she was intrigued by her old pal. She looked around, still struggling to stifle her giggles. "Where is Emma?"

"Her grandmother took her to buy some clothes. The excursion was girls only, so I thought I'd grab a coffee while I wait." He grinned. "I'm warning you, though. She mentioned something about getting Asher some kind of outfit."

"That's sweet." She pictured him at the carnival with tiger tail ice cream smeared around his lips. He said it made him strong and roared like a lion for the next five minutes, trying to prove it.

She had to stop these reminiscences, which were just too darn adorable. He had been such a cute kid. She needed to shove them in the past and focus on the now.

"You look tired. If you watch Asher, I'll pop in and get you a coffee." She had to get away for a second to gain control. "Or anything else you'd like."

"Oh, I can do that. I don't want you waiting on me."

She handed him Asher's leash. "Please, if you watch the pup, I'll get it." She jumped up. "What do you take in it?" She knew his favorite ice cream flavor, what he liked on his pizza, but of course, they never drank coffee back then.

"Black, please."

She took off before he had a chance to say anything else.

"Where's your pup?" Hope asked.

"Chris is holding him."

"Chris Leverton?"

"Yes."

"Oh." Her eyebrows raised. "A friend of yours?"

"Not really."

Hope poured coffee in a mug. "Here, I know he takes it black and also I'll add a brownie. His favorite."

"Thank you. How much?"

"Still on the house, seeing as he's your guest."

"You are very kind."

Lexy walked back to the table, touched at Chris cuddling the pup.

"Here you go." His eyes lit up at the brownie.

"How much do I owe you?"

"Nothing. A Hope freebie." She took the pup from him, plopped back down, and put him on the ground to continue his sniffing mission.

"Consider yourself special, then."

"Well, I plan on leaving a big tip to cover it."

"Good idea. I'll add to it."

They drank and ate in silence. Lexy still trying to control herself as memories continued to surface of Chrissy wrapped in seaweed emerging out of the water, pretending to be a sea monster, always trying to get a rise out of her. Or scare her, which happened in that case. Or he'd put his water goggles on and jump out from behind a bush, laughing at her screams. Mostly she faked being afraid, wondering how far he'd go to freak her out. Pretty far, she discovered, picturing him in a tree, a gorilla mask on his face.

Sigh. Sure looked like she couldn't get rid of past thoughts of a more joyful time.

"I'm sorry you felt I was using a pick-up line on you the last time I saw you," he said. "It's been bothering me. You see, I really did think I'd met you before."

Oops. She jumped out of her reminiscing. Glad to, as a matter of fact. She was probably grinning like a fool. His gaze was direct, staring at her, willing her to speak the truth. Or that was what she felt. Once again, should she just tell him who she really was?

"Sorry, I didn't really think it was a pick-up line. I was just being an idiot, and it was an unfair accusation." Yep, it was, but nope, she didn't trust him enough to share her real identity and besides, she had already decided to avoid him. Great decision since she was drinking coffee with him the very next day. "But I've never met you." She'd turned into such a liar. She thought changing her name would be just a mild stretching of the truth, without realizing it was just the beginning.

"Have you been in Willow before?" he asked.

"Passed through it a few times." Oh, oh.

"Lovely place." He sipped his coffee. "I stayed here years ago for a couple of weeks one summer."

"Oh?"

Silence. She needed to get off the topic of the past in case he clued in to her real identity. But she still figured she was safe. After all, her signature red hair was gone.

"Are you here for the summer?" Chris put his cup down.

"Yes. You?" Good, a focus on the present.

"I'm actually moving here. We had the cottage winterized."

"The same one you stayed at before?" Of course, she knew the answer but wanted to appear as if she didn't. She needed to throw him off the trail every chance she could.

"Yes." He popped in the rest of his brownie and chewed slowly. "Best brownie in the world, next to my mother's. Back to you. Where are you from?"

"Toronto. You?"

"Smytheville, a city a few hours from here."

Lexy almost laughed out loud. Both of them obviously didn't want to share too much about themselves and were trying to get the other to open up. Or that was how it seemed to her. How futile. She wasn't giving an inch. Apparently, neither was he. But she didn't like the way he looked at her. Had he figured it out? Nah. She really did look different. And what was with his hair? Even with a shorter haircut, it could never stay in place, still flopped over his forehead, and she still wanted to brush it away.

"Hey, Asher. How are you doing?" She looked down at her feet. He was fast asleep, resting his head on her shoes. She figured she'd deflect from his questions by showing attention to the pup.

"Emma loves your dog."

"The feeling's mutual. Your daughter is very sweet with him."

"Niece, not daughter."

What?

"Oh, sorry."

"Well, she's like a daughter."

"Are you giving her parents a break by bringing her here?"

"Not really."

Silence. He didn't offer any explanations, and she didn't want to press him for one. If he wanted to share, he would. Anyhow, she still hoped to avoid him in the future. Most of the time, at least. Might be difficult, she now realized, considering they lived next door to each other and this town was small.

A loud ringing cut through the air. Chris' phone. He looked at the screen.

"Gotta go. The shopping spree is over."

Whew.

He put some bills on the table and left fast, but she lingered, eventually taking the cups in and leaving a tip under them, running out before Hope noticed.

Driving home, Lexy sneaked another look at the recreation center, deciding to pull in.

"Hey, Asher. Humor me. Let's just walk around a bit."

He trotted beside her as they slowly made their way around the building. Climbing the stairs to the front door, they sat. She remembered the annual carnival every summer, a fundraiser for the center to help upkeep the many programs. Both the beach and the center held numerous events that day and she'd volunteer to help, loving meeting all the people who came from all over to join in the fun. She wondered if they still had it. It had once been a huge highlight for her.

And what happened to Chrissy?

Back then, he was so fun-loving. Now he seemed hardened somehow. Oh, sure, he still seemed super nice and obviously loved his niece, but a lot of pain radiated from his eyes.

She knew this for a fact, because they matched her own.

He tugged at her heartstrings, but too bad she'd never find out why. He was off her list of people worth knowing. He was just too much of a draw for her, and she needed solitude and peace. She also needed no extra interruptions that would get in the way of her writing.

Hmmm... so he wasn't married? Maybe?
Forget him. She had to stop thinking of him.
"Come on, Asher, let's get home to our safe place."
Writer's Bliss was where she needed to be.

Sixteen

Was Lexy pretending she didn't know him?

Once again, Chris was confused.

He thought he'd try jogging her memory at the cafe and was sure he saw a hint of recognition in her eyes. At least, just before she dropped them, looking down, an aura of mistrust circulating around her. Of course, that could have just been only in his mind.

Chris hit the steering wheel in frustration.

He'd given her every opportunity to tell him who she was. Again. After all, he still had the same name, the same color of hair, stayed in the same cottage, but she kept throwing it back to him.

Sadly, she must really not remember him. He had to face the fact those two weeks had only meant a lot to him.

"Are you okay?"

Chris glanced at his mother. "I'm okay." Her eyebrows knitted together. He was sure she'd grill him later. Then again, probably not. She was great at not interfering.

"Unca Chris, can we sing?" He glanced at Emma in the rear-view mirror. She was practically glowing these days. His mood instantly lightened.

"Sure. You pick the song."

"Goody. The wheels..."

They sang all the way home. Chris was glad of the reprieve from his racing, scattered thoughts. After all, Lexy had the right to go by a different name and being incognito was really none of his business unless she made it so. And she didn't.

"Can we go swimming now?" Emma asked as he pulled to a stop, jumped out, and released her from her car seat.

"Of course. You've turned into quite a dolphin."

"Yayyyy ... I like dolphins."

"Let's go get changed." He led the way to the cottage.

He never grew tired of seeing Emma's joy at Yellow Rose. What a different person she was these days. It soothed his heart and eased his own pain. A lot.

After changing into swim clothes, he hurried to the living room. No sign of Emma yet, but he was surprised to see Meredith still in her long skirt and blouse.

"You're not joining us?" Chris asked.

"No. I want to try out a new recipe for supper."

"But I don't want you to feel you have to cook all the time. I can always whip up something when we get back."

"Actually, I enjoy cooking."

"I know. But I don't want you overworked."

"Don't worry. I don't feel that way at all. I find it rather healing." Emma came flying out holding her duck floaty. "Now skedaddle, the both of you."

"Skedaddle?" Emma giggled. "Cool, I like that word."

Chris opened the door for Emma to go out first. "So does your nana apparently."

He looked over at Meredith, who gave him the thumbs up, then hurried to keep up with his niece. She was pretty speedy these days, as if she'd never learned how to walk, only run.

"Let's dog paddle out." She took off into the water, Chris right behind her, again enjoying her exuberance. Suddenly she looked up and flipped on her back to float. "Do you see that?" She pointed toward the sky.

He joined her, eager to see what had captured her attention.

"That cloud looks like a monkey," she screamed.

"Sure does." A long cloud tail reached out from a clump of clouds and stretched across the sky.

Content to float a while and watch the clouds, Chris' thoughts flicked again to Alex, or Lexy. He'd have to start remembering to call her that. Fascinating also, that someone he hadn't thought of in a long time claimed his thoughts. Memories surfaced he thought he'd forgotten. He used to make fun, in jest of course, of his friend's incredible zest for life but chose plain vanilla ice cream instead of something more exotic. She hated pepperoni but always ordered it on her pizza, picked it off and gave it to him, knowing he loved it. She'd chase waves and sunbeams, laughing, always laughing. And then ... her tears. Yes, he had seen her cry. He recalled finding her sobbing her eyes out one day. He'd been shocked but touched when she had confided in him. Come to think of it, she really was the best friend he'd ever had. He'd never connected with anyone like that ever again. The closest he'd come to having a similar deep bond was with his sister.

And she was gone.

And Lexy was here.

How strange. How wonderful.

Fate?

But instead of sharing memories and hilarious stories about their past and growing close again, she was hiding out. He felt he was walking on eggshells around her, especially if she felt he was getting too close to her secret. That was, if she remembered him at all. And again, he still wasn't sure she did.

He wished he could recall her last name, but at ten years old, it just wasn't important. Too bad because he could have done a Google search. Or checked social media, searching for answers.

"Ahoy, there." Meredith waved. "Supper's ready."

Chris pulled himself out of his thoughts and waved back. "We'll be right there."

Another item on his list. To get better at cooking. He knew how to concoct a few things; however, he was always on the run and would usually pick up take-out. But he didn't want his mother feeling she had to cook all the time, even though she enjoyed it. She had work of her own to do and he needed to pull his weight. She did way too much.

"C'mon, Emma, time to get out and towel off."

"Okay. I'm hungry."

They all walked back through the path in the trees to the cottage.

Beep. Beep.

Was that a car horn?

Startled he looked over and sure enough a car was pulling in. They weren't expecting anyone. As they drew nearer, he saw the driver. Oh, no. He knew her.

Jenny was here.

Driving a car he hadn't recognized.

"We got company." Emma pointed.

"Yes, we do. How about you run inside with Nana."

Meredith raised her eyebrows. "Yes, Emma, let's get ready to eat. You need to wash your hands and change out of that wet bathing suit."

"Okay. My belly's growling."

Good. He was glad she was hungry because otherwise she'd be wanting to know who it was.

Chris walked over as Jenny got out of the car.

"What are you doing here?" He couldn't even summon up an ounce of joy, not sure at all how he felt about seeing her. Hurt? Maybe. Indifference? Could be.

"What? No hug?" Her lips pursed into a pout.

He stepped back. "No hug. How did you find me?"

"Don't be silly. You showed me the picture of this place up for sale which included the address. I remembered it."

"Right."

She grabbed his hand, but he pulled it away.

"I made a mistake, honey." Her eyes darkened with an emotion he couldn't read. "When I saw you the other day, I realized that. I miss you. I want you back."

He was stunned.

Typical Jenny. Blunt and to the point. But all he could think of was the night she had appeared at his door, refused to come in, and stated, *"We're done."* She had turned and taken off, leaving him there shouting her name, begging her to come back so they could talk. He would never forget her ending things at a time when he was dealing with such horror in his life.

Could he forgive her?

Well, might as well listen to her. After all, she'd driven all the way there.

"Come join me in the back yard." He motioned to two chairs off to the side.

"Love to."

So she was ready to talk now. After weeks of trying to get her to meet with him.

More important.

How did he feel?

Did he even want her back?

A few weeks ago, maybe.

But now?

Seventeen

Lexy was disgusted with herself.

She couldn't get Chris off her mind.

Chrissy, actually. Not the adult Chris. Lexy didn't know that guy at all. He was a whole other story and not one she wanted to read.

But Chrissy. She hadn't thought about him in years and now he occupied her mind full time. His face loomed before her and one memory in particular haunted her. A place, actually.

She wondered if it still existed.

Was it even real?

Or was it just one of those memories that intensified over time, soaring out of imaginary status into reality.

She had to know.

"C'mon, Asher. Time for a walk."

He ran over, tail wagging, eager eyes, and once again, she was so grateful to have him in her life. Instead of her BFF, he was her

BFFF—best fur friend forever and game for anything. Lexy hooked his leash to his harness, he grabbed his lamb, and she headed out the door. Her pup took off toward the beach.

"Whoa, sweetie. Not that way." She turned towards the woods, making sure he followed. "Another new adventure."

Her pup trotted ahead, stopped in his tracks, and sniffed. He then dropped his toy on her feet, his signal for her to carry it, and went back to sniff again.

"What did you find?" She was always amazed at his discoveries. Sometimes they were gross, like a smelly stick washed up by the lake, but often he'd find a treasure such as a uniquely colored pebble.

Squatting, she stared at a huge butterfly. One she'd never seen before. Now, this was definitely a treasure. But what was it? The insect had an orange body and big wings with crescents on them. She wished Emma was there to see it, as she snapped a photo and couldn't resist scrolling on her phone to see its name. Aha. A moth. A cecropia moth. And so gorgeous. But they needed to let it be.

Standing, she scooped up Asher so he wouldn't bother it, but continued observing. It blew her away how unusual this was for her. When had she ever taken the time to just watch a moth or butterfly or bird and enjoy its beauty? Normally she'd walk by stuff, always absorbed in herself or her phone. And here she was, enjoying a stunning creature who obviously didn't feel too threatened by them, because he/she certainly wasn't taking off.

Amazing.

In the short time she'd been in Willow, she registered again that life sure had changed. She even felt like a different person – carefree, livelier, and more peaceful. Reaching up to toss her hair, a habit of hers, it hit her: she no longer had long hair. She'd forgotten. So she tugged on a curl instead.

"Okay, Asher. Let's not bug the insect anymore. Let's move away and leave it to get on with what he or she is doing."

After all, they were on a sleuthing mission.

Did it still exist?

Pushing branches out of their way, they continued walking, Lexy making sure Asher had a clear path. Drawing closer, she searched for an opening off to the right, wondering if she was right about the location. Was she?

Wait.

Lifting a large branch purposely blocking the way, and stepping over a tumble of weeds, she came to a stop.

Her eyes grew bigger. Her mouth dropped open.

It existed.

Her small refuge was real.

Exactly the same as she remembered it. Even better.

She sniffed. Yep, it still had the most glorious perfume arising from tiny blue flowers that circled the small clearing. And in the center was the big grey rock she used to sit on.

It wasn't just *her* place. Chrissy knew it existed and it had once been their secret hideaway.

She had one more thing to check out.

"Sniff away, little one." While Asher kept busy, she pushed more branches aside and there, carved into a tree, once again as she recalled, were their initials - A & C. Below were the words, 'Best Buds'.

Overcome with emotion, she picked up her pup and sat on the rock, closing her eyes. It felt like yesterday when she had awakened and found her mom gone. Her grandma explained how she'd gotten bad news from her doctor and went back home for treatment. Lexy had wanted to leave and go to her immediately, but her grandpa said her mother felt it best she stay with them. Upset, she had raced into the woods, wanting to hide away, and stumbled upon this place where she finally let loose all the tears she'd held in.

Somehow, Chris had found her.

Sitting beside her, he had taken her hand. She remembered being startled—after all her eyes had been closed—and she had looked up into such compassion that she could summon it all up even now.

"You okay?" he had whispered.

"No."

"Cry all you want. I'm here for you."

Asher squirmed in her lap, so she set him on the ground, still lost in memories.

That day, they had sat there a long time, and she had finally told him about her mom. That was when she discovered he was way more than just a fun friend, and had a depth of empathy about him, older than his age.

Before they had left, Chris had pulled out a penknife and carved their initials on the tree. When he finished, Lexy read aloud, "A and C, Best Buds."

Chris slipped his baby finger into hers signaling a pact, and said, "Always." She had repeated the word, cementing their friendship.

He had then got all excited saying, "Hey, how about we call this our 'Always' place. Our secret meeting spot. I've wanted one forever."

She had agreed, and when they left, they had eased down a branch to guard the entrance. From then on, they had met there frequently. Sometimes she talked, sometimes he talked, and it seemed to be good for the both of them. Plus, they loved the whole mystery surrounding it. Often, they'd leave little gifts for each other. One time, he had left her a package of red licorice, another a pretty blue stone, and a bag of toffee. She remembered it all.

Asher pulled on his leash and let out a little bark. "Okay, sweetie, guess you're getting bored. Let's continue."

Tossing off thoughts of her past, although hard, they walked further into the woods and a few minutes later, she could see the cottage where Chris stayed. It looked like it had a fresh coat of paint – still yellow but a softer hue - and a brand-new swing and slide set appeared off to the side.

Wait a second. Whoa. Someone was sitting there. She squinted, recognizing Chrissy and a woman. Ducking behind a tree, she peeked out. They were talking and gesturing, but she couldn't make out their words. Suddenly, they both got up and hugged.

She didn't realize he had a girlfriend, and a wave of sadness washed through her. She shouldn't be spying on them, though. Turning away fast, she retraced their steps, and they continued walking along the lake.

"Lexy, wait up."

She turned to find Emma running toward her, Meredith trailing behind.

"I got a present for Asher."

"You do?"

Meredith stood back, allowing her granddaughter to have center stage.

Emma held the bag out to Lexy. "I was on the way to your cottage to give you this."

Lexy looked inside and pulled out a blue doggy coat wrapped in plastic.

"This is gorgeous. Thank you."

"Chelsea, at the pet store, said this coat is very special. You see, you put it in cold water, wring it out and the dog wears it when the sun is really hot. It'll keep him cool. Can we try it on now? Please? To see if it fits?"

"Of course." She handed it back. "I'll give you the honors of unwrapping it."

"And can I go and wet it down? The water is cool. I checked."

"Go for it."

Excited, Emma pulled the plastic off, took it out, and ran to soak it, Asher right beside her.

"I hope you don't mind," Meredith said.

"Not at all." And she really didn't. "Emma is very sweet and Asher sure loves her. Besides, socializing with young children is good for pups."

Lexy noticed Meredith watching her. Intently.

"How are you doing? You were quite upset the other day." The older lady continued to stare. Maybe staring wasn't the word. After all, she was a very sweet person. More like looking at her with concern.

"I'm okay."

Pause.

Silence.

"By the way, I know who you are." Meredith reached over and squeezed her hand.

Eighteen

Lexy whipped her head around, yanking her hand away.
"What do you mean?"

"I heard you speak once at the Bluebell Bookstore in Toronto. I know you're the author Alexandra Ayers."

Her voice was quiet and gentle, rendering Lexy speechless. Should she deny it? Lie? Pack her bags and run?

"Sorry, dear," Meredith continued. "I'm just finding it hard to pretend. I recognized you right away in the pet store and even with the hat, glasses, and different hair color, you can't fool me. And I've read and loved all your books. I'm a huge fan."

Panic flared. "You won't tell, will you?" Lexy took a step back. "Of course not."

"Promise?"

"Promise. I've been trying to decide if I should let on I know or not, because I figure you have a good reason to be incognito. But I also sense you might need some help or at least someone in your corner rooting for you. A friend. Not to mention, I almost blurted your real name out several times."

Whew.

Lexy relaxed.

She intuitively believed this woman. After all, she was a therapist and used to confidentiality. Maybe it would be good to have a pal nearby. Someone she could talk about real things with.

"Have you seen the reviews of my latest?" Lexy asked.

"I have."

"Such a complete downer."

"*Fairy Tale Crushed* is just part one, right? I'm looking forward to your next book. Part two."

"Well, thanks." Lexy moved closer, worried her words might carry in the wind. "But that was made up after critics tore it apart. My agent calls it good public relations. Part two is to correct what she calls my error, making it look like I planned all along to have two books about the same characters."

"Do you feel you made a mistake?"

Nobody had ever asked her that.

"Well, I changed my original ending to suit my then fiancé. So yeah, I was an idiot."

"You're definitely no idiot and you're an excellent writer, Alexandra, or I should say Lexy. Don't forget that."

A tear dripped down at how kind she was. Darn. She was a mess these days. At least she was dealing with a lone escapee, not an onslaught. Wiping it away, she saw Emma running back and also Chris headed their way. He was by himself. Was the woman he was with earlier waiting back at the cottage?

"Oh, please don't tell your son."

"I won't." Once again, Lexy believed her.

"Here's the coat." Emma held it up. "All ready."

Asher was all wiggly and not too pleased at the prospect of wearing something. Lexy helped Emma put it on while Chris grinned, mouthing 'thank you.' The pup at first tried to pull it off but then got interested in a treat Emma pulled out of her pocket and completely forgot he had something on his back.

"Can we take it off now?" Emma looked up at Lexy. "I just wanted to see if it fits."

"Yes, go ahead."

One thing for sure, Lexy remembered that Chrissy was incredibly kind at such a young age. Looked like he was passing that trait on to his niece. She was very sweet and loving toward Asher, even concerned about leaving the coat on too long on their first try.

"How's it going with the pup?" Chris asked.

"Great. We're starting our first obedience class in about an hour."

Emma looked up. "Oh, can I come? Please?"

Lexy looked over at Chris. "As long as Lexy agrees."

"For sure. I'd love the company. Emma, why don't you just come with me right now. I'm picking up his stuff and leaving shortly."

"Yayyy..." She picked up Asher's leash. "Can I lead him back?"

"Of course you can. You've very good at this."

"I'll go get her car seat and meet you there," Chris said.

"Oh, right. I forgot I needed one."

"Yeah, I'm still little," Emma said. "Oh, I need my knapsack too. I'll go get it."

"Don't worry. I'll bring it too." Chris headed back to the cottage.

"Hey Asher, I can sit in the back seat with you." Emma clapped her hands.

"Yes, you can," Lexy said, answering for Asher. "He has a car seat too."

Emma squatted beside the dog. "I'm going to school with you."

His little tail wagged hard. Lexy thoroughly enjoyed watching the little girl talking to the pup. She did the same, so he was used to it and seemed to like hearing their voices. He didn't know what her words meant, but Lexy loved that he really responded to Emma. Looked as if she might need a friend too, noting her leaning over to hug him.

Lexy walked back to the cottage, trailing behind Emma and Asher. She felt as if she were still in a trance. Wow, she just couldn't get over the fact that Meredith knew who she was. Now that was unexpected and scary. She trusted her new friend would keep it quiet, but still felt nervous about the whole thing.

Hey, what was that noise?

A rooster crowing?

On the beach?

"What's that sound?" Emma stopped and looked around.

Oh, right. Her new ringtone. She'd forgotten she'd changed it from a love song.

"Oh, sorry. My phone." She pulled it out of her pocket. Okay, a rooster crowing is kind of weird, very jarring, but at least love lyrics weren't spouting off. She checked to see who the caller was. Her agent.

"Hi Ingrid."

"Any good news? Is the book finished?"

"Not yet. You'll be the first to know."

"I need it soon."

"I'm trying. Hate to end this fast, but I gotta go. Off to puppy school."

"You got a dog?"

"Sorta. He found me."

"Well, who knows. Maybe he'll inspire you."

"Maybe. I sure hope so. Talk to you later." Guilt surged. "Oh, and thanks again for always standing by me. I can't say that enough."

"No problem. I believe in you. Always."

At least someone did. Oh, and it looked like Meredith did too. Lexy sure wished she could believe in herself. But she really had to finish that book. If not for herself, for Ingrid. She deserved her full support.

First things first. She hurried to catch up with Emma and Asher who had forged ahead to the porch.

"You wait here, I'll just run in and grab my purse." Lexy hightailed it in the front door, tossing treats, water and a bowl into a tote. After locking up, she turned to see Chris installing the car seat right next to Asher's.

"Thanks." After he eased Emma in and buckled her up, Lexy slid Asher in. Her two babies.

"It's nice you're taking her," Chris said. "She's beyond excited. Oh, here." He reached in and handed Emma her pink knapsack. "Just some snacks and stuff."

Lexy looked up at him just as a blond lock of hair fell across his forehead. It took enormous control to keep her hand down.

"No problem. I enjoy her company." She jumped in the driver's seat fast, before she made a fool of herself. "See ya."

He waved, turned, and walked back toward the cottage.

Whew. A narrow escape.

So much for avoiding him. Guess that plan was a total bust.

Nineteen

Lexy pulled the directions to the dog school out of her purse, checking them one last time.

"You're not using the talking lady?" Emma asked.

"You mean the GPS?"

"Yeah, that's it."

"Well, the last time I did, Asher freaked out looking around for the other person. So, I figure I'll wait until he's older before I try it again."

"Oh, okay. I freaked out the first time I heard it too."

"It definitely takes some time to get used to it."

Lexy started the car and off they went.

"Can we sing?" Emma asked. "Unca Chris and I always sing in the car."

At first, she thought Emma said, 'Hunca Chris' and she agreed. He sure was a hunk. Then she clued in. Oh ... Unca. She was glad she hadn't said anything.

"Sure, go ahead."

"Old McDonald..."

Lexy joined in, singing as loud as she could. What fun to feel free, not caring if she was in tune or not, just having a blast. Asher joined in with an occasional little howl which left them both in stitches. She drove down a country road, turned right, and headed down another one, slowing when she saw the sign, Pamela's Dog School, with a sweet golden retriever performing a 'sit pretty' painted on it. Turning into the laneway, she drove up to a house with an arena attached to it.

"Look Asher. School." Emma bobbed up and down in her seat, her head twisting back and forth, taking it all in.

Three cars were in the lot, so she pulled in beside them and parked. After unhooking and helping Emma and Asher out, she led Asher to a grassy area for a potty break, then into the arena. A slim brunette hurried over.

"Hi, I'm Pamela. You're Lexy, right?"

"Yes, and this is Emma."

"Hello, welcome Emma, and this must be Asher."

The little pup wagged his tail when he heard his name.

"Sure is."

"Well, come join us. Each of you has your own station to work in."

She led them past a border collie, golden retriever, and a chihuahua, to an area where a small red cot sat beside several chairs.

"This will be your workplace and please direct Asher to sit on the cot. That will be his special place to hang out on."

He was so little he could barely get up on it.

"I'll help him." Emma gave him a gentle push while Lexy sat back looking around, wondering how she ended up in this world—a dog world—so foreign to her and right out of her comfort zone. But she was curious over how to train a pup and how the class was structured. Her heart revved up and the palms of her hands got all sweaty, as she registered how nervous she felt.

Could she do it?

Train a dog?

No, you can't.

Calm down. Doctor Dan loved all animals and wouldn't have given her Asher if he didn't think she was capable.

She could do this.

Maybe.

Oops, listen. Pamela was speaking.

Their instructor began the session by explaining her rules of etiquette. Lexy tried to take in the fact that dogs must always be on their cots, unless released by their owners, only one dog at a time enters and leaves, no interaction. Everything was set up to keep the dogs and owners safe so their pups could learn manners in a healthy environment. She glanced over at Emma and was startled to see she was writing it all down in a little notebook, which must have been in her knapsack. Lexy hadn't even thought of doing that. What an amazing little girl.

So, the first job of the evening was to teach the pups to stay on their cots, using treats to award them when they did. Easy-peasy, Lexy thought, until Asher discovered how much fun he could have if he just kept jumping off and running around the cot, thinking he'd created the best game ever. When directed back on it, his tiny legs worked hard but he seemed to love Emma helping him and he'd bounce around on the cot as if on a tiny trampoline.

Lexy glanced around and all the other dogs were sitting nicely. Oh, no. They were failing already.

"He'll figure it out," Pamela said. "Don't worry."

She must have read Lexy's mind.

And sure enough, he did. Learning eventually that if he stayed put, he got lots of treats. Lexy didn't know who was training who, but it all seemed to work out.

Next, the command 'sit.'

"This is fun," Emma burst out, sliding a treat over Asher's nose and head until he had no choice but to sit. Eventually she just had to say the word and down he went.

"Look, he's doing it when I tell him to." Emma clapped her hands.

"You're doing such a good job." Lexy loved seeing the little girl's eagerness and also loved seeing the spark in Asher's eyes when he 'got it.'

"You try it." Emma handed her a treat.

"Okay." She held the cookie up. "Sit."

To her surprise he did, and she joined Emma in clapping. Forget about being nervous, this was fun.

Next, 'recalls.' Lexy had no idea what that meant.

"This is extremely important," Pamela said. "Our dogs must learn to come to us when called."

Emma and Lexy worked as a team.

One held Asher back while the other crossed the room and called the pup. A couple of times he veered off but eventually learned he got a treat if he came right to them. Lexy felt exhilarated watching her little imp of a dog quickly learn how to do things on command.

She finally got it herself.

Dog training was more about training the human how to deal with their pet. How to raise a mannerly dog, communicate with them, build their relationship and create a strong bond. She enjoyed strengthening this connection, but what she loved the most was that Asher pulled her out of herself and all her issues. He gave her reprieves from her paranoias and fears. And having Emma as her sidekick was a huge bonus. Her enthusiasm was infectious, her joy pure, and Lexy found herself just as excited.

She'd have to thank Doctor Dan for suggesting this.

By the end of the hour, Asher was fast asleep, and Lexy carried him out.

"He's such a smartie," Emma said.

"Well, I think you're the smartie for helping him so much."

This time they didn't sing so as not to disturb the sleeping pup. Instead, they chomped down on peanut butter cookies which Chris must have added to the knapsack. When they arrived back at the cottage, they had to wake Asher to get him out of his seat.

They walked over to Emma's cottage where Chris and Meredith were sitting by the beach.

"Look it. Look it. I can make Asher sit." Pulling a treat out of her pocket, Emma said firmly, "Sit.' And he did.

"Way to go." Meredith clapped.

So that was where Emma got her love of clapping, Lexy thought. From her nana. An act of pure delight. She also noticed the little girl was yawning.

"Looks like you're tired," Meredith said. "And your bedtime is soon. Since tonight is my turn to read you a story, how about you say goodnight to the pup, Lexy, and of course your uncle."

Emma yawned again, kissed Asher on the head, hugged Lexy and Chris, and went to the cottage hand in hand with her grandmother.

Lexy was sad to see them go.

She didn't want to be left alone with Chris.

Or did she?

Twenty

"How did it really go?" Chris asked. "You were very kind to let Emma tag along. I hope she wasn't a bother."

"Oh, not at all. She was a big help. The class was loads of fun and for one whole hour, I was caught up in teaching Asher and didn't think or worry about anything else."

Was she babbling? She babbled when nervous. Oh, no. She thought she was.

"Are you worried about something?"

His concerned gaze almost undid her, but nope, she was keeping her secret. "Not really."

"Well, Asher sure seems content."

She looked down and her pup was fast asleep, his head resting on her shoe. She picked him up, cuddling him close.

"Would you like some lemonade?" Chris asked. "It's homemade by my mother. I have lots here."

Chrissy's favorite as a kid. Looked like it still was.

Should she stay? After all, she was avoiding him. Sort of.

Yes, no, yes, no.

"Okay." She sat, placing the sleepy pup on her lap, not being able to resist Chris' sweet face. Avoiding him was a great plan, but in reality, hard to do. Besides, having company was nice for a change, natural even, as if twenty years hadn't sped by.

"Would you like wine instead? I can run up to the cottage and pour you a glass. I haven't indulged much since Emma came to live with me."

"Oh, no. Lemonade is the best." Hmm ... why was Emma living with him? Should she ask? No, she shouldn't poke around. Then he'd feel he had the right to ask her more questions.

"Better yet. The sun's about to set. How about drinking it in a canoe?" He pointed to a red canoe tethered to their dock. She hadn't noticed it before. "The boat's Emma's, well her mother's. I brought it here the other day. We don't have to travel far. I mean, we can just paddle out a bit and drink while watching the color show. Asher will probably sleep through it."

Oh, it sounded wonderful. And she hadn't been out on a boat in years. They used to have an old rowboat they'd paddle around in until her grandpa declared it unsafe. Once upon a time, they'd had big plans to build a dock and get another one, but never got around to it. But she loved being out on the water.

Should she?

No. Yes. No.

"Yes." Once again, she couldn't resist.

Chris untethered the boat, helped Lexy in, and placed a sleeping Asher on her lap. He put a basket holding the thermos of lemonade and glasses in the center of the boat, then climbed in, paddling out a few feet. He poured and handed her a glass.

"Cheers." He reached forward.

"Cheers." She clinked her glass with his.

They drank in silence. Lexy leaned back, trailing her fingers in the water, enjoying the sun receding in a mixture of vibrant colors. Everything was quiet and still, with only the occasional tweet of a bird highlighting the show. Total paradise.

"It looks like a master artist took a paintbrush and colored the sky," Lexy said softly. "I love how it's different every time. Tonight features so many shades of purple. Just breathtaking."

Was she babbling again?

"Sure is."

"And we have the best view out here. Thanks for suggesting this."

"Thanks for joining me."

Was he staring at her? She wasn't sure in the dark, but she thought he was.

"You know, speaking of paint." Chris put his glass down and leaned forward. "The cottage you're staying in needs a coat of paint. I'm surprised the owners rented it like that."

"The building is a bit run down." She didn't want to admit she owned it because he might clue in as to who she was. "I've been slowly fixing it up, bit by bit."

"And the owner doesn't mind?"

"Nah. I think they're grateful."

"Well, if you need any help, I'm available."

"Thanks. I might take you up on it." Not ever.

"This sure is a peaceful place." Chris pointed to the sky. "And now the stars are peeking out."

"Stunning." Emma sipped her drink. "I can't take my eyes off them." Or to be honest, him. More than anything, she wanted to move closer, drawing comfort from him, like she used to with young Chrissy. Of course, back then she was a kid seeking solace from her worries about her mother. Now, a whole lot of attraction was going on, at least on her end. If she were looking for a touch of romance to inspire her book, this was it. A canoe, the sun setting, stars emerging, and a handsome guy close by. Swoon.

Stop it.

He has a girlfriend.

"You know, even though I was here for only two weeks years ago, I always remembered it," Chris said. "Private and peaceful. Just about perfect."

She was glad he was talking. It pulled her out of her thoughts of how much she wanted to run her fingers through his hair. Ugh. Get a grip.

"I used to hang around a tough little redhead back then," he continued. "You remind me of her."

Oh, oh. "Really?" She almost stood up to run, then remembered she was in a boat. "That's strange. My hair is black."

Did he know?

Did his mother tell him? No, she wouldn't do that. Time to go, though.

Chugging down the last of her lemonade as fast as she could, she put her glass down. "Well, I better get back. Asher needs to go to bed, and I need to do some..." Oops, she was about to say writing. "Reading."

She glanced at him, noting how sad he looked. Guess she'd been too abrupt about leaving. She felt like taking him to their 'Always' place, where they could be themselves, and asking him what was wrong. She'd love to give back to him what he had given her all those years ago.

"Oh, okay. Sure." Chris cut into her thoughts. "I'll get you home." He paddled them back to shore where Lexy almost jumped out, then reached back to get Asher.

"See ya," she said, as she hurried away, ignoring his raised eyebrows.

Don't think about him.

She wasn't capable of a good relationship. Even a friendship. Especially not when all she wanted to do was touch him. She had to keep reminding herself that he was not available but felt exhausted from wanting to be near him, then running from him, all at the same time. Besides, she didn't want him to know who she really was. What a great friendship that would be, using a fake name, and pretending to be someone else.

Guilt surfaced, remembering the hug she had witnessed with that woman in his yard.

She mustn't ever forget that. Not to mention she had been spying on him.

Hard to recall all that, when looking into his eyes.

Whoever that lady was, she was one lucky girl, though. Chris the adult seemed as wonderful as Chrissy the kid. She'd bet on it.

Twenty-one

What was wrong with him?

Why couldn't he just leave it alone.

All he did was scare her away.

Chris quickly tied up the canoe and watched Lexy walk to her cottage, until he couldn't see her anymore. Picking up a few flat stones, he started skipping them over the lake. It helped him think.

Really, what was he doing?

He needed to stop pushing her by hinting about their past. He was being selfish. But somehow when he was with her, he was transported back to that carefree ten-year-old kid and Alex was his best friend. He found himself relaxing around her and finding it hard reining in his thoughts and feelings when all he could think about was reconnecting with her.

He also couldn't stop worrying about her.

What was going on?

Once again, he wondered why she was pretending to be someone else. Why was her hair black, not red? Of course, she obviously had the right to dye her hair, but it seemed more like a disguise than a fashion statement. And he was sure now that she knew exactly who he was. As soon as he mentioned the redheaded girl she ran.

He looked for more rocks and kept on throwing. Wait. Why was he doing this? It only reminded him more of Lexy and their contests as kids to see who could skip a stone the furthest.

Anyhow, if she didn't want him to know, he should stay out of it. He kept telling himself that and then the next time he saw her he started digging again.

He had to put an end to trying to jar her into telling him the truth.

She had the right to hide if she wanted. She had the right to not acknowledge him. He needed to respect her wishes and boundaries.

Yawning, exhausted, he had enough. Time to turn in. Crazy how he felt drawn to go see Lexy even now, but he knew that would be ridiculous.

He walked back to Yellow Rose and when he opened the door, he could hear Meredith's voice. Emma had probably begged her to keep reading story after story and his mother was indulging her. He grinned when he heard them both imitating elephant sounds, knowing Emma was obsessed with elephants at the moment. Last week, it was tigers.

Opening the fridge, he pulled out ham, cheese, mayo and made a sandwich, carrying it into the living room, plopping on the couch that faced the window. This was his favorite spot, while his mother preferred to sit on the nearby rocking chair. They took turns reading to Emma and then the two of them would wind up here. Meredith loved ending her night reading fiction. "It's relaxing," she'd always say. Looked like she had one ready to dig into on the coffee table, but there was still room for his plate.

Putting it down, it slid right into his mother's book, heading for the floor. Grabbing the sandwich he managed to save it but ... bang.

The book fell.

He had meant to fix the uneven table legs but hadn't gotten around to it yet. He was glad they had a rug, so the noise didn't disturb his mother and Emma.

Reaching down to retrieve the book, his mouth dropped open. His heart thundered.

Lexy's face stared back at him.

He picked it up, staring at the photo on the back cover.

Long curly red hair, all smiles. Was he imagining it? He touched it with his fingers.

No, the photo depicting the author really was her.

Who wrote this?

Flipping it around, he found the name.

Alexandra Ayers.

His Alex.

He leaned back, still holding the book.

So, Lexy was an author. And his mother was reading her book.

Did Meredith know?

Well, if she did, she wouldn't mention it. She was good at keeping confidences and also, he had never told her of his suspicions about their neighbor. She also didn't know he had hung around a redheaded girl way back when, since he had never told her. He had been at Yellow Rose with his grandfather while his mother finished up a court case she was involved in as a witness. She'd have no need to hide the book from him because if it wasn't for the fact he knew her, he wouldn't have even given the photo a second look. The red hair really stood out.

Lexy also looked content.

Putting the book back on the table, he grabbed his phone, doing a search on her name. To his complete shock and utter surprise, hundreds of articles appeared, and he was able to read all about her last book and the bad reviews. Also, he found a ton of ridiculous articles speculating about her life but several of them appeared real. Her fiancé had apparently dumped her on national TV. Unbelievable. Chris wasn't one for gossip or messy stories, so he hadn't known any of this, even though it seemed like big news in the literary world.

No wonder she was incognito. She was probably hiding out from reporters. And critics. And maybe her ex. And all people in general.

And he didn't blame her one bit.

Now, it made sense.

He needed to back off. She didn't need him sleuthing around, trying to get her to own up to their past relationship.

Relationship?

Not really.

Barely an acquaintance.

But it had meant so much to him.

He was also convinced she knew who he was but probably didn't trust anyone these days.

But he'd love to help her. To hold her hand like he had so many years ago and tell her everything was going to be okay. Then again, he didn't even know if she needed anyone's assistance, and he shouldn't presume she did.

Maybe if she trusted him more, she'd confide in him. He sure hoped so. But that would be her decision. He was bowing out. Leaving it alone. Still hoping they'd reconnect at some point but not pushing.

He glanced over at the bookcase, seeing several other titles by Lexy. He checked to see which one was her first, pulled it out, and began reading. This might be the only way to feel close to her again.

Twenty-two

The end.

Lexy closed *Fairy Tale Crushed*, tossed it on the side table, and sat back in shock.

She wanted to jump up and down, scream her head off, and rip the book to pieces. But not with a wee pup attempting to jump up on the couch and not being able to make it. She reached down to help him, and he curled up on her lap, probably sensing how upset she was. But she could still scream on the inside.

What was she thinking?

Her main characters—Sarah and Nick—were in a toxic relationship. A horrible one.

Why hadn't she seen that before?

And to think she was going to end part two with declarations of love between them and a wedding. That was the usual way relationships ended in her books.

"Can you believe that Asher?"

He looked up, yawned, and she leaned down to give him a kiss. He was the joy of her life. To think if she hadn't come here, she would have never met him and now she couldn't even envision life without this little guy. He had captured her heart. His whole existence was all about love.

Love?

Fictional Nick couldn't love.

He was a complete and total narcissist.

Yes, her main male character was a narcissist. And she hadn't noticed. In the process of research over the years, she had read about narcissists and Nick Lorel was definitely one. He was an awful person. How had she thought he was the hero of the story? She had made him completely self-involved. And of course, narcissists 'love bomb' you – making you feel you're the most important person in their lives. When they feel they 'have' you, they slowly destroy you. That was what was happening in her book. The love relationship was all about what the male wanted. The female was just an accessory in his life, until she no longer fit the bill. Then she was discarded.

Restless, she placed Asher on a comfy pillow, stood and began pacing. Back and forth. Back and forth.

Woof!

Did Asher want to join her?

Placing him carefully on the floor, she continued to pace while he ran and picked up his stuffed bunny and followed her all around the cottage, tail wagging, having the time of his life. They looked like a small parade, a game to her pup. At one point he ran in front of her, pretending she was chasing him.

Back to her writing.

Throughout her book, Nick had suggested several times that Sarah change her hair and clothes to suit him. And to make it worse, Sarah had done what he said. When her character was upset about the possibility of losing her job, she turned to Nick for comfort. He pushed her away saying he had more important things to do than spend time comforting her. "You need to grow up and face the fact life is hard," he spouted off. He eventually took a job overseas and fully expected Sarah to drop everything and go with him. She said no. Smartest thing she ever did, except in Lexy's current first draft of her new book, she had her join him.

Her ex's idea was to have them end in a break up in *Fairy Tale Crushed*. Not because he read the book, of course. Just his jaded look on life about all relationships. But maybe the reason she decided to go along with his suggestion was a subconscious realization that her characters didn't belong together. Maybe? She'd like to think that somewhere deep in her heart, she couldn't allow this couple to stay together.

Except now her second book was bringing them back as a couple.

No, she couldn't allow that.

And to think she had insisted they print *Fairy Tale Crushed*, against their advice, eventually calling it part one. Part two was that Sarah sees the errors of her ways, marries Nick, and moves with him to provide readers with a happy ending. Guess her publisher didn't want to lose her plus her agent believed in her, pushing her book even though Ingrid wasn't a fan of it, and Lexy had promised her it wouldn't happen again.

She couldn't afford another flop. It would be career suicide.

Maybe the heroine could escape to a cottage like she did. Nope, her readers really did expect happy endings. That's why they hated her latest book. Maybe Nick could go to counseling, but nope, she had read an article about how narcissists don't do well in therapy. How could they? They believed nothing was their fault.

A great big groan rose out of her. Asher stopped and looked back, making sure she was okay.

"I am, sweetie. Just perplexed." Totally messed up was more accurate.

Next step: re-read her current manuscript and see if she could salvage this story. She needed to get a grip on it. But first she had to clear her head.

"C'mon little one. Let's walk."

He ran to the door, tail wagging, already understanding that special word.

Just as she was about to open the door, a knock hit hard, making her jump. Her heart pounded as Asher started barking, already showing signs of being a good watch dog. But who was here so early in the morning?

Lexy peeked out. Chris was pacing back and forth. She opened it fast.

"Is Emma here?" he burst out, hair sticking up all over as if he'd run his fingers through it many times and his clothes were wrinkled, thrown on.

"No, sorry, she isn't."

His hands flew up in the air. "I can't find her. She said she was going out to play on the swings, the next second she was gone and everything's my fault because I wasn't out there with her. I stayed inside making pancakes to surprise her."

"To surprise her? Is today a special day?"

He rubbed his eyes. "Yes, her mom's birthday and they always had pancakes on her birthday. I thought I'd continue the tradition."

Aha. A thought hit her.

"I know where she is," Lexy said.

"You do?"

"Yes, I'm pretty sure. Follow me."

Snapping a leash on Asher, she led him out the door, Chris right behind her. She hurried down the beach to Chris' picnic table, turning left at the tree. Sure enough, Emma was there, fast asleep. Just like she thought. She motioned to Chris to come nearer.

He hunkered down beside her. "Honey, are you okay?" Asher ran up and licked her face.

Emma blinked, reaching out to hug the pup.

"Oh, hi. Yeah, yeah, I'm okay."

Chris opened his mouth, Lexy figured to tell Emma off, so she touched his hand. "Shh... not now," she whispered. "Just wait." She knew she had no right telling him what to do, but this was Emma's special place, and she didn't want it ruined for the girl.

He whispered, "Okay," and quickly called Meredith to let her know where they were and that all was well.

Emma sat up. "Look it. Look it." She pointed to a large beautiful yellow and black butterfly sitting on a leaf beside an open cocoon. "I knew it. I just knew it. I knew it would be today."

Lexy squatted down to get a closer look.

"I knew Mommy would send me this today on her birthday. A swallowtail, right?"

"Yes." Lexy and Chris spoke at the same time.

"A tiger swallowtail," Chris added.

Once again, Lexy wondered what happened to her mom. But she knew this wasn't the time to ask and watching tears pour down Emma's face, had her joining in. Couldn't help it. She brushed them away, mesmerized by Emma's big wide eyes. This was really important to her.

"What d'ya think, Unca Chris?"

"Definitely from your mom. And so beautiful." Chris also wiped his eyes. "And a swallowtail too. This place is known for them, but I haven't seen one in ages."

This was the kind of stuff Lexy wrote about in her books. Things worked out, miracles happened, so it blew Lexy away to see it firsthand. The fact the butterfly appeared on Emma's mom's birthday was indeed one of those special marvels.

Chris leaned over and whispered in Lexy's ear. "Thank you. Obviously, you knew about this."

"Yes. She showed me the cocoon the other day."

Meredith joined them, hugged Emma, and they sat in silence until the butterfly flew away. Emma stood and waved.

"Say hi to Mommy for me."

More tears. Asher seemed to sense Emma's emotions and never left her side.

"She really is a sweetie," Lexy said.

"Thank you." Chris smirked, adding some humor to a tense situation.

"Not you." She pretended to be indignant. "Your niece."

"Unca Chris is sweet too."

"You're right."

He gave her a thumbs up. "So, is everyone ready for breakfast? I'm making pancakes with chocolate chips."

"Just like Mommy did."

"Right. Just like Mommy." Chris took hold of his niece's hand, probably afraid she'd take off again.

"You'll come too, right, Lexy?" Emma asked.

"Sure. Sounds good." How could she resist.

They started the walk back to the cottage.

"Promise me one thing, Emma."

"Okay, Unca Chris."

"Please never take off again. You scared us. Why did you never tell me about the cocoon?"

"I didn't want to make you sad again."

Perceptive child, Lexy thought. Pretty amazing.

"Well, I'm just glad you're safe."

"Me, too." Meredith grabbed Emma's hand and gave it a squeeze.

"How did you find it?" Chris asked. "I would never have even seen it."

"Mommy and I used to look for them on our walks. And I saw it when I was playing with my red ball and just kept watching it."

And kept it quiet.

Lexy was amazed she had been the only one to see it, all because she wore a shirt with a butterfly on it. Definitely an honor and she was going to treasure that shirt forever.

Chris whipped up pancakes and along with fresh Willow syrup, they were delicious. Conversation was light and airy with nothing said about Emma's mother. Was she still alive? Traveling somewhere? Working out of the country? Lexy's head was spinning with possibilities. As soon as they finished and dishes were done, Chris and Emma left for town to sign her up for swimming lessons.

"Would you like another cup of coffee?" Meredith asked.

"Um, sure." Asher was asleep so she might as well let him continue snoozing.

"How are you doing?" Meredith added milk, already remembering the way she took it.

"Well, I'm still stuck on my last chapter. I just can't figure out which way to go." She took a sip. "I seem lost and really doubting my thoughts."

Meredith sat, stirring her own coffee. "Well, interestingly enough, my book club is reading your very first book."

"Really?"

"Yes, we started way before you arrived. I suggested it because I love your books. But I was wondering if you would like to join us at our next meeting. Incognito, of course."

"You don't think they'll recognize me? After all, you did."

"No, I'm sure they won't. I mentioned that I had attended one of your signings and I was the only one who had been to one. It might be good for you to hear what your readers have to say."

Not a bad idea.

"But of course, you probably read all your reviews," Meredith added.

"I do, even the bad ones, but I'll think about it. I've never been to a book club, but the discussion would be interesting."

Meredith nodded.

Somehow this woman soothed her heart, and she seemed to be really supportive. She was helpful in a non-pushing way. Interesting how she had never met her when she hung with Chris that summer. She knew he adored his mom, and she also knew his father passed when he was young. Of course, he was with his grandpa, and they never visited inside each other's cottages but just played away the days, riding their bikes everywhere. After all, two weeks was such a short time, and it flew by.

Should she go to the book club?

Maybe.

Simply because she liked being around this woman. Maybe it would help her figure out where she stood on the writing circuit. Or at least help her find a suitable ending. She'd have to think about it. Lexy was at the point where she might try anything to pull herself out of her confused state when it came to ending her book. Somehow, she had to finish it.

With what ending, though?

Twenty-three

"Go on in, sweetie. The water won't hurt you."

Lexy chuckled watching Asher dip one paw in the lake then pull it out fast. This was the first time he had shown any interest, usually so preoccupied with all the sniffs on the beach. She slid off her sandals and waded in, loving the feel of the warm sun-kissed water and the soft sand squishing between her toes. She turned to face him.

"Here." She'd been practicing her pup coming right to her when he heard that command. Could he do it when water was involved? She watched with interest as he let out a few barks and started jumping around. He'd never seen her walking in the lake and this time he courageously put two paws in, then jumped back fast. He was so darn cute but not ready to plunge right in.

"No hurry. We'll try again later."

She walked out, shook the water off her feet, and stepped into her shoes. "Good boy, Asher, for trying something new." She patted him on the head and turned to head back to the cottage.

What?

She froze.

A tall woman carrying a child walked toward her.

A blue baseball cap covered her hair, and large sunglasses smothered her face.

Who was it? Why was she here? Didn't she see the no trespasser signs?

Did she have a camera?

Was the child a foil? So, Lexy wouldn't suspect a reporter?

Her muscles clenched as she immediately swung into fight or flight mode.

Definitely flight.

"Asher, come here," she whispered, picking him up, starting to turn to run fast to Chris' cottage. She figured they wouldn't mind if she visited them for a while.

"Lexy, stop. It's me, Wendy."

What?

She stared.

Her best friend was here?

No way.

Lexy had just spoken to her the night before and she hadn't mentioned coming.

The woman put the child down on the sand and pulled off her cap. Her long blonde hair fell around her shoulders.

"See? Me."

She also recognized the dinosaur T-shirt the child was wearing. One she'd given Jacob. Oh, thank goodness. She relaxed.

"I can't believe you're here." Lexy headed toward them.

"And look, he's walking." Wendy pointed and sure enough Jacob was taking a few small little steps. Pretty amazing considering he was trotting on sand, sometimes hard to stay upright on, but at least provided a soft cushion if he fell.

Smiling, Lexy put her excited, wiggling pup back down.

"I decided to surprise you, especially since the hubby got called away for work for a few days." Wendy threw her arms up in the air. "And to think all I did was scare you. I should have known better.

Lexy pulled her close into a hug. "So good to see you. I didn't recognize you at all. I've never even seen you with a baseball cap on. What a terrific surprise."

Jacob wrapped his arms around Lexy's legs. "Doggy?" He pointed at Asher.

She disentangled herself from Wendy's arms. "Yes, this is Asher."

The pup approached, tail wagging, and Jacob plunked himself down on the sand, mouth open in delight. Lexy hunkered down beside them, making sure their interaction went well.

"Asher is adorable." Wendy bent down to pet him. "I just never pictured you with a dog."

"Me neither and now I can't picture myself without one."

"And I barely recognized you." Wendy straightened up, eyeing Lexy up and down. "Could you remove your hat for a minute?"

Lexy got up and tossed it down on the sand.

"I know you said you cut and dyed your hair but wow, what a change." Wendy moved in a slow circle around her. "Looks good, though."

"Not really. I've left a lot of uneven sections. Maybe you can snip a bit here and there?"

"Actually, you've done an amazing job. It makes your green eyes pop."

"I pop all right. If I don't get those extra pounds off soon, I might pop all the buttons on my clothes." She picked her hat up and put it back on.

"Don't be ridiculous. You look great. Oh, and I've brought rollers and brushes to help you paint. You said you were going to attempt it tomorrow, so I thought I'd give you a hand."

"Thank you. I'd love the help. Your hubby David went away at a convenient time. Where is he off to this time?"

"Vancouver. Some kind of snag in one of his plans."

"Well, guess marriage to a famous architect in demand is never dull."

"I'm getting used to it. It means more time to spend with you." Wendy grinned.

"Asher, Asher."

Lexy looked behind to see Emma running down the beach screaming his name, Chris and Meredith in tow. She introduced them all and watched as Emma sat with Jacob, who grabbed her hand, giving off one of those cute big gummy grins with a few teeth sprinkled here and there.

Chris moved closer and whispered, "We were coming down for a swim and I saw you turning toward our end of the beach, then stop." His eyes darkened with concern. "Is everything okay?"

How sweet. Chrissy at his best.

"Yes, yes, everything is okay. I didn't recognize who this person was at first. She's my best friend."

"Good." He backed away; the worry lines etched across his forehead dissolving fast. "I think I heard the word painting as we were walking over. Words travel fast in a breeze. If you're talking about the cottage, I'll help too, if that's all right with you. With three of us, it'll be done in no time."

"That'd be great." Surprisingly, Lexy was thrilled. He'd offered before but she hadn't felt comfortable accepting his invitation. She was still worried he'd figure out who she was, but with Wendy there creating a diversion, it would be nice to have the cottage looking good and besides, who was she trying to kid, she really liked being around him. But she would never forget he had a girlfriend. Not that she was interested in him as a boyfriend. No way.

"Who is that?" Wendy asked watching them leave after a few minutes of small talk. "He was like a cowboy riding in on a horse to save you."

Lexy snorted at the visual image. "Just my neighbor. I told you about him. The one I met as a kid."

Wendy picked up a tired Jacob, carrying him in her arms. "Amazing. Just like in the movies. You move to a cottage next door to a hottie, and he's someone from your past. Isn't that how you said the romance movies go?"

"No, they're usually an old boyfriend. I barely knew this guy and I was just a child. Two weeks only, and shush by the way. He doesn't know I'm that girl."

"Really? Hope I didn't ruin any of your plans. Maybe you would have liked painting, just the two of you."

"No, I'm glad you're here. Definitely."

Jacob squirmed to get down, somehow not so tired anymore, and promptly fell. Lexy went to grab him but Asher was there first, licking the little boy's hand.

"Don't worry. The sand is soft, and he'll get right back up," Wendy said. "Besides, he has a furry friend watching out for him."

Sure enough, he stood and started walking again, this time his hand on the pup's back. They were both that little.

"Looks like he has a walking partner," Wendy said.

"Asher comes in handy in so many ways." An idea hit her. "By the way, would you like to go to a book club meeting tonight? I kinda said I'd go."

"You joined a book club?" Wendy's mouth dropped in shock. "That's not like you."

Lexy nodded. "You're right, but Meredith figured out who I am, and apparently their club is reading my first book. They started it before I even arrived, so an interesting coincidence. She wants me to hear how others view me. Incognito, of course."

Wendy's eyes lit up. "Hmm … not a bad idea. It might help. I keep telling you, your books are inspiring, and your characters come alive. Every time a new one comes out, I feel like I'm having a lovely visit with my best friends."

"Thanks for saying that."

"Well, truth is truth."

"And then my last one was so horrid."

"Well, the writing was great but the story didn't have your expected romantic ending. But you're changing that in your new one, right? Part two."

"Hopefully."

Wendy's eyebrows raised.

"Yes, yes I am."

"Well, let's go. A book club sounds fun. and with two new people the emphasis won't just be on you. Do you think Jacob will be welcomed?"

"I'll call right now." Lexy pulled out her phone and hit the numbers for Meredith. They chatted a few minutes, then she hung up. "Yep, Jacob's a go. Um, Wendy. When you read *Fairy Tale Crushed*, did you notice the relationship with Sarah and Nick was not a good one?"

Silence.

"Ah … yes. But I was afraid to mention it. I didn't want to stomp all over your creative process."

"Oh. Next time feel free to stomp."

She was halfway through re-reading her current work and hating Nick even more. How she was going to turn them into a loving couple was even more of a mystery.

What was she going to do? What strategy could she use?

All she wanted to do was kill off Nick in some unfortunate accident. Now that plot twist would be a joy to write.

Twenty-four

"We brought food, by the way," Wendy announced, raising her eyebrows several times in fun, as they reached the cottage. "I baked your favorite chocolate croissants and picked up pizza from Momma's Pizzeria. I know you loved it the last time we had it at my house. Found out they have a store not far from here. We just have to heat it up."

"With olives and pepperoni?"

"Of course."

"Heaven. Haven't had pizza in ages." Lexy shook her head slightly, trying to shake out the dark place she'd entered when thinking about her book characters.

"Well, you've certainly done a good job of beating back those weeds." Her friend swung her head back and forth. "I see a huge difference from the first photos you sent. Bet you'll be glad to have this place painted."

"Sure will. What a mess."

"But definitely intriguing and very sweet. A real rustic look."

"I agree. I love it here."

"I can see why. You're on a lake." Wendy spun in a circle, taking it all in. "How cool is that, but I bet you haven't even been in swimming."

"Not much of a swimmer."

"Baloney. You hate wearing a bathing suit. Admit it. You think you're too fat."

"You know me well." Lexy was loving the banter as she helped unload Wendy's car. Jacob and Asher were hanging together in the grass having a little lovefest, so they were free to get the stuff she had in the trunk, onto the porch.

"I bought the pizza frozen and packed it in that cooler surrounded with ice. It'll be mostly unthawed by now, so we'll have to stick it in the fridge."

"No problem." Lexy opened the front door and ushered them all in, carrying the cooler right to the kitchen, and placing the two pizzas in the fridge. She hurried back to the living room.

"Quaint and unique. I love it." Wendy walked around, holding Jacob, Asher leading the way. "David would be beside himself here, admiring how old the cottage is, loaded with all sorts of memories and traditions. What's under those sheets on the wall?"

"Mom's paintings. I haven't been able to look at them yet."

"Oh." Wendy stared at her, knowingly. "I get it. Best to wait until you're ready."

"Yep. Let me show you your room. Luckily, I cleaned and aired it out the other day. I've been working hard at getting rid of all dirt and grime."

She led them up the stairs, carrying their luggage. Wendy's hands were full with Jacob in one arm and dragging a portable cot in the other.

"This is the sand dollar room." Lexy opened the door.

Wendy walked in. "Right. I remember you telling me each room had a name. How beautiful. I love that I can stand at the window and look out at the lake. Love the sand dollar display too."

"Yeah. My grandpa was quite the collector." The dollars were showcased under glass in a picture frame on the wall. They were of various sizes and quite stunning to look at.

"Well, I'll let you get settled and I'll get supper ready," Lexy said. "Here, Asher, you come with me."

Her pup seemed reluctant to leave his new pal but finally trotted behind her. Lexy got to work heating up the food, filling Asher's bowl, setting up Jacob's portable high chair, and they all piled around the kitchen table getting caught up with each other. Jacob was so enthralled with the pup that as soon as he finished, he wanted to play with him. Once again, Lexy gave thanks that Asher was great with children, after all his best friend was Emma, and especially loved playing chase the ball. How sweet to see little Jacob sitting on the floor throwing a ball and Asher bringing it back. A baby's laughter was definitely pure music to the ears.

Finally the dishes were done, everyone was cleaned up, and they walked over to meet with Meredith. Just before they knocked on the cottage door, Lexy said, "Remember. Chris doesn't know who I really am."

"Got it. My lips are sealed."

"Thanks." Lexy knocked, Meredith let them in, and Emma ran over to Asher.

"You be a good boy, okay?" Lexy patted Asher on the head. Meredith had phoned earlier to say that even though Asher was welcomed at the book club, Chris and Emma would love to dog sit. Lexy agreed, knowing Asher would love it too.

But why was she doing this? Going to a book club?

Her legs trembled at the possibility of hearing bad feedback on one of her books. Especially since she felt so vulnerable and confused these days. Fragile, even.

"We'll take good care of him," Emma said.

"I'll make sure of it," Chris added. "I may have to protect Asher from my niece, though. Do you want to leave Jacob with us too?"

"Really?" Wendy asked.

"Sure. The more the merrier."

"Yeah, he can play with us." Emmy clapped her hands.

"How tempting. I'd love to have an evening on my own. It's been a long time." Wendy paused for a second, looking like she was mulling it over. "Okay, I'll take you up on it."

Jacob was too engrossed in Asher and Emma to even notice they were leaving.

Off they went. Meredith was driving and in no time they were in town and parking right on the main street.

"Tonight's meeting is at Hope's place and she lives above the bakery."

"Bakery?" Wendy moaned. "One of my most favorite places in the world."

"You'll love this one," Lexy said. "I know your weakness is chocolate chip cookies and hers are the best."

"She'll probably have some tonight. They're a staple of Hope's." Meredith led the way to a side door, opened it, and headed up the stairs where their host greeted them at the door.

Lexy loved how large and airy the apartment looked. Walls were painted an off-white, featuring multiple gorgeous seascapes, and the furniture was a light beige, highlighted by pops of color in the form of cushions in various bright hues of blue and green. It all came together to look inviting, warm, and cozy. Definitely a snuggling place.

"Grab a seat." Hope pointed to the couch and love seat.

To be safe, Lexy kept her hat on, hoping no one would think she was weird. A smile tugged at her lips. But she was weird so they'd be thinking correctly anyway. She was surprised to see Chelsea from the pet store and Helen from the vet clinic. She knew them all and was glad the group was a nice mixture of ages as she wondered again what they all thought of her book. Introducing Wendy, she noted how friendly everyone was as they welcomed her friend. Willow rocked.

"Coffee?" Hope asked.

"Sure." Lexy started to get up.

"Stay put," Wendy whispered in her ear. "Don't draw any attention to yourself. I'll help her."

"Oh, good idea."

"Here, I'll pour." Wendy popped up. "I'll get yours too, Meredith."

"Why, thank you, dear."

Wendy truly was the best friend ever. Lexy was so thrilled she was there, as she watched her, along with Hope, make sure everyone had a drink, then bring coffee over to them. Her buddy always managed to fit in, no matter where she landed. Sometimes even taking over.

"Thanks," Lexy whispered when she sat back down.

"No problem. It gave me a chance to scope out what goodies I'm going to eat." She licked her lips and rubbed her tummy. "Yummm..."

Always the joker. Lexy loved how much fun her bestie was.

Hope passed around plates and then a huge tray of cookies, brownies, and muffins made the rounds. Lots and lots of sweets, and hard to choose. Small talk ensued as everyone oohed and aahed and ate.

"Now, let's begin," Meredith said.

To Lexy's surprise, her neighbor appeared to be the moderator.

"We've all read the book," Meredith continued. "Did everyone enjoy it?"

Trying to be discreet, Lexy looked around, relieved to see nods of approval.

Hope put down her coffee cup. "Well, I loved this book. I am a sucker for mushy endings and this was one of the best."

Once again, everyone agreed.

"What do these types of endings mean to you?" Meredith asked. Lexy leaned in, curious about the answer.

"Well, there are a lot of feel-good moments," Hope said. "Just what I need at the end of a long day of hard work. I can finally relax with a glass of wine and a book that inspires me. I looked forward to reading chapters of this book all week, practically racing upstairs when the bakery closed."

"I agree." Chelsea jumped in. "Sometimes life is tough and good fiction simply makes you feel better. When my husband died, books like this kept me going. They gave me a respite from my pain, transporting me to another world. I wish I had read Ayers then. Oh, and I love the humor and antics too. That scene where Violet adopted a baby goat had me in stitches."

"I'm sorry about your husband," Lexy said, feeling her pain.

"Thanks. I didn't mean to make you sad. My marriage was a good one and I was lucky to have had George in my life for the length of time he was."

Such a beautiful thing to acknowledge. Lexy wished she could feel that way about her mom, but her loss still hurt, even though she knew her mother would want her to get out there and live her life the best she could.

Helen flipped open a page that was bookmarked. "Listen to this. 'Violet felt safe in Chad's arms. He promised to be there for her and he kept his promise. All is right with the world.'" She looked up. "Well, I'm single and still looking for love. I know this is fiction but I like the idea of finding someone who keeps their promises. This book gives me hope that maybe in life sometimes it actually mirrors fiction."

Good to know, Lexy thought.

"What do you think, Lexy?" Hope asked. "You're so quiet."

Warmth flooded Lexy's cheeks. Unbelievable, but she was blushing. She hoped no one else noticed.

"Oh, I enjoyed it."

"Well, I read this a while back when it first came out," Wendy said, jumping in, mouth still full of cookie.

Her friend saved the day again, Lexy thought.

"And I still go back and read it over and over," Wendy added, swallowing fast. "It makes me want to stand up and cheer when Violet, hurt by who she thought was her first love, dumps evil Joseph, and finds true love with Chad. I'm a total sucker when it comes to love ever after and I especially like a plucky, courageous heroine, not afraid to stand up for herself."

Everyone clapped, giving Lexy another warm glowing feeling.

But evil Joseph? She frowned. She'd forgotten about him. He was a lot like Nick, her current main character. Once again, why had she never noticed that before?

She was also surprised how fast the hour flew by filled with much hilarity and excitement as they discussed all the characters. Sure, she'd heard people talk about her books before but never so intensely and so positively. How fascinating to hear Violet and Chad come alive. She'd read so many bad reviews, it was cathartic hearing good ones.

"Well, how about we read Alexandra Ayers' second book?" Meredith asked.

Everyone agreed and as if they were all spurred on at the same time, they started to clean up. Time to go and Lexy was really glad she came.

While Meredith and Wendy chatted all the way home, she was quiet. She had a lot to think about. Finally, they arrived to retrieve a sleepy Jacob and Asher. They were all curled up with Chris and Emma on the couch. Chris was awake of course.

"Thank you, Meredith." Lexy surprised herself by reaching out to hug her. "Your book club helped me enormously."

"Figured it would. Just remember. Believe in yourself."

"Wish I could."

"You'll get there."

"Everyone I've met here seems so nice," Wendy added.

"They are. Kind and helpful too."

"And the best chocolate chip cookies ever." Wendy yawned. "Guess I'm beat."

"Thanks for coming," Meredith said.

"Thanks for the invite." Lexy cuddled her sleeping pup in her arms.

"I'll carry Jacob back, if that's okay." Chris picked him up. "He's right out of it."

"Why, thank you." Wendy looked relieved. "I appreciate the help. He's quite heavy."

They walked back to the cottage in silence, not wanting to wake up Jacob. Chris carried him right up the stairs and put him in the cot. Then he left. Lexy had hoped he'd stay for a while but knew he would never do that, assuming she'd want to be with Wendy. Seems he was always considerate. Now, and back then.

Her friend was exhausted. The long drive to get there and the busy day sent her straight to bed. Lexy made sure Wendy had everything she might need, then headed out to the porch and to Granny's rocking chair, Asher on her lap. She had a lot to think about.

So they loved her book.

Lexy had a hard time with praise, never thinking she was good enough.

You'll never amount to anything.

Deep down, she really believed she'd live life as a loser. One of those creepy mean people who sat on porches and screamed, "Get off the lawn" all day.

She wrote from the heart and never realized the impact of happy endings. She had always figured a massive fluke made her books hit the bestseller lists and not that she earned it and people enjoyed them.

Writing them was her own respite from the world. She always wrote whimsical little stories as a kid but started writing her first novel one night when she was sad. Her fingers flew over the keyboard trying to create the world as a better place.

On the surface she appeared content. Privileged. Like she had it all.

Underneath she was a hurting little child.

Basically, that she was no good.

Like Meredith said. She needed to believe in herself.

But how?

How could she fix this?

How could she learn to have faith in herself when she thought of herself as a failure. Even below a loser in the pecking order.

Hopefully she could gather the positive energy she felt tonight, hone it, and produce something good.

She crossed her fingers willing it to happen, but when she sat down at her computer, longing for inspiration, nothing materialized. No words appeared.

Sigh.

Twenty-five

Bang!

Lexy jerked her head to the side in time to see Asher jump off a chair with a paintbrush in his mouth. She'd forgotten he was getting a lot better at climbing up on stuff. He took off into the living room, Lexy in hot pursuit.

"Asher, stop, give it back."

He kept on running around and around, through the living room, back to the kitchen, even stopping a few times to make sure she was behind him. She'd catch up and he'd take off again.

Roaring at his antics, not to mention the comical look on his face as if he'd pulled off the greatest heist, Lexy collapsed on the floor. Concerned, Asher ran over.

"Gotcha."

She grabbed him and managed to wrestle the brush out of his mouth.

"You're lucky you're cute, but remember, you have to be good today. We're painting."

She chuckled more when he tilted his head as if struggling to understand what she said, then grabbed the brush which she had stupidly put on the floor behind her. He took off fast. Again.

"You little scamp. You're way more intelligent than your own good."

Chasing didn't work, so this time she called his name to get his attention, then took off in the opposite direction hoping he'd follow her into the hall where she could corner him. Trying to be one step ahead of him proved to be challenging. So far her pup was winning.

"Did you lose something?" Turning she stared at the comical vision of Chris holding the struggling pup with one hand, the brush with the other. He was followed by Emma and Meredith.

"Sure did."

She ran over and took him out of Chris' arms.

Whoa. Her heart picked up speed.

Being near him was not helping her remain aloof. His hair was slightly wet and whiffs of soap and a pleasant-smelling cologne rolled off him. Feeling the need to get away fast, she turned, put Asher on the floor, and snapped on his leash. "Aha, you're not escaping now."

"He only wants to help," Emma said, moving closer and placing her hands on her hips.

"You're right." How sweet that she was sticking up for the pup, as Asher ran to greet his buddy.

"Hope you don't mind that we walked in. I knocked but could see you were busy chasing Asher," Chris said.

"No, not at all."

"I brought the troops."

"Is that okay?" Meredith added. "I thought I could help watch the pup and Jacob. And I brought lemonade. Figured you'd be hot as the day wore on." She opened the fridge door and placed the pitcher in it.

"And I brought donuts." Emma picked up the box she had put on the chair when petting Asher. "And I can play with Jacob and Asher. They're so much fun."

Lexy's eyes widened. "You are all so kind."

"Well, this way, we'll get it done in one day and then you don't have to worry about it," Chris said. "I brought over two ladders as well."

"Hey, am I missing the party?" Wendy trotted down the stairs holding a cranky, crying Jacob who brightened up when he saw his visitors. He held his arms out for Chris. Lexy didn't blame him, she felt like doing the same thing, watching him snuggle the little guy in his arms. How sad that she felt jealous of a baby.

"We ate breakfast. But Jacob wanted to wear his pajamas all day so we got in a bit of a tussle." Wendy frowned, looking exhausted already. "I don't mind most of his choices but today is going to be hot. He needed something lighter."

Emma walked over, pointing a shaking finger up at him. "Yeah, your mommy's right. You need shorts."

Jacob beamed. "Okay."

Chris looked at Lexy, eyebrows raised.

Emma might be the biggest peacemaker around these days, she thought.

"Well, let's get started." Lexy led the gang out the front door. Luckily, she had helped paint it before with her grandpa who had taken great pains to teach her techniques. In the past week, she'd slowly peeled off paint strips, sanded, and all that was left was to paint the walls and trim. She had chosen a beautiful rose color for the cottage and grey for the trim, just the way she remembered it.

Ladders out, paint mixed, they were ready to go.

"I'll start on the front, if that's okay," Wendy said. "That way Jacob can see me and not freak out. Although he doesn't seem to care now that Emma is here. And how about Lexy and Chris start on the back."

Lexy glared at Wendy, whom she knew was throwing them together on purpose. Wendy's wink made her chuckle though. She was as much of a rascal as Asher.

She carried her ladder, Chris did as well, and they leaned them up against the back wall.

"After we do the top part, we can come down and use the long rollers my grandpa had." Thank goodness. She never looked forward to being on a ladder. Up high for extended periods were not her thing. She'd barely survived when sanding.

Chris scooted up, but she hesitated.

"You afraid of heights?" Chris yelled down.

"A bit. But I can do it. Luckily the cottage is not too high."

"I can do the top part and you can stay on the ground, if you'd like."

"I'm all right." Sweet of him to offer, though.

She started to climb and was surprised to see Chris hurry down and hold her ladder.

"Thanks," she said.

"No problem." After making sure she made it, he went back to his and climbed up again.

Lexy was amazed at how fast Chris was. He'd definitely done a lot of painting. He was probably the one who painted Yellow Rose, toning it down a bit.

They finished the top part in no time at all, climbing down to use the longer rollers. After several strokes, Lexy leaned over to add more paint and felt something on her back. She turned.

Chris smirked. "Sorry. I got you mixed up with the wall."

"You painted my back?" She picked up a brush, ran it down his T-shirt, then started to run.

"I'm faster than you," he yelled. "Longer legs."

Lexy remembered all their races on the beach and yep, he was faster. He caught up and swiped her with more paint. She got him back.

"Lunch time," Meredith yelled, coming around the corner. "Whenever you two have finished painting yourselves, of course."

Yikes. Meredith must think they're crazy, but she did have an amused expression on her face.

"Lunch already?" Lexy was amazed so much time had passed although her stomach was rumbling, signaling she was really hungry. Managing to wipe off paint the best they could, they joined the rest of the gang.

"Did you get any on the walls?" Wendy whispered as Lexy sat beside her.

"Yes, we did."

"That guy is a keeper." Wendy nudged her. "I heard you screeching back there. You sure a romance isn't going on?"

"Nah, not interested. Besides he has a girlfriend."

"He does? But he can't keep his eyes off of you."

Lexy glanced over and sure enough he was looking at her. Chris nodded. She could hardly keep her eyes off of him as well. She took a bite of her sandwich, chewed slowly, buying time to answer Wendy. "Well, all I'm trying to do is finish up my new book and sort out stuff from my past that I've been running away from."

"You're dealing with past issues?" Wendy's eyebrows rose. "Now that's interesting and about time. But I'm sure you'll figure out your book."

"Thanks for your vote of confidence." Wendy had always been such a good friend. They also had a paint history. They had met in kindergarten when Lexy had accidentally spilled pink paint all over Wendy's brand-new white T-shirt. Instead of being angry, Wendy had hooted with delight and kept doing it until Lexy joined in.

"You know, I wanted a pink shirt," Wendy had said, "but Mom made me buy this white one. Looks like I won, after all." And they'd been besties ever since, both opposites, with Wendy seeing the good in everyone and everything and Lexy expecting the worst.

"Hey, you're ganging up on me," Chris shouted.

Lexy looked to see what was going on and was surprised to see Jacob, Emma, and Asher on top of Chris, who was stretched out on the ground. They were playfighting and tickling him, with Chris pretending to push them off. He was such a nice guy. All these years later she could still remember how she felt when he was so supportive after finding her crying. She had discovered that she had the best friend in the whole world. Someone who would always be there for her. Too bad they hadn't kept in touch.

"Lunch is over. Back to work." Meredith interrupted her thoughts and shooed them all away. Good. She shouldn't be thinking of Chris like that. Then again, it would be nice to acknowledge their past and maybe she could have her best childhood buddy back. Did he remember her? She suspected he did.

"Lexy, that's so pretty."

She swung around to find Emma pointing at her grandpa's homemade wooden trellis that she had cleaned up, anchored in the ground, and planted flowers at its base. They had grown tall, twisting around the wooden frame and were now in full bloom.

"The flowers are called pink clematis, my mom's favorite."

"Where is your mom?"

"She's in heaven, so I planted these for her. They make me feel good and remind me of her."

"In heaven, huh?"

"Yes."

"Do you miss her?"

"Yes, very much."

"Lexy," Chris called. "Where are you. Are you slacking off?"

"Coming." Reluctantly, she left Emma still staring at the flowers and wondered what that was all about. Maybe in time, the little girl would open up more.

After the walls were painted, Chris tackled the trim, being the most expert among them. Then he did something really sweet. He gathered Emma and Jacob together, handed them each a brush, and had them help paint the door.

"If I wasn't already happily married, I'd fall in love with him," Wendy said. "Listen to those kids squealing in joy."

"I know, they're having a blast." Lexy stood in awe at how patient he was, taking the time to show them how to paint properly. Of course, Emma appeared a pro but Jacob was pretty good himself. Mind you, Chris was propping him up from behind while Asher bopped around between them all.

Her decision was made.

She was going to talk to him, reveal who she really was, and see if he remembered their time together. She was ready.

They eventually finished, cleaned up, and Meredith got ready to leave with a sleepy Emma.

"Thanks for all your help," Lexy said.

"You're very welcome." Meredith squeezed her hand. "That's what neighbors are for."

"You've still got paint on your face," Chris said.

"Where?" Lexy reached up and brushed her face with her hand.

"Right there." He leaned over and swiped her nose with his brush.

"Hey, no fair. You caught me without my own brush." She reached up, touched her nose hoping to get paint on her finger—yay, she did—and ran it down his cheek.

"Well, while you two kids are playing, Jacob and I are going in to get cleaned up in the cottage." Wendy winked for the second time at Lexy. "Fine examples you are."

Lexy exploded with laughter. "I haven't had that much fun in years."

"Me, too. Hey, if Wendy agrees, I was wondering if you and Asher would take a walk with me."

"Go ahead." Wendy rolled her eyes. "I'm going to be busy bathing a squirming Jacob anyway."

"Are you sure?" Lexy tried sending out signals to her friend. Please say no. Please say no. Her decision was new and she needed more time before she spilled the beans, so to speak. If she was alone with him, she'd blurt it out with little thought and probably mess it all up. "Don't you need some help?"

"Nope. Go." Wendy took hold of Jacob's hand and walked into the cottage.

Well, that was quite a statement. Of course, Wendy definitely approved of Chris. Then again, even though incredibly nervous, Lexy was curious about what this walk might entail.

"So where are we going?" she asked.

"You'll see."

Twenty-six

Excited, but also nervous, Lexy followed Chris as he led them away from the beach, into the forest, stopping for a few minutes here and there for the pup to sniff.

Was he taking her to his cottage? The fast way?

For some kind of surprise?

Or...

Suddenly he veered off.

Oh, oh.

He lifted the large branch that led to the 'Always' place, pushing it off to the side.

No way.

Sitting on the rock, he patted the empty space beside him.

Startled, Lexy debated running away, but his compassionate eyes got her.

She sat, leaving Asher to sniff.

Silence.

"We always told the truth here, Alex." He turned and their eyes locked.

Alex. He called her Alex.

"So you know." Her head dropped. She had suspected but wasn't sure. She should have known she couldn't fool him.

"Yes. Do you know who I am?"

She raised her head. "Of course. Chrissy."

He took hold of her hand just like he had all those years ago. "I admit the black hair threw me off at first. Your bright red braids had been burned into my memory."

"Well, underneath this black dye, the red still thrives." She took in a deep breath at the gentleness of his touch. "When did you figure it out?"

"Breathe." He sucked in a big breath and exhaled, waiting for her to do the same. "The first time we met. I never forgot your smile, a combination of joy and mischief. And then, of course, your kindness. Adopting a stranded pup is so you, as well as being incredibly nice to Emma. Not to mention your fear of heights on that ladder. I remember how terrified you were on the Ferris Wheel."

Images of screaming in fear, clasping his hand tightly and closing her eyes as the ride soared high flooded her. She was amazed he remembered.

"I'm sorry. I should have never tried to keep my identity from you."

You're an idiot.

"Don't be. You had your reasons. Did you recognize me right off?"

"Took a few minutes, but yes."

"I hoped so. I hinted several times to see if you'd say anything." He squeezed her hand. "But I was finding it hard to pretend, especially since I almost called you Alex today so many times. And then I wanted to remind you of all the fun we had back then. So I took a risk and did what Jeremy did."

"Jeremy?" What was he talking about?

"Yes, your fictional character Jeremy in your first book, *Sunrise*. He found out a friend's secret and confronted her. It all worked out, so I was hoping to have the same success tonight."

Lexy was amazed. "You read my book? And reenacted one of my plot lines?"

"Yes." He looked quite proud. "And I brought you to the place where we could always be ourselves. I figured I'd have this conversation while Wendy was here, so if you were upset, she would be there for you."

Kind, thoughtful Chris. The way he always was.

"You remembered our place."

"Yes. You?"

"Of course. I was here a few days ago."

"Me, too. We must have just missed each other. I hope you don't mind that I forced this reunion."

Asher put his paws up on her knees, signaling he was tired. She lifted him up and he curled into a ball on her lap, falling fast asleep.

"No, I don't mind at all. I was planning to talk to you about it too, and the fact you emulated Jeremy is pretty cool. I've almost called you Chrissy a few times as well. Not to mention coming close to pushing your hair back the way I used to, so you could see what you were doing."

Was his face really turning red?

"You remember my long always-in-my-eyes hair, and you were the only one I let call me Chrissy, by the way.

"Yes, I remember your hair. And I even let you call me squirt a few times. We had such fun back then."

"We did."

"Do you remember carving our initials? They're still there."

"Really?" He jumped up and pushed aside a few branches. "Amazing they held up all these years."

"Sure did."

He sat beside her again, reaching his baby finger towards her. "Always."

She took hold of it. "Always. You remember that too."

"I do." He released his finger. "Did you just not want me to know who you are?"

"I didn't want to burden you, plus I find it hard to trust anyone these days."

"I understand. After all, we haven't seen each other in years."

"Twenty to be exact. You know, you look so sad these days." This time she grabbed his hand. "Can you tell me about it?"

He stared off in space. Lexy stayed quiet, wondering if he'd share or if he'd write her off as being too nosy.

"I lost my sister in the space of seconds." His words were soft, so much so she had to lean closer to hear. "All because a drunk driver decided to go down a one-way street, hitting her car head on."

What?

"Oh, I'm sorry."

They sat in silence. Shocked, Lexy was struggling to take it all in. She did wonder if Emma's mom had passed away, but really didn't want to think of that. This news was so heartbreaking. She pulled her hand away and wrapped her arm around him.

"So that's why Emma is living with you now?"

"Yes. My sister was a single mom, so I took custody of my niece, which was what my sister would have wanted, and my mother moved in to lend a hand."

"You are amazing." Lexy had never met his sister. That summer, she had apparently stayed in town with her mom, having a job she couldn't take time from. She was a lot older than Chris. "How wonderful that you are there for Emma."

"I wouldn't have it any other way. Luckily my mother is a psychotherapist and has dealt with a great deal of grief and is a huge help. Of course, she lost her daughter, too."

So that was why Meredith was so easy to be around. She was a therapist and used to listening. She also radiated an aura of peace.

But no wonder he appeared sad.

"That's a lot to happen."

"Yes." He wiped his eyes. "Sorry, I'm not ready to talk much about it yet."

"That's okay. Well, did you become the teacher you always wanted to be?"

"Yes ... I ..."

He stopped mid-sentence, gazing off into space. Lexy stayed quiet, sensing all sorts of turmoil radiating through him.

"I just hope I can give Emma a good life. The way her mother would."

His pain made it obvious his chief concern was for his niece.

"I think you're doing a good job. More than good. A great job. She's seems very happy and content."

"Thanks. I appreciate your observations. But enough of me. Your turn. When did you start going by Lexy?"

She wanted to hear more about him, thinking it would be good for him to get it all off his chest, but guessed that was all he could share at the moment. Then again, he always was the type who highlighted others, not himself.

"A few months ago. I go by Lexy Errol now, not wanting people to know who I really am."

"Alexandra Ayers, a bestselling author."

She squirmed, waking Asher. "Sorry dude. Go back to sleep. You even know that?" She pulled her arm away, as if attempting to disappear.

"Google has everything. I never knew your last name until I saw your picture on a book flap. Apparently, my mother is a big fan because one of your novels is on our coffee table. She probably figured I'd never look at it, not reading women's fiction at all, but also she never knew we had met before. I'm thrilled you followed your dream and became an author. I remember you carrying around that notebook everywhere, but I'm sorry to see reporters giving you such a hard time and even lying about stuff."

"You knew they were lying?"

"Of course. I know first-hand you're not a selfish person or any type of person they're trying to make you appear as."

"Thank you."

That darn tear again.

Chris reached over and brushed it away. "The old Alex would have flicked her braids, stuck out her tongue, and challenged them all to a duel."

"Yeah, guess I was once like that."

"According to the articles, you changed your original ending in your last book. Is that true?"

Restless, she got up and walked Asher around. Should she tell him the truth? Staring into his eyes, she had her answer.

Yes.

"In a nutshell, my boyfriend Jake mocked my books and suggested that ending, so I changed my own. Why? Simple. He was my fiancé and I wanted him to keep loving me. I didn't want conflict. To rock the boat, as that old saying went. How ridiculous. I messed up my writing career, all because of a boy."

His eyebrows rose.

"Yeah, I know. The old me would have smirked in his face."

"Well, you always were sassy." He cocked his head. "Remember that time the circus guy said the park was closed and you pointed out ten minutes were left and marched up to the merry go round and insisted they take you for a ride or you'd report them? And they did."

"And you came too, looking all embarrassed. You know, I liked who I was back then."

"But you always had a softer, more vulnerable side. Especially when talking about your mother. I'm so sorry to have read that she passed away not that long ago."

Tears rolled. Lexy brushed them away, sitting again. "Around the same time your sister did, as well."

"Yes. I also recall you talking about how much your father hurt you."

Just hearing his name made her ill. She felt like throwing up.

"You remember that?"

"Of course. I remember everything you said."

"Well, my father is definitely in my past. I never think of him at all. Looks like we've both had a lot happen, though. Mine pales in comparison to yours."

"Yours is just as hard. I know how close you were to your mother."

"Yeah, I was. I really miss her."

They sat in silence for a while.

"You know, despite all our issues, we had such a good time that summer," Chris said. "Maybe we can help each other discover those fun kids again."

"I'd like that." She felt like leaning in and kissing him, but turned away instead. What was she thinking? "Guess we should get back. I don't want to leave Wendy much longer."

"Yes, of course. By the way, are you still with that guy? The guy who mouthed off about you on TV?"

"Absolutely not."

Did he smile? She wasn't sure. She wanted to ask him about the woman she saw him with but couldn't bring herself. She didn't really want to hear about someone else making him happy. Selfish, but true.

He took hold of her hand as they walked back to the cottage. She liked that. As friends, of course. They were both quiet and she was grateful, not quite sure how she felt sharing so much. She wasn't sure if Chris the man was the same sweetie as Chrissy the boy was. But she was honored that he shared as well.

"Oh, one more thing. Does my mother know?" Chris asked.

"Yes."

"Figured. Hard to fool her."

Lexy was thrilled at how trustworthy Meredith was. She had never said a word.

A quick hug and he was gone. She felt they both had enough of baring their souls and needed time alone. She sure did. She quietly opened the door and walked in.

"How did it go?" Wendy asked, looking up from her iPad.

Lexy put Asher in his crate and motioned Wendy to join her on the porch.

"I want to know everything." Wendy grabbed her hand as they settled on the steps. "Every single word."

Lexy spilled away.

"So, he figured you out." Wendy hooted. "I knew it. Are you okay with that?"

"Yes, kinda. Well, maybe. I just hope he keeps it quiet. It might be just one more complication I don't need." She didn't want to tell Wendy she'd considered telling him too, or her friend would be all over her convinced she was in love.

"I'm sure he will. You like him, don't you?"

"Yes."

Wendy threw her arms around her, hugging tightly. "He seems kind, caring, and fun. Look how sweet he is with Jacob, Asher, and his mother. Any kisses tonight, by any chance?"

"Stop it. He's not available." Lexy also left out the part about how much she wanted to kiss him.

"Oh, I was hoping he didn't and like in the movies, you just thought he did."

"Actually, the topic never came up."

Wrapped in each other's arms, friends forever, they stayed quiet for a while until Lexy noticed Wendy's eyes closing.

"Hey, you need to go to bed."

"Yeah, I should. I'm beat." Wendy yawned. "You coming in, too?"

"Soon. Just need a few more minutes out here."

"Well, see you tomorrow."

Stars shone, a sweet breeze washed over her, and peace reigned. Lexy and her buddy Chrissy were together again. Yes, she was worried about it, but for now, it sure felt good.

You'll never amount to anything. You're stupid and ugly.

Trembling, Lexy sat straight up.

Who said that?

Twenty-seven

Terrified, Lexy looked around.

Of course, no one was there.

Usually, she'd ignore these hurtful words shooting through her psyche. They arrived to bring her down when she was happy, and lingered when she was upset to keep her locked in that state. She'd stuff herself with food, get super busy, have an extra glass of wine – anything to block them out.

Not anymore.

For the very first time, she acknowledged exactly who had said them.

Her dad.

She actually sensed him standing there, ghost-like, spewing his hate.

Over and over and over.

Horrible words that hurt.

Hard to believe his mantra about her was so negative. And unfortunately lived on inside her.

Yes, she had talked to Chrissy about her dad one day in their secret place – the first and last time she had ever mentioned him to anyone.

Chris bringing it up tonight must have really hit home. Opened her mind and heart to face the truth.

She was also much more peaceful in Willow, her racing mind was quietening down, making her aware how many times hateful negative thoughts raced through her. She had never realized how often she criticized herself throughout the day and had certainly never clued in before that they came right from her dad's playbook. Her negative thoughts really belonged to him. She thought she had just ignored his comments but now realized they had taken up residence in her mind, ready to jump out at any moment. And they still stung. After all, he must have said she was worthless, or variations of the same, hundreds of times. His painful words always remained with her, eroding her self-confidence and her sense of worth.

You're stupid.

There it went again. She heard it loud and clear. Her dad's words. Occupying her heart. Day after day after day.

Her father.

Allen was his name. He was tall with short red hair. At times he was fun. One day on a shopping trip, he pretended to be walking an imaginary dog who kept pulling on his leash. In those moments he was hilarious and she would relax, feel safe, and then ... almost immediately he'd hurt her again. She'd learned never to unwind in his presence and that name calling was his big thing. His only thing. Stupid, dummy, ugly, fat, rolled off his tongue at any given moment.

Her mom kicked him out when she was seven and he died in a car crash shortly after. He was drunk. Lexy even went to his funeral and every time someone said something nice about him, she wanted to puke.

Jumping up, she paced back and forth across the porch as she realized blocking him with various addictions only allowed him to fester inside her, making her feel if he couldn't love her, no one else could. How sad. How tragic.

Plopping back down on the chair, she also realized that was probably why her bad reviews really hurt. Awful comments were part of a writer's life, because no matter what, some people were not going to like her books. She didn't mind constructive reviews, but often comments would be intentionally personal and hurtful. And they underlined her father's cruel words and made her doubt herself again.

You're a lousy writer. You're no good. Your face is too round. Your hair too red. Too curly.

Yep. Her father's words again.

Although her books were very positive, where she created a world she longed for, her outlook on life was negative - born and nurtured by her dad.

Not anymore. She was tired of it all.

Enough.

She closed her eyes, slowly breathing in and out, calming her mind.

Instantly an image of her grandmother took over.

One day she was helping her plant flowers and her granny said, "The perfect garden has no weeds. We have to pluck them out so that all of the beautiful plants have room to bloom and blossom."

Lexy's eyes popped open.

An idea threaded in and out of her thoughts.

She was no longer a little kid smacked down by words. As an adult, aware of what was going on, she could take charge of herself.

What if she did this?

What if she viewed her mind, heart, and soul as gardens of beautiful flowers of every color imaginable. And she needed to tend to these gardens by pulling out any weed that managed to take root. In her case, weeds represented hurtful words.

That was exactly what she was going to do.

Follow her grandmother's advice.

Every time a negative thought emerged, she'd figuratively pluck it out and throw it away. So the goodness, the kindness, the beauty inside her could bloom.

Yes, she could do that. Not only could she, but she also really wanted to. She'd had enough of negativity.

Somehow, she felt lighter, more peaceful, joyful. Possibly on the path of healing.

She fully believed a breakthrough in her quest to find herself had emerged.

And she had Chrissy to thank for this.

Life was looking good.

And getting better.

She was sure of it.

Twenty-eight

Chris peeked into Emma's room.

The night light cast a glow, and he could see she was fast asleep, Betty the bunny and Larry the lamb, curled up in her arms. The two stuffed animals were the last gifts given to her by Elizabeth and she slept with them every night. Interesting how she had given Asher a bunny and lamb toy too, as if sensing how scared and vulnerable he was.

Tiptoeing in, he kissed her gently on her forehead, then sneaked out again. He noticed a light on in his mother's room. She was probably reading Lexy's books, no doubt. He was still impressed at how she had kept his friend's secret. Of course, she wasn't aware he had known the author as a kid, but she was not a gossip either. Holding onto to someone's innermost thoughts was a huge part of a psychotherapist's life and Meredith was one of the best. She had been a well sought after counselor with a busy practice until she retired, and he was lucky to have her as a mother. She was helping him enormously as he navigated caring for a young child. He needed to remember to thank her more than he did. She was truly amazing.

Restless, he grabbed a cold drink and left, heading down to the lake. He seemed to be going there most evenings. Often he jumped in the canoe for a ride, but he dragged a chair closer to the water and sat, leaning back, enthralled with the multitude of stars showcasing a glorious moon. He felt peace for a change, a calmness that rippled through his whole being. The fact that years ago he'd had such fun here with a spitfire redhead provided the foundation for feeling good today. He was convinced of that. And now they'd reconnected. Truly a miracle.

It felt good pouring his heart out to Alex, or Lexy – he had to keep calling her that, her choice for now at least. It seemed natural, the way he used to. Of course, back then he hadn't as many problems as Lexy, who was coping with an ill mother and still hurting from her father. He had always admired her mixture of strength, openness, vulnerability, and courage.

But tonight, he had actually talked to her about his sister.

A huge step.

Normally he avoided questions about Elizabeth and would change the topic. But he instinctively knew Lexy had a depth of compassion and would understand, and besides they were meeting at their 'Always' place, a place of truth. It felt cathartic to let his pain out, very freeing. He hadn't said much, but at least made an attempt.

And what a reaction she had to the fact he was raising Emma.

So different from Jenny.

Jenny.

Restless, needing to move, he got up and walked along the beach.

They'd had a lot of good times together. He was a bit more routine-oriented and he admired Jenny's spontaneity when she'd call him up and suggest a bike ride, or a jazz festival, spur of the moment. She was quick-witted and he had enjoyed being with her. When they first broke up, he always thought he'd jump back in a relationship with her in a flash, if given the chance.

And then she arrived at Yellow Rose wanting him as a boyfriend again.

Begging, actually.

Seeing her on his turf was an eye opener and made the decision for him.

He was over her. Done.

In fact, he might not have ever been into her. He had a job, and it seemed fitting to seek out marriage and possibly children as the next step. Sure seemed he had just drifted along, in fact, going nowhere.

Did he ever love her?

Guess it didn't matter. Sure, it hurt, but he couldn't get off his mind the day she showed up at his apartment when his mom and Emma were out, and stood there, hands on hips, screaming,

"Why can't your mom raise Emma? Why does it have to be you?"

All he needed to know about her was contained in those words.

Jenny wanted life her way and was not prepared for any twists and turns. Couldn't say he blamed her. He found it difficult at times raising a young girl, becoming a father/mother overnight. But he would never change a moment of it because Emma had changed him. And he liked the changes he saw in himself.

So, he said no.

Surprisingly, her tears had no effect on him. He wished her all the best, but he had seen who she really was and wanted no part of it. Of course, it didn't help that she was sitting beside Emma's swing set in Yellow Rose's backyard. He felt choosing Jenny was not choosing Emma and he'd rather be pushing his niece on her swing than anywhere else. He couldn't spend his life trying to forget that Jenny didn't want Emma in her life, especially when his niece was his whole life.

And now Lexy was back.

Right away he noticed how different it felt when he was with her. Like coming home and being with someone he felt comfortable with.

Of course, his feelings for her now were different from when he was a kid. He had almost kissed her. And not on the cheek this time.

How ridiculous.

He shook his head; sure she'd run far from him if he did that.

Turning back, he headed to the cottage.

Lexy.

The most important thing was not to ruin the friendship that was beginning again.

He didn't want to lose her.

Ever.

Twenty-nine

Lexy kept waving, long after Wendy's car disappeared. Her heart ached. She was really going to miss her, as well as Jacob. As always, they'd brought a lot of excitement with them and promised to come back soon. She hoped so.

A tug at the leash. She looked down at her pup, raring to go. Anywhere.

"Asher, time for dog school." His little tail wagged hard as if he knew what that meant. Maybe he did. She was really enjoying training him and found herself looking forward to classes. Who would have ever thought that?

After grabbing her bag of treats and training clicker and putting them in the car, they started to walk over to pick up Emma. They were early, but Emma had phoned to say she and Meredith had baked cookies and to come and get some. The sun always felt so warm and inviting on her face and arms and once again she gave thanks for coming here. Slowly, she was healing her wounds.

Cutting through the trees, she was tempted to stop at their special place, but didn't have the time. Arriving at the Yellow Rose, she knocked.

The door swung open and Emma waved them in to the kitchen table where a plateful of cookies sat.

"Can I give Asher a treat too?" she asked.

"Just a tiny one. He'll get lots in class."

"Oh, right. Can I take him out to the yard?"

"Sure, go ahead."

"Come, sit with me." Meredith pulled out a chair and then sat across from her. "Here, help yourself." She pushed the plate closer. "Lemonade?"

"Sure. And the cookies look delicious." Lexy took a bite. "Yum...."

"Hope gave me the recipe she uses at the bakery." Meredith poured them both a drink.

"Lucky you."

"You don't mind taking Emma along again? To dog school?" Meredith asked.

"Not at all." Sipping her drink, she looked around, disappointed not to see Chris.

"He's out."

Lexy felt her cheeks heating up, signaling she'd blushed. Nothing seemed to get by Meredith, definitely the sign of a good therapist.

"Oh, I wasn't looking for him." Okay, she lied. Imagine lying to a therapist? "I was wondering if you have any thoughts of my last book that might help me fix the one I'm working on now. I just can't seem to finish it and my deadline is drawing nearer. As a matter of fact, I'm late sending part of it in already."

Silence.

"What do you, as the author, want to do?" Meredith's gaze was direct.

"I'm really not sure, but I respect your opinion."

"Well, one thing I really love about your writing is you go deep within your characters. They come across as real people with problems we can all relate to. Did you actually change the ending to suit your boyfriend? I read that in an article, but nowadays you often can't tell if you're reading truth or lies or fiction."

"Yes. Unfortunately, I did."

"Hm... you know, I don't believe that. You were originally going to have your two main characters marry?"

"Yes."

"Well, for whatever reason you did it, have you ever thought that you chose the best ending?"

Lexy sat up, eyes widening. She'd been thinking the same thing, but hearing it from someone else hit home. "What do you mean?"

Meredith's eyes were as blue as Chris' and they seemed to grow larger. "Well, maybe not marrying each other was a good thing."

No one had ever said that. Everyone seemed to be angry they didn't marry and have a happy ever after like her other books.

"You see how toxic their relationship is too?"

Meredith sipped her lemonade, then put her glass down. "I don't want to say too much. I'm hoping you learn to believe in yourself. Trust your instincts. You need to figure this out in your own heart. But when you do, I'd love to talk to you about it more."

"Thanks, but my characters have to marry, or my agent will flip."

Meredith said nothing. She probably figured she'd said all she needed to. Lexy knew enough about counseling to know that a good therapist never tells you the answer. Their job is to guide you so that you can figure it out yourself. She sure hoped she could one day soon. Lexy glanced at her watch. "Well, time to go."

They trekked back to her cottage. Lexy had already installed Emma's car seat, so she got them all buckled in the backseat and began the drive to the arena.

All she could think about were Meredith's words.

What did she mean?

Was she suggesting Sarah and Nick never marry? Then again, why should they if their relationship was so horrible? How could she fix this? Sarah deserved a happy ending.

"Unca Chris said I might get a dog too one day." Emma's words pulled Lexy out of her thoughts. Thank goodness. She was in a state of confusion and needed to snap out of it. "Jenny has a cat. I liked him too, but I like walking a dog even better."

"Jenny?"

"Yeah. His girlfriend."

Aha. It really was true. Chris had a girlfriend and Emma just confirmed it. She was probably that woman she saw in the back yard. Interesting to note. She was sure glad she hadn't initiated a kiss the other night and faced being rebuffed. Whew. She wanted to ask Emma more questions but figured that was not a good thing to do. She shouldn't be snooping about her friend and putting his niece on the spot.

"Well, Asher loves you, so please feel free to think of him as yours, too."

"I love him back."

They sang the rest of the way and Asher barked his excitement when they arrived. Today they were practicing walking with their pups heeling beside them, stopping, starting, and learning more commands such as 'down' and 'stand.'

Lexy led Asher across the room and at one point their eyes locked for a split second. She registered her pup's eyes twinkling and he looked like he was having the best time of his life. He literally took her breath away and all she could think about was, *What a blessing he is in my life.* They had become a team. Partners. His delight flew out to her, enveloping her, and she was no longer leading, but accompanying him through a great adventure. Why had she never gotten a dog? Every day she loved him more.

Emma next took her turn walking Asher and Lexy felt the same thing watching them. This little girl had filled Lexy's life with such enjoyment, and reminded her of how exciting life could be. A feeling she was striving to get back. Writer's Bliss cottage had definitely been another blessing for her, leading her to Asher and Emma. Her heart was so full tonight.

Class always seemed to rush by fast, and on the way home, they drove by the center. She was startled to see a sold sticker stretched across the for-sale sign.

That was interesting. She wondered what was going to happen to it, fearing it might be torn down, or made into offices. She sure hoped not.

After singing all the way home, she pulled into her laneway, then walked a tired but exhilarated Emma next door. Chris appeared as if waiting for them.

"How did it go?" he asked.

"Great." Emma clapped her hands. "Watch." She turned to Asher. "Drop." And he did. She walked a few feet away. "Here." And Asher ran right to her and sat down beside her. "Yay ... good boy."

Chris' jaw dropped. "Well, I'm impressed. I guess he's doing well."

Not tired anymore, Emma skipped off with Asher to Meredith's room to show her what the pup had learned.

"Thanks for letting her go with you. She's having a lot of fun."

"I'm the lucky one. She's a delight to be around."

"Do you have time to join me?" Chris pointed to the back yard. "I want to discuss something with you."

"Sure."

They sat at the picnic table where a nice cool breeze trickled by.

"So lovely out here. What did you want to talk to me about?" Lexy fixed her eyes on him, liking what she saw. His blue T-shirt matched his eyes, making them pop even more.

"You mentioned that Asher came from a litter left on the beach."

"Yes."

"Have the rest of the pups found homes?"

"I'm not sure. Why?"

"Well, seeing how much Emma loves Asher, I was thinking of adopting one of his brothers or sisters for Emma."

"Wow." Such a kind and loving gesture. "A terrific idea. I can call Doctor Dan and see."

"I'd like that. Thank you but shh, I'm keeping it a surprise."

"My lips are sealed. Hey, did you see someone bought the center?"

"Yes." He looked serious. "And I happen to know the owner."

"You do?"

"Yes. Me. I didn't say anything before, because I was waiting to close the deal."

Excited, she grabbed hold of his hand, then pulled back fast.

Remember the girlfriend, who was now confirmed as Jenny.

"Really? Are you going to run it the way we knew it?"

"Sure am. That was what drew me even more to this town. The center was for sale, as well as this cottage."

"We had such fun times there."

"We sure did."

It felt good talking to someone who knew her from way back. Who knew that girl who appeared strong on the outside but was vulnerable on the inside. Good to know that someone had liked her just the way she was, flaws, weaknesses and all.

"It's a new dream and I'm thrilled for you."

"Thanks. My life changed fast but I'm liking the path ahead."

"Me, too."

Staring into his big blue eyes, she wondered if she was falling in love.

No, she wouldn't allow that. She couldn't.

He was with someone else.

Besides, their friendship was too good to ruin.

Ever.

Thirty

Ah... silence. Lexy never knew how much she craved it.

Deep breath in, deep breath out.

Back sitting on the porch, now her favorite place, Asher asleep on her lap, coffee on a little table beside her, the sun rising in a glory of pinks, reds and blues, she felt life couldn't get any better.

Except her book wasn't finished. She was still re-reading her current draft right from the beginning, slowly, but almost done. She'd deal with this issue later.

Lexy was continually stunned at how different she felt from that stressed-out city girl. Actually, different wasn't quite the right word. More herself seemed more apt. She felt she was letting go of that person she used to be in Toronto. The one who tried to be who everyone else wanted her to be. The one who lived behind thick walls protecting herself from getting hurt. Or trying to.

It hadn't worked. She got hurt anyway.

Jake.

How had she ever gotten involved with him? Why had she let her defenses down? Why had she allowed him to chip away at her walls?

She wished she could stop thinking of him.

Then again, maybe she should.

Maybe instead of shoving him away, squishing him, trying to ignore all thoughts about him, she should confront her feelings. Or lack of them. She didn't feel much at all about him now, but once thought she had what she figured was a terrific boyfriend, one she'd spend her life with. Okay, to be honest, she had a gut feeling all along that the relationship wasn't good, but she ignored that and eased the ramparts guarding her heart.

What a mistake.

At first, he seemed perfect, and she had felt loved, but as time went on he began criticizing her relentlessly and resenting the time she spent writing.

"You care more for your made-up characters than you do for me," he'd say repeatedly.

He was probably right, especially near the end.

What Jake liked the best was – what he called – the fame she received as a bestselling author. The parties they went to. The so-called prestige. None of that meant anything to her. All she wanted to do was write.

Write.

She sat straight up, making sure she didn't wake Asher.

She wished she felt the way she used to. When she would wake up with a story idea and rush to jot it down. That was what her writing used to be all about. It filled her heart, nurtured especially by her grandpa, and was her whole being.

Where had it all gone wrong? It seemed so commercial now. After all, she began writing what was in her heart and was shocked to find an agent and readers who loved her first book. Then the tension erupted to create another bestseller with everyone watching and reading and judging. Instead of coming from her heart, she found herself poring over reviews – the negative ones especially – trying to write for them. To make them stop saying bad things about her.

And then Jake got involved. And she was afraid of losing him after investing so much emotional time into him. Especially, thinking she was in love. He never showed interest in her work, until he was bored one day and flipped through one. He mocked the romance element, and it haunted her every single day that she had changed it.

Why did she really do it? And so fast?

Meredith had challenged her on that.

Maybe the problem ran deeper than just trying to please him.

You'll never amount to anything. You're useless.

Oh, no! There went that negative tape that played over and over in her head.

Enough. Get lost, Dad.

Another weed to pull out.

Several, as a matter of fact.

Time to practice some healing.

Lexy closed her eyes and imagined a field full of red roses, her mom's favorite flower. She also added lilies and sunflowers, tulips and daffodils. She sniffed, feeling she could smell all the aromas mingling together into a perfume she'd want to wear forever. Her 'heart' garden was beautiful, and she wanted to keep it that way. Then, she noticed the weeds. Big tall ugly ones sprouting up, threatening to destroy everything. Nope, she wouldn't let it. She imagined moving in and out of the flowers, pulling every single rotten weed and throwing it away. And once again her garden was gorgeous. Her eyes popped open.

Yes, this was going to work. The weeds of her father had been tossed aside. She liked this imagery and what it meant to her. She needed to keep beauty alive in her heart, soul, and mind. Forever.

Whew.

But now she needed a break. Thinking of Jake and her dad simply wore her out.

"C'mon, Asher. Let's go into town."

She grabbed her purse, buckled him in the car and they took off. First visit, the pet store.

"How is it going?" Chelsea asked.

"Great. Always looking for new treats."

"Try these." She handed over a bag of liver ones.

"Thanks, I will." She also loaded up a few more toys, keeping in mind that Emma might be having her own pup soon.

Next stop. The café.

Sitting outdoors, a latte on the table, a pup at her feet, she relaxed. Somehow her horrid thoughts had flown away, and peace reigned again.

"Hello there."

She leaned back on her chair and almost fell over.

"Sorry. Didn't mean to startle you."

Lexy looked up at Chris. A disheveled Chris wearing a wrinkled tee, paint stains on his jeans, holding a coffee. She noticed his hair was growing longer too. Don't touch it, she admonished herself.

"Oh, just deep in thought. I see you've been painting. How are the renovations going?"

"Good." He reached down to pet Asher. "Hey, would you like to come see them?"

"I'd love to."

"C'mon, then."

Lexy was excited to have the opportunity to step inside the building again. While walking to the center, a flash of bright red sped by. She turned her head fast to see a car in the distance. Red? Jake drove a red car. Was that him? No, couldn't be. She'd been thinking of him that morning so she must have just conjured him up. He wouldn't even know where she was.

"So, here we are."

Chris opened the door, and walking in set off memories. Glorious ones of kids playing together, sports, art, crafts. So much fun.

"Lots of cleaning to be done, but I have big ideas." Chris circled the room, pointing out things he'd already started, like adding missing floorboards, painting walls, replacing the broken hardware on doors and cupboards. His eyes literally glowed. She envied him.

"You know, seeing you with your dream makes me want mine."

"I thought writing was yours." He squinted, staring at her.

"I thought so too, but now I'm not sure what to write about. Something more serious maybe? Frivolous? Lighthearted? I can't even finish the one I've been working on for months."

"My mother loves your books. She feels they are more than just romance, with profound messages for readers to savor. Don't doubt yourself. I'm on your second one and I like that you really get into the human psyche, making your characters come alive. I'm enjoying them and understand completely why they are bestsellers."

"Really? You're reading another one?" She was stunned.

"Of course. I always admired your writing, even as a ten-year-old kid. I'm planning on reading every one of them. You're a really good storyteller."

Lexy was so touched she could barely speak. Instead, she threw her arms around him. To have someone she respected care enough to venture into her creative world meant a lot. Oops, she pulled away fast. She shouldn't be doing this. It made her feel things she shouldn't be feeling.

She spent about an hour there before leaving for Writer's Bliss. Chris followed behind her in his car and waved as he drove into Yellow Rose's laneway.

Pulling up beside her own cottage, she was alarmed to see a red car parked there.

Oh, no.

Jake was sitting on the porch.

She wanted to vomit.

Thirty-one

People often describe having butterflies in their stomachs when nervous.

Butterflies? Forget it.

Freaking big birds were stomping all over Lexy's insides. Nausea rose again, panic moved in.

Should she just back out and take off?

No, Jake would go after her, and thoroughly love the car chase. He'd be in his element, terrorizing her.

Groan. Might as well deal with it.

Lexy slowly eased out of the car and opened the passenger side to retrieve Asher.

"You got a dog?" Jake stood and walked down the steps. "That's not like you."

She held her pup in her arms, keeping him safe. She had never seen Jake around animals and had no idea how he'd react. Glancing at him, her heart skipped a beat. Unwillingly. She had to admit he looked good. He always did. Dark chestnut hair perfectly styled; casual clothes tailored to fit his gym-induced physique. She also noted he didn't reach out to touch the pup. Unusual. She didn't know many people who could resist the cuteness of a little ball of fur.

Just ignore him. But how do you do that when he was standing right in front of her?

"What do you want?" She ignored the whole dog comment. Her current life was none of his business.

"To see you." He opened his arms. "Now give me a hug."

Lexy backed away. "How did you find me?"

"You told me about this place. I figured you might be here. See? I know you well."

No, he didn't. But she did recall telling him about the cottage one night when they were sharing past stories. When he was nicer.

"Asher, Asher," Emma's voice rang out.

Lexy turned to see Emma running toward them, Chris trailing behind. Jake backed away when she put the pup down and Emma knelt to hug him.

"Sorry," Chris whispered. "We were out on the beach and I saw a car here. Thought I'd see if everything is okay."

"Who is this guy?" Jake bellowed. "Your bodyguard? Did you hire someone to protect you?"

"Chris, this is Jake Montgomery."

"Is everything okay?" Chris' eyes were wide and worried.

"Yes." Lexy nodded for emphasis.

"All right. Come on, Emma. Let's keep walking."

"Okay." The little girl reluctantly said goodbye to Asher.

Watching them leave, Lexy felt like calling them to come back but the fact was, she didn't want Jake around any of them. She didn't want her messy old life to intrude on her new peaceful one.

"Can I come in?" Jake tapped his foot, looking at his watch. "I've been waiting here for over an hour."

Too bad. Should she tell him to just get lost? Should she at least listen to what he had to say? After all, he'd driven all this way.

"Well, okay, but you can't stay long. I'm busy."

"Doing what? Writing another dud?"

Outraged, she considered running into the cottage and locking the door behind her, but she knew he wouldn't leave until he had his say. And she didn't want her neighbors to hear anything coming out of his mouth. Ignoring his words, just wanting to get this over with, she opened the door, stood back to let him in, then followed. He ignored the pup, so she let him down. Asher just stood there, as if in a trance, staring at their visitor while Jake strutted around.

"Sure, looks like a hovel to me." He stopped, hands on hips. "I can't believe you'd stay in such a dive."

Same old Jake. No appreciation of tradition. No respect for the fact this once belonged to her grandparents whom she loved. Always negative.

"I love it here." Her chin rose to meet his eyes.

"You never did have the best of taste." He smirked as if finding his own hurtful words funny.

"Are you going to make me some coffee?"

"No. What do you want?"

He reached out again to hug her, but she backed away again. He shook his head. "I don't know why you aren't welcoming me more. Oh, and thanks for mailing the ring." He pulled it out of his pocket. "Today's your lucky day, I want you back."

The ring that never seemed to fully disappear.

She stared.

Her lucky day.

Yeah, right.

She had loved him. Or thought she did. Once upon a time, she couldn't believe this handsome man wanted her and she felt proud to be by his side. He also used to say such sweet things to her. Then it all changed. Almost overnight. Insults were hurled at her, sarcasm, demands. And here he was again, still the same.

Sadly, part of her wanted to run into his arms.

To the life she once had.

The days when she had a fiancé, when she felt part of a couple, a team.

Involuntarily, Lexy took one step toward him. Asher growled. She stopped, sweeping her pup up in her arms, where he licked her face, bringing her back to reality.

She saw it all clearly now.

An invisible line was drawn between Jake and herself. On his side stood ridicule, deceit, hurtfulness. On her side was a life she was building in peace, with Asher, and good friends, some who lived right next door.

She missed what she thought she had with Jake. Had hoped to have. Not what she really did have. Which was nothing.

"That's not going to happen." Stepping back, she glared, holding firm.

"Oh c'mon. Are you still sore over changing your ending? I was only joking." He shook his head. "I couldn't believe you'd do what I said anyway."

Of course, he knew she would. At that point, he was controlling almost everything she did.

"You almost ruined my life."

"I did not. We were a good team together. You loved having me at all your functions."

Yes, she did. Back in the days when she had loved him. Love? Probably not. More like under his spell. He'd gaslighted her so much she had believed him – that she was nothing without him.

"You dumped me on national TV."

"Look, they paid me big-time money. I didn't mean it. C'mon, put the ring back on."

Of course he meant it. He had refused all her phone calls after that.

Enough. She was done. For good.

She said nothing. Not responding and not taking the ring was her answer. She let a wiggling Asher down, and he continued to stand beside her, growling.

"C'mon, you're not a good writer," he sneered. "Face it. Your bestsellers were just sugar on a stick and won't last."

And there it was. What was that saying? Oh, right, same old, same old. Jake threw out love, then reeled it back in.

To her surprise, she could feel that ten-year-old redheaded child rising inside her. The kid who never backed down.

"Get out," she screamed.

To her surprise, Asher started barking the loudest she'd ever heard. Of course, he had never heard her scream.

"Oh, honey, you don't mean that." He went to hug her just as Asher raced over, jumped up on him, still barking, trying to push him away. Even her pup knew how rotten this guy was. "Get lost, dog." He actually looked afraid as he backed away.

Scooping Asher up in her arms, Lexy marched to the door, pulling it open. "Get out," she repeated.

To her surprise, Emma stood there, Chris running up to join her.

"Is Asher okay?" Emma asked. "I heard him barking." She ran in, reaching up to pet him. Lexy put him down to be with her.

"Sorry." Chris looked at her, then at Jake, then back at her. "Emma was upset hearing Asher bark. She took off running. Is everything still all right?"

"Yes. Jake is just leaving."

Jake eyed him up and down. "So, you do have a new boyfriend. Is that it? Definitely a step down."

"What I do is none of your business. Now, go."

Lexy could feel Chris tense up beside her, but admired the fact he said nothing. It felt like a standoff until Jake finally walked out the door, passing Chris. Then he turned around, pointing his finger.

"You'll come crawling back to me. I'm the best you'll ever get."

"Go," she said firmly. She wanted to scream but figured if she did, it would set Asher off again and right now he was having fun playing ball with Emma.

Finally, Jake got in his car and drove away. Chris swung an arm around her shoulders. It felt good.

"Was that your ex trying to get you back?" Chris asked.

"Yes."

His eyebrows rose.

"But I channeled my redheaded kid and told him to get lost."

Chris lips tugged at the corner. "I remember that fierce little kid well. Here, let's sit. You're swaying and I'm afraid you'll fall."

She hated that he removed his arm, but it felt good to curl up on her grandma's chair.

"You know, I never realized before that he is just like my father. I think having him in this cottage made me really see that. Insults roll out of him, he's constantly demeaning me, making everything my fault."

"I hate seeing you treated like that."

"Guess I was used to it and accepted it as normal. My mom and grandma always told me to ignore my father, but I found it tough to hear I'm useless and will amount to nothing. It makes you wonder if he was right."

"He wasn't."

"I'm slowly figuring that out, but the feeling is hard to shake when something is so rooted in my head. And then I go and choose a fiancé just like him. Someone who treated me the same way."

"I'm glad that you are at least seeing that this type of behavior is wrong." He pulled his chair closer and reached out for her hand.

"Me, too." She appreciated Chris' confidence in her and loved the warmth of his hand. Her nightmare with Jake was over. Put to rest. Finally. That was then, but this was now. And her now was quite pleasant. Her now just needed to shake the past. To let it go.

She could do this.

Another gigantic weed gone out of her life.

Thirty-two

"Are we done? Are we done?"

Chris smiled. Emma's eyes shone as bright as the sun washing over her, illuminating her excitement.

"Almost."

"Goody. I can't wait. I'll go get Nana." She ran into the house.

He stood back and looked, remembering a phone call he'd had from his sister several years back. "Emma has always dreamed of a little treehouse of her own," she had said. "Nothing elaborate. Just big enough to read in, but large enough so a friend can join her. Will you help me build it?"

Of course, he'd agreed. Had even purchased the materials needed, but they'd never gotten the chance.

Elizabeth.

Gone way too soon, and he missed her so much.

He still reached for the phone to call her.

Ever since talking to Lexy, his sister had been on his mind more so. This time he allowed his thoughts to surface, not burying them as usual, granting himself the opportunity to grieve. He also got the courage to ask his niece if she wanted to help him build her treehouse. To be honest, it took a great effort on his part because he'd rather just store the materials away, never thinking of them, feeling guilty that he hadn't run over to his sister's that same day and helped her put it together. Instead, he'd waited, thinking they had all the time in the world. How quickly life could change.

Chris had thought of doing it himself and surprising Emma, but decided having her input would strengthen their bond. Besides, she was so much like her mother; he figured she'd enjoy putting her own stamp on it all. Her enthusiasm was like a meteor shower he'd once witnessed. Shiny, bright, with hundreds of shooting stars circulating her joy as she helped hammer, saw, and paint. Surprisingly, her mother had been teaching her such skills since a tiny child and she even had her own kid-size tools that she was very proficient with. The whole time, he had felt he was fulfilling a promise to his sister, feeling closer to her as he worked on it, as if he honoring her memory nail by nail, board by board. He knew Elizabeth would have loved it and also would have enjoyed Emma's precious ideas. It even looked a lot like the one he and his sister used to play in as kids, minus the bright color.

A smile edged across his face at his all-time funniest moment during this project. He had asked Emma what color she wanted. He figured brown and green, to blend into the tree. Emma had other ideas. Much to his shock, she had startled him when she raised her tiny fist in the air and screamed, "Pink. Pink. I want it pink."

Pink?

And, as it turned out, fluorescent pink. The brightest in the paint store.

So pink was the chosen color.

Leaning over, he checked the ladder again, making sure of its sturdiness, just as Emma ran out pulling Meredith by the hand.

"Are you ready?" he asked.

"Yeah. Yeah."

"Go to it. Make sure you grab the railings."

"Great job," Meredith said. "The pink is Elizabeth all over again."

"Sure is. Emma definitely is a lot like her mom, growing more so each day." He was watching his niece closely, making sure she made it up okay. He'd even consulted with a colleague from his old school about how to make it secure and sturdy. The treehouse boasted not only a platform but four walls, a roof, doorway, and window. And of course, not too high up.

"I made it. I made it." Emma peered out the window. "And I love my pillows."

More pink, of course. She'd wanted it simple, but with lots of fluffy things. Pillows, she meant. They'd gone on a shopping spree one day and she'd discovered pink outdoor ones that qualified.

"Do you want to join her, Mom?"

"Is there room?"

"Sure is."

"Well, yes. I'd love to be up there too." She climbed up, agile as ever, and now he could see both their heads out the treehouse's window.

"Look it. Look it." Emma pointed. "I see Lexy and Asher coming."

Chris whipped his head around. He hadn't seen his buddy in a few days. His heart sped up at her smile and he found himself just standing there staring, grinning back.

"I came a bit early. Hope that's okay?" Lexy asked.

"Yes, of course."

"Hi." Emma waved.

"Hi there." Lexy waved back. "Love the pink. Emma's choice, of course?"

"Of course."

"Come on up," Emma yelled. "Bring Asher. Unca Chris has a surprise for him down there and I have another one up here."

"First, I'm coming down." Meredith swung her legs over and climbed down. "Your turn, Lexy."

"Thanks. Does Emma know yet?" she whispered.

Chris shook his head.

"Good."

"And here's Emma's surprise." Chris picked up a knapsack laying on the picnic table. "Asher will fit in this and you can attach it to your back. That way the pup will make it to the treehouse safely."

"Pretty amazing. Thank you, Emma." Chris helped her strap it on and put Asher in it, his little head sticking out, taking in everything.

He had invited Lexy and Asher over a few days ago to take part in another special surprise for Emma. He was glad to see she seemed contented and well-rested after the whole Jake episode. He also noted that the comfort he felt around her the other night was still there. Knowing she understood his grief was a wonderful support.

He chuckled as Emma squealed in delight at having her best furry friend up there with her. Along with Lexy. She had made sure the walls would keep the pup safe.

"Here's another surprise. A special doggy bed just for you, Asher."

Emma had definitely thought of everything.

"So beautiful," he heard her say. Asher barked out his approval, which had them all laughing.

Meredith went indoors to finish up a few things, and Chris got to work cleaning up, getting ready for the next big thing he'd planned. Enjoying hearing the chatter between Emma and Lexy, he waited about thirty minutes before yelling up, "How would you all like to go for a drive? I have a surprise for you too, Emma."

Emma poked her head out the window. "Ice cream?"

"That, too."

They joined him on the ground, rounded up Meredith, and piled in the car, singing at the top of their lungs. At one point, it got quiet and he heard Lexy ask Emma if pink was her favorite color.

"Nah," Emma said. "Blue is. Mommy liked pink. So now that the treehouse is the brightest pink ever, she'll be able to see it from heaven."

Chris never knew this. He was also shocked, since she rarely mentioned her mom. Wiping away a tear, he glanced at his mother's eyes, wide in surprise. He also caught Lexy staring at him through the back mirror. How touching. How thoughtful. And he was so glad he hadn't talked his niece out of that bright color. She knew exactly what she wanted.

Arriving in town, Chris pulled up next door to the vet's office.

"Where are we going?" Emma looked around.

"You'll see." Chris helped her out of her car seat and led all of them into a large red brick building behind a sign saying 'Animal Haven' on it. A tall, pleasant looking woman rose from behind her desk. She looked down at Emma. "Hello there, I'm Sandra."

"I'm Emma and this is Nana, Unca Chris, Lexy, and Asher."

"I've been expecting you."

"You have?"

"Yes. Follow me."

The lady led them out a door to a large area out back. A little white pup was romping with a toy inside a fenced-in unit.

"Asher. Look." Emma pointed. "A puppy just like you."

He squirmed with excitement, so Lexy put him down fast. He ran to the crate door, pawing at it.

"Emma, would you like to visit with the pup?" Sandra asked.

"She's a girl."

"Yes, please."

Lexy held Asher back while Sandra opened the door and ushered in Chris and Emma. She shut the gate behind them.

"The best thing to do is to stand still," Sandra said. "And just let the pup approach you."

Chris was surprised to see the little one run right to Emma, placing her tiny paws on her knees. Emma plopped down and the pup climbed on her lap. She hugged her while the dog licked her face.

"What would you call her?" Chris asked.

"Angel." Not even a moment of hesitation.

"Really? Well, guess what. Angel is yours."

To his surprise, Emma started to cry. She looked up. "You mean it?"

"Yes."

Emma got up and wrapped her arms around him. "Thank you, thank you, thank you."

The little pup put her paws up on her again, and Emma dropped to her knees and hugged her. "Hey Angel, you're coming home with me. Lexy, can Asher meet her?"

"Yes, of course. Angel is Asher's sister."

"She is?" Chris didn't think Emma's smile could get any bigger.

"She sure is." Sandra opened the gate, and the two pups sniffed each other, then began tugging on a toy dinosaur together.

Emma couldn't stop smiling and clapping her hands.

Warmth spread through Chris, producing a huge grin, probably as big as Emma's.

He had his final answer.

Moving here was a good decision.

He glanced over at Lexy.

And he was sure he was falling in love.

Thirty-three

"Ruff, ruff, ruff..."

Asher looked up and let out a woof.

Darn. Lexy should have anticipated setting her pup off when she changed her ringtone to a dog barking sound. She made a mental note to try again. No love songs. No animal sounds.

Checking the name, she was surprised to see her mother's lawyer calling.

"Hello, Jim."

"Hello there, Lexy. How are you doing?"

"Surprisingly well."

"Good to hear. I figured it'd do you the world of good to be there. Now, do you remember an Edith Chamberland?"

"Yes, of course, Mom's best friend."

"She wants to see you. Can I give her your number?"

"Certainly. Is something wrong?"

"Not that I'm aware of. She just wants to get in touch with you. I'm rushing off to court but give me a call if you ever need anything."

Jim, a man of few words.

"Thank you, I will."

Click.

"Ruff, ruff, ruff."

Asher barked.

Lexy glanced at the phone.

Edith.

Jim worked fast.

"Hi, Edith."

"Oh, hi, Lexy. You knew? Oh, right, you saw my name on your phone. Um, I was wondering if I could come see you."

"Yes, of course. I'd love that."

"Later today?"

That fast? Something must be up.

"Sure."

"I'm not too far from you. Around one o'clock?"

"Certainly. See you then."

Nerves exploded. Or the heebie jeebies, as she used to call them as a kid. The stomping birds were back wreaking havoc.

Why the urgency?

Was Edith sick?

And why hadn't she kept in touch with this woman? She'd meant to. After all, Edith was close to her mom, having attended high school and college together. She glanced at her computer, quickly deciding to give up her daily sit down and try to write a few words. She was still getting nowhere with that book. Then again, she hadn't finished reading over what she'd already written. Close, but still had several chapters left.

"Let's get our walk in, Asher."

Somehow her pup managed to get two stuffed toys in his mouth, hanging onto them by their ears.

"Really? You're bringing the lamb and the bunny?"

He ran right to the door.

"Well, okay then. You're sure getting the hang of it."

Walking out on the sand, she was thrilled to see Meredith with Emma and Angel. The two pups ran toward each other. Stopping in unison, they watched as Asher dropped the bunny on the sand and carried the lamb over to Angel.

"Ruff," Asher barked. Angel picked it up as Asher wagged his tail.

Seriously? Was Asher really giving the lamb to Angel? The stuffed animal was like a security blanket for him. Guess he figured Angel needed it more.

Emma ran over.

"Mommy would love her," she said.

Lexy squatted beside her, surprised to hear her mention her mom again.

"Yes, she would."

"Your mom too, right? She would love Asher?"

"Yes, definitely."

She was touched that Emma felt a bond with her, both having lost their mothers. She watched the pups carry their toys and run up to Emma, crawling into her lap, licking her face. The joy on the little girl's face was breathtaking. Lexy jumped up and quickly snapped a photo, wanting to remember this moment forever.

"Pups that share," Meredith said, walking over. "Sweet."

"So sweet."

"How are you today?" Meredith asked.

"I'm doing okay. Still not writing much, though."

"You'll get it done."

"Sure wish I had the faith in me that you do."

"I have complete faith in you. Your writing is such a gift, and I look forward to your next book."

"Well, thanks. I'm still searching for a proper ending."

Meredith's eyebrows jumped up. "Or maybe a beginning."

Lexy loved this about Meredith. She said few words, but the ones she used made her think. Guess she should be viewing her last chapter as a beginning for the young couple. Instead, she thought of it as an ending, even worse, some kind of deathtrap or something. That alone was awful, yet very telling. Why was she thinking of her fictional couples' union as a deathtrap?

"Look it. They're sleeping," Emma said.

Such cuteness. The little pups could barely keep their eyes open. All that playing had worn them out.

"Gotta take Angel home for her nap," Emma said.

How sweet watching the good care this little girl took of her pup. Lexy waved goodbye as she carried Asher into the cottage, putting him in his little home. She decided on the spot to do something she hadn't done in years. Bake. She had even purchased all the ingredients for chocolate chip cookies a few days ago, just in case.

She remembered from her days baking with her grandmother that she always kept her favorite recipes, as well as ones she wanted to try, in a notebook in a drawer Lexy hadn't checked out yet. She pulled it open and found it – blue cover, worn, pages dog-eared – just as she remembered. Picking it up, she pressed it against her heart, closing her eyes, remembering all the times her grandmother flipped through it, searching for an oldie but goodie or deciding to experiment with a new one. One time they even tried out a Christmas cookie in the middle of a heat wave and laughed and laughed as they created little snow people and reindeer, still in their bathing suits. Then they'd eat them.

"Save room for supper," her mother would say. Then her grandma would sneak her another. Such good times.

Finally opening her eyes and the book, Lexy flicked through the pages finding the cookie recipe she wanted. She had it almost memorized but checked just in case, and then got to work mixing, rolling, enjoying the feeling of producing something edible. Hopefully.

They turned out lopsided and in many twisted shapes but tasted good. That was all that mattered.

A knock on the door.

Lexy opened it. A small elderly woman stood there. Squinting, she barely recognized her mom's friend. Her hair was greyer, she was stooped over, and pain radiated from her eyes.

"Edith. Welcome."

She was carrying a large flat package. Looked like a painting.

"Here, I'll take this."

"Okay, dear."

Lexy took the package and leaned it up against a wall.

"What's that delightful smell?" Edith asked.

"I've made cookies just for you."

"Why, thank you." She looked around. "I was here once years ago with your mother. I remember it well. A well-loved home."

Well-loved. Lexy liked that description, feeling embarrassed that she still hadn't removed the covers from her mom's paintings. Oh, well. One day.

"So, who do we have here?" Edith was looking at a wiggly Asher, fully awake, sitting up in his crate, tail wagging.

Lexy quickly opened the latch, and he came bounding out to greet his guest.

"This is Asher."

"Oh, how cute."

"That, he is. C'mon out to the kitchen. I've put some coffee on."

After cookies, coffee, and small talk, Edith burst into tears, seemingly out of the blue. Lexy was startled. "Are you okay?"

Her pup put his little paws up on their visitor's knees. Guess he could sense where he was needed as Edith lifted him up on her lap.

"I have something from your mother." She wiped her eyes. "When she got sick again, she was worried she wouldn't have time to give it to you. I promised I would. But then my husband got ill unexpectedly."

"I remember. You couldn't come to the funeral because of that."

"Yes, true. But I totally forgot to give you your mom's gift."

"That's okay." Lexy touched her hand. "I understand."

"I know you do, dear. You're as compassionate as your mom." She dabbed again at her tears. "Well, Stan passed away and I decided to move into a retirement home."

"I'm so sorry." Lexy hadn't known that, then again, she was so lost and wrapped up in her own issues, it probably just flew past her. She had met Stan once and thought he was such a nice man. That was probably why Edith looked so tired. Not only had she lost her best friend, but her husband in such a short space of time.

Once again - why hadn't she kept in touch?

"Well, I found this while I was packing up." She pointed toward the other room. "The gift from your mother. A painting, of course, with a letter taped to the back of it."

Lexy was shocked. A letter? A painting?

"Again, I'm so sorry." Edith put Asher back on the floor and wrung her hands. "I meant to give this to you a long time ago."

"Don't worry. I know you've been through a lot. Thank you for bringing this now." She considered opening it right then, but couldn't find the courage. They chatted for a while longer before Edith got up to leave.

"Promise you'll keep in touch?" Edith asked.

"Promise." And she meant it.

Lexy and Asher walked her to her car and waved goodbye as their visitor drove off.

Back in the living room, Lexy stared at the package.

She needed help. Picking up her phone, she hit some numbers.

"Chris, I know this is selfish of me, but can you meet me at the rock? Emma can come too, of course, and the two pups can play together."

She held her breath.

Thirty-four

"Yes, of course."

"Whew." Lexy exhaled. "Thank you. When are you free?"

"You sound panicky. Mom is teaching Emma how to knit, so I can go there now. Would that work?"

"I'm on my way."

Lexy quickly harnessed Asher and attached his leash. Balancing the painting tucked under one arm, and leading Asher with the other, she walked to their rock. Her pup seemed in tune with her urgency, because not once did he veer off course to sniff. She felt herself relax when she saw Chris was already there. Just seeing his smile set off a warmth from head to toe, easing her wild birds into gentle butterflies. Nervous, but not as bad. She smiled back.

"Thanks for coming."

"Sure, no problem."

"What's this?" He pointed to the package.

Sitting beside him, leaning the painting up against her legs, she let Asher explore the surroundings, as she explained.

"Aha. A letter and a painting from your mom. Have you looked at it yet?"

"No." The stomping birds were back. "I'm afraid to. That's why I called you. For moral support."

He wrapped one arm around her. "Take your time. Don't do it until you're ready."

"I think I am." She reached down and pulled the tape releasing the envelope, moving the painting over so it leaned up against a small bush. Her hands shook as she opened it and pulled out a sheet of paper. She stared at the familiar handwriting, feeling as if her mother was standing right there. "Do you mind if I read it out loud?"

"Go ahead."

"Here goes."

"Dear Lexy,

I didn't expect to get sick so fast and fear I have little time left. In case you can't get here quick enough and I don't get to tell you in person, I asked Edith to give you this letter and painting. There are a few things I want to say to you before I go."

Lexy paused, a tear drifting down. Her mother's presence enveloped her, soothing her, yet making her heart ache with sadness.

"I know you don't like to talk about your father, but I can tell he still hurts you even after all these years. Oh, I understand you try to hide it, and your grandparents and I tried to compensate, but I know the awful things he said to you linger. I see it in your self-doubt, your hesitation, your refusal to believe in your own gifts."

Hmm... so her mother was a lot more aware than Lexy thought. Her hands shook. She handed the letter to Chris. "Do you mind reading the rest?"

"Of course not."

"My biggest regret was that I should have kicked him out sooner and I'm sorry I didn't. He was so nice to me in the beginning, then became very moody, but I kept hoping he would get over that. I never realized the cruel things he said to you, until one day I came home early and heard him, and that was the moment I told him to leave. I still remember him walking out the door and how he stopped and hurled more hateful words at you. I saw your face – stoic – realizing you were used to it, but I also saw you flinch as if in pain. Of course you were. Mental pain. And I'm so sorry. You did nothing to cause this. Nothing at all. I was his meal ticket and he obviously pretended to care for you when I was around. I have tried to be supportive of you but fear I'll be leaving you soon and I won't be here to say everything I always want to say to you.

Most important, please, never forget that you are beautiful and talented and amazing. Your creativity leaps from the pages of your books, spreading love out into a world that needs your special touch. You soothe the souls and hearts of everyone you meet.

My dying wish for you is that you embrace life with all your heart. Throw your arms out and hug the world. Give love, but also let love in.

I painted this for you, showing more of how I feel in the best way I can, through my artwork. I hope it brings you joy every day.

I will love you forever, always hoping that one day you will learn to love yourself.

Forever in my heart, Mom."

Tiny paws appeared on her knees. Once again, Asher always knew when he was needed. Lexy pulled him up on her lap and they all sat in silence.

"Thank you," she finally said. "Thanks for being here."

"I'm always here for you." Pause. "So, he terrorized you behind your mom's back."

"Yes. And he told me not to tell anyone."

"Any physical abuse?"

"No. But verbal cuts like a knife."

"Definitely. How confusing it must have been."

"Sure was. Unfortunately, I blamed myself for everything."

"And none of anything he accused you of, was your fault."

"Mentally I know that, but my heart hasn't figured it all out yet."

He squeezed her hand. "You will."

"I'm ready to look at the painting now," Lexy said.

"Would you like me to pull the paper off?"

"Yes, please."

After unwrapping it, Chris stood in front, holding up the painting. Lexy melted. Her mother had created the most beautiful sunrise she'd ever seen. Truly a masterpiece. She feasted on brilliant swatches of violets, reds, purples, oranges that danced across the canvas. A redhead, arms outstretched, embraced the scene in all its glory. Of course, the redhead was her.

One word was painted in the bottom right corner. Joy. Her mom's signature flowed below it.

"Stunning," Chris said, leaning it against a tree, and coming back to join her on the rock.

"It truly is."

"It's like a great big apology from your mom."

"Yes. But it was never her fault. It's also a reminder of all the beauty there is in the world."

"Sure is. I'm so sorry you father was like that."

"You know, I kept busy writing and with book signings, and I never realized until I slowed down that all these negative tropes running through me, all came from my dad. I'm stunned by this. I'm also trying to root them out." She explained the analogy of pulling out weeds in her beautiful rose garden.

"Super idea."

Silence.

"Speaking of rooting out, I debated whether to remind you or not." Chris took hold of her hand. "But do you recall the box we buried?"

"Box?"

"Do you remember one movie day at the center where the characters wrote down bad memories and burned them. You liked that idea and when we came back here, you jotted down hurtful memories of your dad. We pulled the pages out of your notebook, and you wanted to burn them like we saw in the movie, but figured our grandparents would flip if we started a fire. So, we wrapped them in plastic and buried them in a box."

Way back, buried under cobwebs, Lexy remembered.

"I'd forgotten. Or blocked it out."

"I figured that and wasn't sure whether to bring it up again. But how about we dig it up and burn them like we wanted to. It might make you feel better and help put things in the past."

Lexy thought about it. "I'd like that."

Using a stick to dig with, Chris had it out in no time. An old tin box that once held tea leaves.

"How about I get some matches and wood and meet you at your place," he said.

"Good idea."

After they dragged the branch across the opening, he pulled out a bag from his pocket and handed it to her.

Taking it, she looked. "Caramel fudge, my favorite."

"I know. Remember we used to leave little presents here for each other?"

"I sure do."

"You used to make me things. A bracelet, a paper tie, and once even a little story."

"And I still have the pretty blue rock you gave me."

"You do?" His eyes lit up.

"Sure I do."

He grinned. "Great. Well, hey, I'll meet you back at your place in a few minutes."

"Okay, see you then."

She hurried to her cottage, rushing inside to put an exhausted Asher in his little home, and leaned the painting against the couch. After arranging cookies on a plate, she walked out the front door to find Chris was already there, near the beach, piling pieces of wood together to create a fire.

"You baked?" he asked.

"I did. Don't look so surprised."

"They look good."

He lit the fire, pulled over the two lawn chairs he'd brought, and handed her the box.

Lexy opened it and pulled the pages out of the plastic. Hurtful memories stared her in the face – the time her dad destroyed her garden, ran over her sandcastle with a bike, called her fat and ugly in front of her friends.

He was not a nice person and always seemed repulsed by her. She had always made excuses for him, but truth is truth, and to hurt a child was despicable.

Time to let it all go and not let him impact her life any further.

One at a time, she burned each slip of paper.

No more weeds.

"And since Jake was just like him, I'm letting him go too," she added.

"Good." Chris handed over a pen and notepad. "I brought this in case you wanted to add anything else."

"Smart thinking."

She jotted his name down and tossed it in, feeling it was time to be her true self and to take down her walls. This ritual was very cleansing.

They sat by the fire eating cookies for what seemed ages. She ran in a few times to check on Asher, but mostly just sat there watching the paper curl and burn, finding it cathartic. Lexy felt freer, happier, peaceful, and oh how she wanted to snuggle up in Chris' arms.

Even kiss him.

Stop it.

"It sounds like Emma likes Jenny, too." She had no idea she was going to say that, but his ever-present girlfriend was always on her mind.

His head swung around. "You know about her?"

"Yes. Your niece mentioned liking her cat. I'm glad you found someone."

Silence.

"Well, I haven't. Jenny is not my girlfriend anymore."

"I'm sorry to hear that."

Was she, though?

Nah, not really. In fact, she was elated.

Stop it. She shouldn't be overjoyed over his sadness. And probably Jenny's sadness too.

He jumped up and started pacing, startling her, but at least pulling her out of her selfish thoughts.

"Jenny, who I thought was a good friend, even considered asking her to be my fiancé, dumped me not wanting the responsibility of a child and the fact she came second."

Lexy was surprised. Emma was the sweetest and how admirable it was to see Chris step right in to raise her. It made her like him even more.

"That must have really hurt." This time she meant it, recognizing his pain, knowing how it felt to be broken up with.

"It did. But like Jake, she arrived at Yellow Rose wanting me back, and I felt the same as you. Seeing her here really showed me she didn't fit in." He sat, grabbed a paper, wrote something, and tossed it in the fire. "I think I'll let her go, too."

Lexy noticed something. "Hey, are you kidding me?"

"Pardon?"

"Are you wearing the bracelet I made you?" She stared at the multicolored beads she'd threaded together all those years ago. She remembered how hard she'd worked on it, wanting it to be perfect. He couldn't have kept it all this time. Could he?

"Sure am." Chris held out his arm. "I still have the tie and story, too."

She was touched. She reached out to hold Chris' hand. "Thank you and you know what? I think it's time we focus on you."

"What do you mean?"

"Tell me about Elizabeth."

Thirty-five

Whistling?

He was actually whistling?

Really?

He hadn't done that in ages.

A sense of contentment rolled through him. His grandpa had taught him how to whistle as a young kid and he had gotten really good at it over the years. It had all ended when Elizabeth died.

What was with him?

He had awoken that morning with a grin on his face, jumped out of bed, showered, threw on jeans and a sweater, hurried to the kitchen, and started making pancakes.

Meredith walked in the door from the back yard.

"Good morning," he said.

"You're in a good mood today." She stood there watching him. "And you're even making pancakes, and this is Wednesday. You usually only do that on the weekend. Are we celebrating something?"

"No. Just felt like something special this morning. Where's Emma?"

"She's still out in the yard with Angel. She'll be right in and thrilled to be having her favorite breakfast. You were out late last night. With Lexy? I hope?"

"Yes." He flipped the pancakes. "And you were hoping? I take it you like Lexy?"

"I do."

He glanced over. "We're not dating, so get that glint out of your eyes."

"I can always dream. But don't worry, I won't bother you with any questions."

"Thanks."

But he felt like screaming out Lexy's name. With joy and gratefulness. She was responsible for his good mood this morning because last night was the first time he had really talked to anyone about his sister. As in, great detail. He had kept so much in about his own grief, caught up in taking care of Emma and concerned about his mother who was dealing with losing a daughter. But he had also lost a sister and along with that, his whole life had changed, and it felt so good talking about it all, getting a lot off his chest. Especially since Lexy really listened, understood, and her compassion once again soothed him. A lot of pain soared from his broken heart and calmness settled in the cracked spaces, filling them up, making him whole.

Elizabeth.

She was his confidant and cheerleader. Grief hit hard when you least expected it, and he was sure it would happen all his life. It really hurt losing her, but lately he saw glimpses of who he was when she was alive and, as Lexy pointed out, his sister would want the best for him as well. She would always be in his heart, but he needed to start living again. Or at least trying to. This way he would be honoring his only sibling, who always had a positive outlook on life and believed in striving to be all that you could possibly be. She had been a hardworking woman who went to law school after having a child so that she could provide a good life for Emma.

Thank you, Lexy.

United in grief, they had nurtured each other, and life suddenly felt much better. Only one problem. He was still fighting that growing attraction toward her.

Should he tell her?

No. Forget about that. It would only ruin their friendship, which was incredibly special to him. Forget the glow in her eyes, the curve of her lips, the way she cared about everyone and everything. He could go on for hours about how wonderful she was.

"Pancakes. We're having pancakes?" Emma shouted as she came racing in the door, Angel right behind. He was glad of the respite.

"Sure are. How about you wash up, give Angel her breakfast, and let's start eating."

Breakfast was fun with everyone in a great mood. Yellow Rose sure had changed them, and now frequent laughter was entering the mix.

"Off you go." Meredith pointed to his room, eyeing him taking his last sip of coffee. "Emma and I will finish up the dishes. After all, you cooked. And I believe you have a meeting to get to in town."

"You know about that? I wasn't going to mention it until I knew the outcome."

"I ran into the mayor the other day and he told me. Good luck."

"Thanks." Chris quickly changed into more formal clothes, threw shorts and a T-shirt in a gym bag, and drove into town. Pulling into the center parking lot, he grabbed his briefcase and walked the short block to the mayor's office. He was nervous. Asking for money had never been his forte, but he really needed the town's support to get his center off the ground. He had discovered they had several grants available to assist programs involving young people and he hoped his dream qualified. He also needed to get permission to reestablish the carnival as a fundraiser. He was asking for a lot, but he needed it all to make things work for the good of the community.

So here he was. Standing in front of the green door that led into the mayor's office, his heart racing.

Courage. He needed courage.

Channeling his sister's strength, he pushed forward and opened the door.

"Hello there." An elderly woman was sitting at a desk typing on a laptop. She looked up. "May I help you?"

"Yes. I have a meeting with Mayor Ellis."

"Of course. You must be Christopher Leverton."

"Yes. But you can call me Chris."

"Okay, Chris. I'm Cathy. He's waiting for you." She led him down a hall and opened a door. "Go on in."

"Thank you, Cathy."

He walked in and the man behind the desk rose. "Mayor Bill Ellis here. You must be Christopher Leverton."

"Yes. You can call me Chris." They shook hands. He took a second to size him up and was pleased to see he had a ready smile on his face.

"Grab a seat, Chris. How can I help you?"

He pulled out the report he had put together, handing the mayor a copy. He explained all about his hopes for the center and how he wondered if the town would contribute like they used to years ago.

The mayor's eyes lit up.

"I'm honored to do business with you, Chris. I had heard about what you're doing and meant to drop in. We need that center back and we will do our best to help funnel money into it. Things are tighter now than before, but I'm sure we can find a way." The mayor smiled. "I remember practically living there as a kid and my folks knew Matthew Willow, the center's namesake."

"Thank you. I appreciate any help you can offer. It made an impact on me as well and I was only there for about two weeks. And by the way, I'm keeping the same name."

"That's good news."

"And do you also approve of bringing back the carnival as a fundraiser as well?"

"Yes, of course. I'd love to see that here in Willow again. It attracted people from all over." Pause. "Is your mother Meredith by the way?"

Did the mayor actually blush? His mother mentioned running into him. Was he single?

"Yes."

"Fine lady. Fine, fine lady. Well, I'll bring everything up at the next council meeting, but I know they will agree. Folks have been talking about the center since you bought it, hoping it would once become the place for young people to hang out, like it used to be. Keeping them busy and out of trouble."

"Thank you."

Chris practically danced all the way back to the center. Only one problem. He couldn't dance. Just like he couldn't skip. He needed Emma to teach him some dance moves, too. He'd attempt it, if he wasn't in the public eye. So he alternated that feeling with one of almost flying, as well. He had gathered all his savings to buy the building, and his mother helped as well, but the town's support would go a long way.

Pulling out his key, he let himself into the center, excitement racing as he pictured all the activities that would be starting soon. Time to get painting. His deadline was coming fast, and he still had a lot to do. He changed into his casual clothes and was halfway through transforming the kitchen from a bright orange to a calming blue when he heard the door open. Walking out to the main room, he was surprised to see Meredith, Emma, and Angel. He wasn't expecting them.

"Why, hello there." His eyebrows rose.

While Emma was busy introducing a sniffing Angel to the room, Meredith rushed over. "Emma has something she wants to ask you. Something she's apparently been planning."

She looked serious, so Chris knew this must be important.

"Okay, just a second." He hurried back to the kitchen and quickly put the lid on the paint can, cleaned his roller, and came back.

"Hi Emma. I heard you have something to ask me. You have my full attention." He directed her to the chairs set up in the corner.

After they all sat, Emma said, "Unca Chris, can we buy a small oak tree and plant it?"

His eyes widened, not expecting this. She had never really shown much interest in trees and an oak?

"Yes, of course." He looked at his mother who winked. If Emma wanted an oak tree, she was going to get one.

"Goody." Emma clapped her hands. "I saw one at the garden center."

She did?

"We can go pick one up now if you want." Like his mother, he wanted to jump on the idea immediately. It seemed important to her.

Emma beamed. "Okay."

They walked to the garden center, just past the bakery, and Emma chose the one she wanted. Surprisingly, the smallest one. Chris carefully carried it to his car and gently laid it down in the back seat.

"I'll meet you at home." He took off behind them, unloading the tree when he arrived.

"Can you put it in my wagon?" Emma asked.

"Okay, sure." Really? Her wagon?

"So now you have to go see Lexy," Emma said.

"I do?"

"Yes. She's waiting for you."

"She is?" He felt completely out of the loop, not knowing what was going on.

"Do what she says," Meredith added. "She's planned this all out and she wants to surprise you. Me, too. I've been told that I am only allowed to assist her in small ways, at her request."

Once again, Emma was definitely her mother's child. Full of surprises. Chris quickly changed then left, walking through the woods to Lexy's.

She was outside playing ball with Asher, and he stood for a moment drinking her in. Finally he moved closer, wanting desperately to hug her and never let her go.

He needed to back off.

"Hi there, Lexy. Apparently, I'm supposed to be here, Emma's orders."

Thirty-six

"Yes, you are."

Lexy wanted to run into his arms and hug him.

Kiss him?

Get it together.

What was wrong with her?

Asher ran over to greet him, giving her time to pull herself together. She had been surprised when Emma had called, asking for a favor. She had no clue what was up, but she had hurried out to pick up groceries.

"Such a cool pup. Love the fact he's so friendly."

Lexy giggled at Asher not leaving her guest alone, as if he were a long-lost friend, even though he saw him almost every day. Chris finally swept him up in his arms.

"Well, he definitely loves you. Oh, and I even made supper."

"You did?"

"Yes, and I'm to keep you here for a specific period of time. So, c'mon in."

"Really?" He followed her indoors and put Asher down on the floor.

She continued into the kitchen. "I'm heating up lasagna and it should be done by now. Hope that's okay. Emma said you liked it."

"Yes, I do."

She turned and he was right behind her. A little too close—she backed away. "Good."

"Can I help?"

"Nope, all done." She pointed to a chair. "Have a seat."

"It smells delicious. I wish I could have brought something. A dessert or rolls, maybe. I didn't realize we'd be eating together."

"Oh, don't worry. I even have lemonade. Not your mom's, though."

"No problem. I'd love some."

Lexy poured him a glass, careful not to get too close. Darn, he had quite the effect on her, and one she couldn't act on. Or rather, shouldn't. She had to remember not to do anything that could wreck their friendship. The oven timer rang out, and she pulled the lasagna out of the oven. "Sorry, not homemade, though."

"I eat anything."

"That's what I like to hear." Letting it cool, she got Asher's food ready and put his bowl on the floor. She then placed the hot dish on a tray in the middle of the table, cutting a piece and placing it on Chris' plate. She also added a roll and did the same to her own. "I did make the salad, though." She put the bowl in front of him.

"Looks good."

Glancing at her watch, she was surprised time was flying fast. "Guess we'll have to eat rather quickly. We are due back at your place in thirty minutes. Emma gave me a note to open, to tell us exactly where to go."

"Definitely a mystery, but I'm enjoying seeing her excited and animated."

"Yes. I've even noticed a huge difference in her since the first time I met her."

Chris told her about the oak tree.

"Interesting choice. She's quite the intriguing little girl."

"Sure is. Her mother was just like that. Precocious beyond her age."

The rest of the meal passed quickly, with Chris sharing more plans about the center.

"You know, we rode our bikes over there almost every day." Lexy chuckled.

"We did. I was glad a trail led there from the beach where we could avoid traffic for the most part. Otherwise, we might not have been allowed."

"Yes, we were lucky." She started picking up dishes and placing them in the sink. "Sorry to rush you. I'll do these later. We better not be late for Emma."

"You're the leader right now."

She handed him a gym bag. "First, Emma left a change of clothes for you. A white shirt and shorts. As you can see, I have a white sundress on, which was her wish, as well."

"Really?"

"Yes. You can change in the washroom upstairs."

After he came back down, Lexy pulled a paper out of her pocket, ignoring how good he looked. Sniff. He smelled good too. She opened the note from Emma. "Oh, we are to meet at the halfway mark between your cottage and mine."

"Interesting."

She leashed up Asher and they headed out. As they drew nearer, Chris said softly, "Wow, look at that." As if in sync, they stopped at the exact same moment.

Twinkly white lights threaded through trees providing a backdrop to a table lit up with candles. Lawn chairs were placed in a circle and as they moved closer, they could see plates of cookies and lemonade on another table covered with a white cloth.

The whole setting was ethereal and stunning. Breathtaking, actually.

Emma emerged from the tree area wearing a long flowing white dress with white flowers twisted in her hair, Angel right behind her. Meredith joined her, also wearing a pretty white dress.

Emma ran to meet them.

"Surprise." Her face glowed. Lexy watched as Chris pulled her up in his arms and twirled her around, while the pups united in playtime. "This is just beautiful." He put her back on the ground.

Angel had a white rose entwined in her collar and Emma quickly pulled out a white bowtie from her pocket and clipped it to Asher's. Everyone looked incredible and completely in sync.

"Did Chris tell you Emma's mother was an interior designer?" Meredith asked.

"No, he didn't."

"Well, my grandchild sure takes after her. Years of watching, I guess, and taking it all in. Everything needs to match and she's quite creative."

"No doubt about that."

"What's this all about, Emma?" Chris asked.

"Well, um, I want to do what Lexy did."

What?

"You do?" Lexy asked.

She did?

"Yeah, you planted your mommy's favorite flowers at your cottage. You said it made you feel good, so look it, look it." She pointed to a red wagon with a tree sitting in it.

"Is that an oak tree?" Lexy asked, pretending Chris hadn't already told her.

"Yep."

"You want to plant the tree here?" Chris asked.

"Yeah. In the middle between Lexy's cottage and ours. I wanna share it."

Lexy looked at Chris, touched at being included.

"Is that okay with you?" he asked.

"Certainly. Go ahead."

Lexy picked up Asher and Meredith picked up Angel, and they walked over to the wagon. Emma pointed to the shovel and Chris got to work. He quickly dug a hole, Emma helped him lower the tree into it, and then they both pushed the soil back in. Emma immediately picked up a watering can and watered it.

"Such a great idea," Lexy said. This little girl had thought of everything.

"I wrote something too." Emma pulled out a sheet of paper from her pocket. "Mommy loved oak trees. She called them the mighty oaks. She said they were strong and brave and have courage. She said we get sad sometimes, but we have to always be like the oak tree, and be brave and strong. I miss her, but I know Unca Chris and Nana do too. I hear Nana crying sometimes and Unca Chris looks sad lots. And I know Lexy misses her own mommy. This oak tree will remind all of us to be strong. My mommy and Lexy's mommy would want us to be that way." She ended with the hugest grin Lexy had ever seen on her face. She was touched that Emma included her and as she looked around - there was not a dry eye among the rest of them.

She watched Chris walk over and put one arm around Meredith, the other around Emma, and the love among them bubbled up in Lexy's heart. How lovely to witness this.

"Come join us." Emma held out her hand.

Lexy did and basked in the good feeling of Chris' arm around her and feeling part of a family.

"This is so beautiful, Emma. Thank you," Lexy gushed.

"Well, I get sad, but Mom was always happy, and she would want me to be happy too. Right Unca Chris?"

"Right. Like your mom said, being sad is okay sometimes. And of course we miss the people we love, but they will stay forever in our hearts. Always. And we still have to live our own lives. They would want us to."

"Yeah. Let's eat," Emma said.

Good idea.

Lexy went over to Meredith, who hadn't said a word. "You okay?" she asked.

"Just surprised. I had no idea Emma was planning this."

"Your daughter must have been an amazing person, and she lives on in her daughter."

"She sure does."

"Nana, do you want some lemonade?" Emma asked.

Meredith walked over to join Emma, but Lexy hurried over to Chris, who had his back to all of them, fussing with the dirt around the tree.

"How are you doing?" she asked.

"Blown away, actually. I'll join you soon. I just need a moment."

Lexy could see the tears in his eyes.

"Take all the time you need."

She understood.

Thirty-seven

After cookies, lemonade, and helping to clean up, Lexy went back to Writer's Bliss. Chris wanted to come and help her do dishes, but she said no. He looked exhausted. Asher went straight into his little home to sleep while she tidied up and finally finished reading her current manuscript. Up to the last chapter, of course, which she had yet to write. She was left with the same old question. One she was tired of.

How to end this?

What would make her readers happy?

What would make her happy?

Pouring her third cup of coffee, she checked to make sure Asher was still sleeping. She plopped down on the couch, her mind spinning.

She had come to Willow to basically 'find herself.'

Leaving the noise and busyness behind, she had actually discovered a lot.

Chris' suggestion to burn away bad memories really helped. She felt freer, loving herself more for a change. Less critical. Her heart garden was blooming and as soon as a weed appeared, she got rid of it. She had even decided she was going to talk to Meredith about a recommendation for a good counselor. The need to continue to heal was strong, and she figured professional help would be the perfect guide.

Her thoughts flung to her mom.

Emma's tribute to her mother was so touching. The way she had included the rest of them showed an empathy beyond her years, and her message to be strong hit home.

The time had finally arrived.

Lexy walked over and pulled the covers off her mother's paintings, ready to see them. Two more gorgeous sunrises, breathtaking actually, that lit up the room. Now, where to put her special one. She took down a water scene hanging in front of her desk and put her new painting there where she could see it when she worked. Sitting, she couldn't stop staring at it. The sunrise was full of glimmering color and she could feel the joy radiating from the girl with the outstretched hands, as she embraced the day. She felt closer to being that person, someone who woke up every morning greeting it with delight.

Wait a second.

She remembered something the lawyer had told her. About a box in the attic.

Making sure Asher was safe in his crate, Lexy pulled open the ceiling door and a rope ladder fell down. Blech. She remembered that ladder and being afraid of it as it swung. Taking her time, she climbed up and gagged from the musty smell, almost wanting to go right back down. But she held on tight. The space was small, just room for a few labeled boxes. She quickly saw the one she wanted and carefully pulled it towards her and carried it back down. Sitting on the couch, taking a deep breath in and out, she opened it.

Memories exploded.

Her mother had kept every card, verse, story she had ever written.

Reminiscing, her heart swelled as she finally cemented how much her mother had loved her, along with her grandpa and grandmother. Why had she never really known that? Or allowed herself to feel it? She was amazed she had let the hurt created by her father color and push away their love. She had always focused on the negative stemming from him, not on the love flowing from those who cared.

No wonder she gravitated to Jake.

Fooled at the beginning by thinking he was the greatest, she now saw how she basically fell under his spell of control and hurt. He slowly undermined her every single day using items she'd confided in him against her, especially the one when she had told him how her dad always said her face was too wide. Jake knew that really hurt her.

So what would he do?

Just before she was off to an appointment or something, he'd say versions of, "Your hair looks ugly like that. It makes your face too wide, too fat." His aim? To squelch her joy. To throw her off balance. She realized that now.

No wonder it felt good being with Chris.

She didn't have to work hard or pretend or try to be perfect to get him to like her. She could just be herself. She could trust him, felt safe with him, and could be vulnerable, strong, silly and every part of who she really was. And he was okay with it all.

So what about her book?

How could this newfound knowledge help her?

She still had to finish it.

Wait a second.

She stood up and began pacing back and forth.

No wonder she still couldn't let her dad and Jake's effect go, even after figuratively burning their memories in a fire. She had one more realization to face.

Her character, Nick, was toxic. Yes, she had figured that out, but never made the obvious connection.

He was just like her dad and Jake.

She had never noticed that. Why had she not linked that thread? Her book clearly mirrored what was going on in her own life.

Not wanting to wake up Asher, she ran to the kitchen and pulled out her phone, hitting numbers fast.

"You okay, Lexy?" Wendy yawned.

"Yes. Sorry to wake you."

"Oh, I'm awake. What's up?"

"Well, when you read *Fairy Tale Crushed,* did you feel Nick was just like Jake?"

"Yes."

"You never liked Jake, did you?"

"Nope. Never did. He never knew you. He only liked what you did for him. To be more honest, I secretly cheered when that couple broke up in your book."

"Really?"

"Really. I never said anything because you were so in love with Jake, and I feared losing our friendship if I opened my mouth. He hurt you just like your dad did."

"You knew about my dad?" Lexy was surprised. "We never talked about him."

"No, but your face scrunches in pain whenever a father is mentioned and I put the pieces together. I also see you watching with envy when David plays with Jacob. I'm thrilled that you're finally clicking it all together. Like finishing a puzzle."

"Thanks, Wendy."

"No problem. Now have Sarah dump Nick and finish that book with some good news."

Easier said than done, because it had to end in happiness. That was what she was known for. Oh, what a mess she was in.

Asher was awake, so she took him out back for a potty break. He went back to sleep, but she just sat there, staring at her mom's picture, taking it all in.

Joy, beauty, colors...

Wham!

Clarity hit hard.

Brandon.

What about her fictional character, Brandon?

She couldn't let her heroine marry that idiot, Nick. But what about Brandon, her best friend? He was also featured in her book. He was always there, watching out for Sarah, holding her when she cried, laughing with her in times of joy.

Brandon was the actual hero.

Why had she never thought of that?

She jumped up, feeling as if lightning had struck, or a veil had been ripped off. She was having her own private personal sunrise in her heart.

She saw truth.

Her character Sarah would finally realize her true love was Brandon.

Time to write.

To write – as Meredith said – a beginning.

For the first time in a long while, she was excited about her story.

Brewing more coffee, she got to work. She now knew exactly how she wanted the story of Brandon and Sarah to evolve. She also had to go back and fix several scenes in earlier chapters to reflect her change of direction.

Her hands flew over her computer. With the exception of potty breaks, coffee pourings, and brief walks with Asher, she stayed writing all night and all day, until she was exhausted. But done. Writing the last word had never felt so good.

Attaching it to an email to her agent, she hit send.

Curled up on the couch with Asher, she finally fell asleep.

Beep, beep, beep...

What was that?

Lexy's eyes popped open. So did Asher's. Oh, right, her new ringtone. Way too jarring. Like a horn honking in downtown Toronto. She glanced at her watch. Five hours had passed. She clicked on her phone.

"You did it," screamed Ingrid. "Perfection. I'm rushing it to the editor."

"Thank you."

And thank you, Mom.

And Emma – for leading the way.

The little girl's gathering of love had pushed Lexy into facing things she'd hidden away.

And a miracle happened.

She had finally finished that book.

Thirty-eight

Lexy felt better than she had in a long time. She turned her coffee machine on and buttered her toast. Asher was eating his breakfast, probably in anticipation of a walk, his favorite thing to do.

She continued to feel grateful.

Thank goodness for Albert the pig farmer, whose search for a wife to take care of him had pushed her over the edge. She wished him well in his quest. Thank goodness for Writer's Bliss with all its glorious memories of her grandparents and her mother, and how being here nurtured her creative spirit. And thanks to Asher, a ball of love in her life, as well as Emma and Meredith.

Most of all, thanks to Chris, who knew the real her and still cared. Total acceptance was his gift to her and how comforting to discover someone with whom she felt safe.

Big breath in. Big breath out.

Sitting at the table, sipping coffee after shoveling in her breakfast, she watched Asher toss around his bunny, reveling in the quiet she had grown to love. Stillness that slowed her down enough to realize three major factors in her life. She repeated them often, hoping to never forget.

First, she had realized the negative vines that twisted through her mind stemmed from her father.

Second, Jake was just like her father.

Third, her character Nick was just like Jake.

She understood it all now.

Yes, she had changed her *Fairy Tale Crushed* ending because her boyfriend wanted her to and she basically wanted him to love her, but deep down she now believed she knew the relationship was not a healthy one. Thank goodness her fictional characters never married in the book, and thank goodness she never married Jake in real life.

All seemed good again. More hopeful. Positive.

Her new book had been edited up to her last chapter, but in light of all the changes she'd made, it needed to be re-done from the beginning. Her editor had promised to start work on it stat. They wanted to get the book out as fast as they could.

Was it time to go home? No. How sad the only one she missed was Fred the doorman. She could still see Wendy and kept in touch with her agent, but she was feeling the cottage was where she wanted to be. Besides, she could do all her edits from here. She just didn't want to leave yet. She loved the fact she had gotten in touch with whom she really was. The person she'd hidden away under a pile of hurts. Another exciting development was that she felt on fire with her passion to write again and to share the many love stories she held in her heart.

"Go, Lexy."

Asher ran over, tail swishing. She hadn't realized she'd spoken out loud and her pup thought she was talking to him.

Wrapping her arms around him, she kissed him on the head saying, "C'mon, sweetie, let's head out. I must ask Meredith something."

Leashing him, she walked out to Emma, Angel, and Meredith, walking down the beach toward her.

"Hi there." What a welcome sight, thought Lexy. They were part of her new found peace and she loved visiting with them.

The two pups greeted each other with wild excitement, tails wagging, paws flying, totally in play mode.

"They're brother and sister and also best friends," Emma said, thoroughly enjoying their antics.

"Sure are." Emma looked even happier having her own pup to take care of. Chris was right about that. Having a fur friend to love had really been a great decision.

"How about we take them both to dog school?" Lexy asked. "I phoned Pamela, and she said to bring Angel along, if you want."

Emma's eyes shone. "Yes. Let's do that."

Meredith stared. "You know, you have a real glow about you today."

Lexy leaned over to hug her. "I finished my book," she whispered.

"You did?" Meredith beamed. "I'm thrilled."

"Um, I was wondering if you would read it. My editor's working on it so I have time to change stuff. I'd love your input." Lexy grinned. "I think you'll like the ending. Or, the beginning, as you called it."

"I would be honored."

"Hang on." Lexy ran indoors and picked up a printed copy. She hurried out and handed it to Meredith. "Thank you. Your comments here and there really helped me dig deeper."

"Oh, I think you had it in you all along." Meredith's eyes twinkled. "I'll get started on this as soon as we get home."

"Wonderful. Where's Chris? I can't wait to tell him."

"He's at the center. He'd love to hear your good news."

"I might just pop over."

After another bout of pup playing, with Emma cheering them on until they tired themselves out, Lexy headed into town.

"C'mon, little one. Let's go see Chris."

First stop. Lunch. After pulling into a spot at the center, she walked down to the bakery, sliding Asher up into her arms when she entered.

"Hi there, Hope." She sniffed. "You should bottle your baking aromas and make them into a spray or lotion. I'd be your first customer."

Hope chuckled. "I'm so used to them I don't even notice."

"Trust me, they're divine."

"Well, thank you."

"So what would you recommend for lunch for two?"

"You and Asher?"

"Nope, me and Chris."

Hope's eyebrows raised. "Hmm... how about two big roast beef sandwiches? I know Chris has bought one here before."

"Sounds good." Her stomach rumbled.

"Ready in two minutes."

Lexy strolled around the bakery, enjoying the local sections displaying gifts. Oops. Her books were there. She walked by them fast.

"Here you go." Hope handed over two large bags. "I added some cookies and water. And of course, a few brownies. Oh, and a couple of dog biscuits. But you're only paying for the sandwiches."

"You are way too kind." This woman was so sweet and caring, Lexy wondered how she made any money. Digging out her wallet, she pulled out her card and swiped the machine leaving a huge tip as Hope got busy with other customers. She waved goodbye and they walked back to the center. The door was open so she went right in, finding Chris sitting at a desk with his back to her. A catch caught in her throat at the very sight of him.

"Knock, knock."

He turned around and, once again, she felt like walking right into his eyes. Was that a thing? The softness she saw there, the compassion, tenderness, moved her.

Stop it.

"I come bearing lunch." She held up the bag.

"Any brownies in there?"

"Of course."

"Great. And thank you. This is a nice treat." He patted a chair beside him. "Come join me." He reached down to pet Asher.

Lexy pulled the food out and placed it on the corner of his desk. "Here, Asher." She'd brought some of his treats, but gave him one from Hope instead. He settled down to chew on it. When they all finished eating, she exploded. "Guess what?"

"You finished your book."

"Did Meredith tell you?" She gathered up their garbage and tossed it in the can off to the side.

"No, but I figured there could only be one reason for that glow on your face."

Oh, she could think of two reasons. One was seeing him.

"I'm so relieved to have finally figured it all out." She sat, still so excited she could barely remain still.

"Congratulations." His face clouded over. "Does that mean you'll be leaving?"

"Not yet. I'd like to help you get ready for the center's opening." The twinkle was back in his eyes. Would he miss her? Somehow, she liked to think so.

"Thank you. I appreciate your support."

Suddenly, he looked all serious again.

"Is something wrong?"

"Well, I'm worried. Money might be a problem. I had someone inspect the building and there are a lot more repairs than I thought or budgeted for."

"How can I help?"

"Well, I know of one thing you definitely do better than me."

"I'm in."

"Could you help write the pamphlet and flyer? I think you'll create better ones than the sample I came up with." He handed her a mockup.

"I would be honored. I'd also like to help organize the carnival, if that's okay."

"Definitely okay. I just wish we had a big draw."

"What do you mean?

"Something people would flock to. Crowds of people."

His eyebrows drew together, his eyes squinted. He looked really worried.

"Maybe we'll think of something."

"Well, I'll keep plugging away at it."

The stress radiating from him startled her. Had she been so wrapped up in her own issues that she had ignored what he was going through?

"If anyone can pull this together you will, Chris. I have total faith in you."

"Thanks."

Should she hug him? Could he feel the same? Should she ask him? Clarify matters?

Nah. He probably had nothing to clarify and besides, they needed to get through the carnival first. Maybe he would remember that he kissed her on the cheek back then, if he really did, and meant it. Yes, she'd wait. The timing was off right now. Besides, she should be thinking of him, not her.

"Well, I'd better go." Before she made a fool of herself.

"I heard you are taking Emma and Angel with you to puppy school tonight."

"Hope that's okay."

"More than okay. Thank you, and thank you again for lunch."

"No problem."

She practically flew out of there, energized by his support. Someone who appreciated her was often hard to find, and she needed to give that back to him. First things first. She planned on creating a pamphlet and flyer that hopefully would help draw crowds out to support his center.

Lexy finished her day at dog school. Emma had worked hard to get Angel up to snuff, so they fit right in.

Such fun.

When she got home, she put a sleepy Asher in his little home but never made it to her room. Exhausted, she fell asleep on the couch; Chris' eyes were the last thing she imagined.

She was in love.

Definitely.

Thirty-nine

The morning sun was at its best as Lexy walked along the beach with Asher. Golden arrows stretched through the sky, rendering everything bright and shiny. The sand was warm beneath her feet and she'd even stopped wearing her huge wide-brimmed hats. She felt safe. That she was among friends. That everything was going to be okay.

"Ahhh ... bliss. Perfect weather, huh, little one?" Her pup was proudly carrying his stuffed bunny, continuing his fixation with taking a toy on a walk. Pretty darn cute.

"Ding, dong, ding, dong..."

Bells ringing. Softly. Her new ringtone and Asher never reacted. Good. She finally had a winner. Pulling it out of her pocket, she glanced at the name.

"Hello, Ingrid."

"Hi, Lexy. Just wanted to let you know I'll be sending you a mockup cover to see if you like it and your first edits should arrive later today."

"Great. I can't wait to see the artwork."

"I think you'll like it. I'm also moving ahead your release date, still trying to stop the negative press."

"Thank you. And as always, thank you for sticking by me. I owe you the world."

"Another book is always good." Her laughter bubbled over. "I have your back always. Talk to you later."

Lexy slid her phone into her back pocket. She couldn't wait to tackle the edits and finish the book for good. Life was certainly looking up.

Picking up a smooth rock, she skipped it across the water. The last time she had done that was her first day there, when she had felt conflicted and confused and wondered if she'd ever finish her current book. Amazing how far she'd come and how good she felt.

Now about Chris. How grateful she was to meet him again and enjoy his friendship.

"Hey, Alexandra."

She stopped in her tracks. Was that him? Had her thoughts conjured him up? Turning quickly, she was momentarily confused by a tall man sporting a blue baseball cap running out of the woods. His black ponytail flew around his face and was that a camera?

Snap, snap, snap.

Yes. Yes, he had a camera.

Her eyes grew large, and her mouth dropped. She'd never seen this guy.

Wait. He called her Alexandra? What was going on?

"How about a smile?"

"Who are you?" she screamed, wanting to run, but also tired of running. She picked up Asher to keep him safe.

"Pete." Snap, snap, snap.

"Why are you taking my picture?"

"Oh, come on. You're a famous writer. Chris Leverton told me."

Chris?

Instant nausea.

"He told you where I live?"

"Yes."

"Did you pay him?" She had to know.

"Of course."

Snap, snap, snap

Time to run.

"Alexandra. Alexandra. Wait. You don't understand."

Ignoring him, she raced to the cottage, pulled her door open, and locked herself in, collapsing on the floor, still clinging to Asher, who licked her face.

Why did this keep happening? The minute she felt safe and content, she was smacked in the face. Why would Chris do this?

She decided to ask him.

Pulling her phone out, she clicked his number. He answered on the first ring.

"How dare you." Hearing his voice set her off. Anger took over and she couldn't stop herself.

"Pardon?"

"Did you really need money that badly?"

"Please, Lexy. I don't know what you're talking about."

"Oh, c'mon. You found a way to make some big bucks. Siccing a reporter on me. Those photos will be sold to the highest bidder. And all you had to do was ask me. I would have helped you out. I even offered, remember?"

"I still don't understand."

"No, you don't. Obviously."

Furious, she hung up.

"We've got to get out of here, Asher."

After tossing some things in a bag, she picked up her pup's crate and loaded the car fast. Running back in, she grabbed her mom's painting, placed it in the trunk, got in and took off.

Her heart snapped in two.

~ * ~

Chris made sure Emma was okay and that his mother was with her, then raced over to Lexy's cottage as fast as he could.

Just in time to see her peel out.

"Lexy, Lexy, wait." But of course, she couldn't hear him.

Watching the car disappear down the road, he wondered if he'd ever see her again. Piecing it together, she must have run into a reporter on the beach and decided he had sicced him on her.

Whatever happened to trust?

Walking back, he met Meredith. Emma was coaxing Angel into the water.

He explained what had happened.

"How can she believe I would do that?" He threw his hands up in the air.

"A hurting heart retreats fast."

His mother was right and obviously knew Lexy well. Chris' anger dissipated. Lexy had been devastated a lot by her father, her ex-fiancé, reporters chasing her. He thought she trusted him implicitly, but could see why she wouldn't.

He'd have to make her understand.

He couldn't lose her for the second time.

Forty

"Please be home, please be home, please be home."

Lexy knocked. No answer. She rang the bell.

The door opened a crack.

"Lexy?" Wendy opened the door wider. "And Asher? What are you doing here?"

Tears rolled down Lexy's cheeks.

"C'mon in." Wendy pulled her inside, sat her on the couch, and while Asher sniffed his new surroundings, she wrapped her arms around her. "What's wrong?"

"I don't want Jacob seeing me like this." She wiped her eyes. Asher hopped up on her lap.

"Don't worry. He's with David and his grandmother. They're shopping for my birthday. Shh... just let it all out."

Lexy sobbed and sobbed, but somehow got the story out about the reporter and Chris.

"I can't believe he'd do this." Wendy's eyes widened, stroking Lexy's hair. "Come out to the kitchen. You need wine and cookies." She grabbed Lexy by the hand, dragged her to the other room, and pointed to a stool. "Sit. I'll get Asher some water and I'm sure I have a few dog cookies hanging around. Jacob likes feeding the neighbors' dogs."

"Oh, I have some in my pocket. I have a portable bowl too. I never leave home without it." Lexy poured water in a bowl, placed it on the floor, leaned down and offered a treat to Asher. Sitting, she watched her friend open the cupboard and take down two wine glasses. She filled one with ginger ale and another with wine. Right, Lexy forgot. Wendy had given up drinking when she first became pregnant and just never got back into it. Her friend added cookies to a platter, put it all on the table, and sat across from her. It felt like back in college when they'd shared many a bottle of wine while discussing their lives. As life got busier, they'd barely had time to squeeze in moments to just sit and chat. She hoped to change all that.

"Keep talking." Wendy raised her glass.

"I just can't believe he'd sell me out." Lexy clinked her glass with Wendy's, took a few sips and helped herself to a cookie.

"But why would he do that?"

"Money. That must be it. He needs money for the center."

Wendy shook her head. They both watched Asher standing one minute then curling up in a ball falling fast asleep on the rug. He was probably beat from all the excitement.

"Are you sure?" Wendy topped up Lexy's glass.

"Yes, I know for a fact he needs money, and the reporter said Chris was the one who let him know where I live."

"He just doesn't seem the type to betray you."

"Money and a desperate need for it changes people. That's what I think." Lexy leaned over to make sure Asher was okay.

"What about Emma and Meredith?"

"I'll miss them. But I just had to get away."

"I don't blame you."

Pause.

"You like this guy a lot, don't you?"

"Maybe."

"Come on, Lexy. Admit it."

"Yeah, I do. But once again I obviously chose someone so wrong for me."

Wendy slugged back the rest of her soda and plopped her glass down on the table. "I still think there has to be some kind of explanation. Chris seemed so devoted to you."

"Well, the reporter freely offered up his name." Her stomach rumbled as she grabbed another cookie. She hadn't eaten since breakfast.

Wendy refilled her glass and started to pour more wine in Lexy's.

"No, thanks. I've got some work to get through tonight."

They sat in silence, chomping on the cookies. Lexy liked that about her friend. She let her talk when she felt like it, not pushing any type of agenda. Finally, she pushed herself off the stool. "I'd better get home. I still need to work on edits. I can't let Ingrid down again."

"Do you want to stay here for a few days?" Wendy asked. "Jacob would love it, especially having the pup around. Me too, of course."

"No, I'm all right. I've got my computer all set up at home."

"Yeah, you'll probably get more work done there than with a toddler running around wanting to be with you every minute. But hey, they'll be home soon and David can drive you. I know you handle your wine well, and actually didn't drink that much, but you're exhausted and emotional and shouldn't be behind the wheel. Then tomorrow I can follow him in your car to drop it off."

"Okay, good idea. Just let me call Ingrid to let her know where I am."

She made a quick call, reassured Ingrid she was on the job, and hung up just as the door flew open.

"You're here." Jacob wobbled over and threw his arms around her legs.

"Hello, sweetheart." She pulled him up for a big hug.

"Puppy." He pointed to Asher, who trotted over to greet his friend.

"Yes." She put Jacob down. "Look at his tail wag. He certainly likes you."

Jacob dropped to his knees, wrapping his arms around the pup. "Me love you." Asher licked his face in response.

"Glad you got a photo of that," Lexy said. "I'd love a copy. I'm going to blow it up and call it 'joy'."

"Sure. I'll send it to you now." Wendy pushed a few buttons on her phone.

"Thanks."

"What brings you here?" David's eyes widened. "Is everything okay?"

"Nah, not really. Wendy will fill you in. Right now, I need to get home."

"Guess you need a chauffeur." He gestured toward the wine bottle.

"Yes, please."

Lexy quickly said her goodbyes and David helped her transfer her stuff to his car. She made sure her mom's painting was in a safe spot.

"Thanks for doing this," she said, getting into the passenger seat, holding Asher on her lap.

"No problem at all. I recall you driving me home after a Christmas party."

"Yeah, true. But I appreciate it."

She also treasured his silence on the drive to her condo, giving her time to calm down. Her mind was still racing, probably not as fast because of the wine and emotional binge, but when she woke up that morning, she had never dreamed she'd be leaving Willow a few hours later.

All the peace she'd gained had fled fast.

David pulled into the visitor parking in front of her condo. Gathering up her belongings, Lexy pushed the door open and entered the foyer, her mom's painting tucked into her side, Asher beside her, David right behind. Home sweet home, but she missed the cottage already.

Fred looked up. A surprised expression on his face. "Good evening, Alexandra. Good to see you."

"Hello, Fred." Lexy was glad to see him too. He always made her feel relaxed. "Thanks, David. I'm okay now."

"I'll make sure she gets home," Fred said.

"Thanks. We'll be back with your car tomorrow." David put down her two suitcases, Asher's crate, large bag with the pup's belongings, petted Asher, then left.

"So who is this?" Fred walked around his desk. "You got a dog?"

"Yes. His name is Asher." She leaned the painting up against a chair.

Her pup put his paws up on Fred, who swept him into his arms. "He's a real cutie."

"That he is." Asher covered his face with doggy kisses. "And he really likes you. I had no idea you were a dog person."

"Sure am." He placed the little pup down. "By the way, I have something for you." He pointed to a large bouquet on a side table. Thank goodness that darn ring didn't appear again.

"Really? My agent must have sent them to inspire me."

"No, a very nice gentleman arrived with them."

Heart pounding, she ran over and quickly opened the card. Four words: Please call me, Chris.

"And you say this guy showed up here? A tall blond?"

"Yes. He was hoping you were here. I gave him a cup of coffee and he waited for a while but then left. Apparently, he needed to get home to take his niece swimming."

What day was it? Monday. Right. Emma had a swim lesson and he always went with her. No way would he let her down.

"That's his niece. She's six."

"He seems like a nice guy. A beau of yours?"

"Never and not so nice."

"Oh." He eyed her, obviously sensing a story, but she was just too tired to say anything more. "Well, let me help you carry all this up to your place. Lovely sunrise painting, by the way."

"My mother painted it and thanks, Fred."

Lexy slid her mom's painting under her arm, picked up the flowers and pressed the elevator button, while Fred grabbed the two suitcases and the crate. When the doors opened, they all piled in. Asher tried to run back out the door, but Lexy made sure he stayed put.

"Everything is okay, honey. You'll get used to your new home." She pulled out a treat from her pocket and leaned down and gave it to him, basically bribing him, hoping he'd associate the elevator with good things.

The doors reopened, and she led the way to her place, sliding the key in, and opening the door. "Thanks, Fred. I'm okay now."

"Certainly, Alexandra." He placed the two suitcases beside the crate. "If you need anything, give me a call."

"I will. You're always there for me."

"Always." He tipped his hat and left.

Not really wanting to be alone with her thoughts, she felt like begging him to stay.

At least she had Asher.

How had she never had a dog?

Closing the door and locking it, Lexy turned to see her pup twisting his head back and forth, his nose up in the air, sniffing.

"This is your home, little one."

She put the flowers on a table by the door, leaned the painting up against it, unleashed Asher, and led him around all the rooms so he could get his bearings.

"Now where should we put your crate? Since I work a lot in the living room, either on the couch or at the desk by the window ... how about right here." She set it down, added his pillow, and he promptly ran in. Guess he was tired from the long day. Wish she could say the same, but she was wired. Busying herself putting their stuff away, she surveyed the living room walls, took down a beach scene, and hung her mom's painting where she could see it from all vantage points. Perfect.

Now, to check her emails. First, she put her phone on vibrate so her ring tone wouldn't wake Asher. Sitting on the couch, she dragged her laptop out of its case, opening it to find Ingrid's email with the edits attached.

Her phone vibrated. Pulling it out of her pocket, she checked to see who was calling, half hoping it would be Chris. Nope. Not that she'd answer his call, anyway.

"Hi Ingrid."

"Did you get your edits?"

"Yes. Thank you."

"You mentioned you're not at the cottage?"

"No. I decided to come home."

They chatted for a bit, then she hung up. Time to get to work. But first, a very important email to Meredith. The carnival was in a few weeks and she wanted to finish what she promised, so she hoped Meredith wouldn't mind being the go between with the pamphlet and flyer she was still creating. Ding. She was surprised her friend emailed back so fast. No mention of her son, but she agreed Lexy could send the finished product to her, no problem. Great news. She also wrote, "I loved your new book. Fantastic job and terrific writing. I'm so proud of you."

This meant a lot. Meredith had a great deal of insight into the human psyche and Lexy was sure she would have said something if she saw anything amiss.

Now, on to the edits. She had to get this right. Her career was depending on it.

Forty-one

Thank goodness for editors.

Thank goodness for Sharon. She was Lexy's editor, and they had yet to meet in person, since everything was sent through computer emails, but Lexy adored her. So caught up in her storyline, it was easy to mess up, but Sharon searched through her manuscript on the hunt for repetition, plot errors, grammar, spelling issues, and anything that might prove a problem. Her goal? To make Lexy's book shine. To be the best it could be.

She was a saint.

The next couple of weeks saw Lexy fully immersed in edits between taking Asher out for walks and potty times. She had also finished the center pamphlet and flyer during brief breaks, and sent them off to Meredith. Thankfully, her friend continued to keep quiet about Chris and didn't ask for explanations. She never mentioned him even once. Good. Lexy had no time to deal with her emotions surrounding Chris. She had work to do.

Then it finally arrived.

The day she finished.

"Yahoo," she screamed, as she hit send.

Asher came running over.

"Let's dance."

She jumped off the couch, picked up her pup, holding him close, as she boogied through each room.

"I'm done. I'm done. That's it. Hey Asher, time for a walk to celebrate."

He licked her face, then stood still as she put his harness on, added the leash, and off they went to the elevator. Arriving on the first floor, she waved at Fred, who was chatting with another tenant.

"Let's try a different park today." Lexy walked out the front door and turned left instead of right. She led him to a bigger park with many new sniffs to delight her pup. After a while they sat on a park bench where Asher could indulge his love of watching people with their pets, joggers, walkers, and anyone or thing that caught his attention.

Unfortunately, now that her mind was clearer, of course, all she could think of was Chris.

Stop it.

She'd pushed all thoughts of him away to get her work done. Or most of them, at least. She didn't want to think of him, since all it did was make her hurt all over again.

She stood up fast. "C'mon, Asher. Let's keep walking." Anything to get her mind off of that guy at Yellow Rose Cottage.

On the way home, she noticed Clem who worked at Phil's Donuts. He was off to the side of the shop, having a smoke.

"Hi there." She waved.

"Hi, Alex." He waved back as they approached. "Who is this?" He looked down at the pup.

"Asher. Hey, when you're finished, I was wondering if I could pay you out here and you could bring me a coffee and donut."

"Right, right. For Fred?"

"Exactly. I know I can't go in with a dog."

"No problem. I'm done now anyway." He took a last puff, stomped his cigarette butt out, and threw it in a metal container. Five minutes later, he came back out with a bag, a coffee, and a small dog treat. "Can I give this to him?"

"Sure."

Lexy chuckled, wondering if Asher ever thought it strange that every human he met had dog cookies on them. Then again, why would he be concerned? He got to eat, which was the best thing ever. And, of course, he didn't think like a human even though she talked to him as if he were a tiny one. In her eyes, he was.

They walked back and into the condo building.

"Is that my obsession?" Fred grinned, pointing to her hands.

"Sure is." She put his treats on the desk.

"Thank you." He reached down to pet Asher, who had scampered over to see him.

"Guess what, Fred? I'm done. My edits are finished."

"Congratulations. That must be a huge load off your mind. So are you going to see that nice young man now?"

"No." Her eyes widened. "I told you what he did."

"Do you think he might have had a good reason? Did you ask him?"

"No. I don't want to know his reasons. He was just being selfish."

"Well, I'm not pushy or anything, but after years of being around people all the time, phony ones too, that gentleman was sincere and also seemed to genuinely care for you. Not like Jake."

"You never liked Jake, did you?"

He shook his head. "Never. He never treated you the way you deserved to be treated."

"And you saw all that?

"Certainly. Clear as anything. He used to rush through those doors, coming close to slamming them in your face every single time. And he never acknowledged me even once."

"Really?"

"Most certainly."

"Well, you were right. He turned out to be horrible."

"Yes, he did."

Several tenants walked in and approached Fred. Time to go.

"Enjoy your coffee and donut. Catch you later."

"You definitely will."

Back in her condo, she sat on the couch, Asher curled in her lap.

Staring at her mom's painting, clear-headed for a change, she let her thoughts flow. This time, she couldn't take her eyes off the little redheaded girl with pigtails enjoying the sun rise.

Then it hit her.

That was exactly how she looked when she was ten, the age she met Chrissy.

Chrissy.

He had been her best friend for two weeks when they were kids. He was kind and sweet and fun and was still like that as an adult. A solid, loyal buddy.

Finally, allowing herself to think of him, a parade of memories marched across her mind. Chris comforting her, listening to her, joking around, being supportive, and someone with whom she had fallen in love with.

And that was the truth.

She really was in love with him. A forever kind of love. The love she wrote about in her books.

Groan.

She sat straight up.

What had she done?

What was wrong with her? Instantly thinking he had betrayed her and rejecting him so fast. Running away to get as far from him as she could, without giving him the chance to explain.

She knew Chris better than that.

He would never intentionally hurt her.

Maybe he talked to the reporter about his center, and her name accidentally slipped out. Maybe the reporter misunderstood.

Anyhow, now that she was calmer and more clear-headed, it hit her that she really didn't care about that anymore.

All she knew was that she really, really missed him. So much.

A plot hatched.

She knew what she should do.

She knew what she wanted to do.

First, she called Wendy.

Next, her agent.

Then she called Meredith.

Finally, she gathered up her sleeping pup and his crate and went back down to the foyer.

"Fred, would you mind watching Asher for a bit?"

"I would love that."

She settled the pup in his crate with his bunny and walked out the door.

Off to the hairdresser.

She needed to find Alexandra again.

She needed to stop hiding.

Forty-two

Today was the day.

Hands on hips, Chris turned his head slowly, surveying the carnival, enjoying the excitement rippling through the air. Hard to believe this moment had finally arrived. He found himself crossing his fingers that it would pull in enough money to help finance the rest of the repairs needed before he could officially open up the center.

Walking around, he watched workers put finishing touches to the rides and do a trial run of the Ferris wheel. He remembered the many times he went on it with Lexy when they were kids, even though she was afraid of heights. She'd hang on to his hand, clenching it to the point of pain, and they'd roar until their bellies hurt.

And to think he'd found her after all these years and lost her again.

Leaving flowers at her condo with a message to please call him had been a bust. He'd never heard from her. Then again, why would he? She believed he had sicced a reporter on her and he didn't blame her, since she'd been under attack for so long and had a hard time trusting anyone. After this day was over, he was determined to seek her out again and beg her to believe him. He'd had nothing to do with leaking any information to anyone. He would never do that. He'd keep on trying to convince her.

He continued walking, checking out the game booths equipped with targets beckoning baseballs to hit a bull's eye. Teddy bears of all shapes and sizes lined the shelves as rewards for good throws. And the smells, oh the smells. His mouth watered as wafts of caramel corn, candy floss, hot dogs, fudge, drifted around him. Everything looked ready.

Except Lexy wasn't there.

He couldn't get her off his mind.

He had looked forward to sharing this day with her. She had a way of helping him relax when things were tense and admittedly; he was worried about the day. Pulling out a pamphlet from his back pocket, he marveled again at the great job she had done describing the many programs he hoped to feature. He was stunned that she followed through on everything she had promised, even if she used his mother as the go between. Her words on the flyers described the day with such excitement he'd received calls from neighboring towns from people wanting to come, and it looked as if today might pull in the biggest crowd ever. Lexy was an amazing person, a treasure, that was for sure.

"Hey, Chris."

He turned to find Meredith walking toward him with Emma, Angel, and the mayor.

The mayor?

"Why don't you go on over and supervise the center ... we'll handle the carnival here." Meredith linked her arm in the mayor's. Both of them were grinning. And blushing?

Were they an item?

Chris' eyebrows rose. Had his mother found love again? She certainly deserved it and the mayor seemed like a nice enough guy. Good for her.

"Yeah. Let's go." Emma grabbed his hand. "Me and Angel will come with you."

"You want to go to the center?" Chris threw his arms up. "Don't you want to go on some rides? Your favorite is here. The Ferris wheel."

"Yeah. Later." She pulled him to get him to move.

That was odd. The center's activities were much tamer than the carnival and mostly geared to educating adults about his plans. Emma would be bored. Oh, well. He definitely needed to check it out and he was glad of the company.

"All right. Off we go. Catch you kids later." He winked at his mother, nodding his head toward the mayor. She smiled, which warmed his heart. Both Emma and Meredith seemed to thrive, which was exactly what he had hoped.

They walked up the sandy path from the beach that led to the center, stopping every few minutes for Angel to sniff.

What the...?

A line up twisted its way down the street. A orderly mob scene. Everyone seemed chatty and to be having a good time. Where was it leading? The café? Was Hope giving out freebies? He followed it down the street and was even more surprised to see it began at the closed door of the center.

"What is going on?" He glanced down at Emma. "Do you know what this is all about?"

"Maybe." She ran her finger over her mouth as if zipping up. "But I can't tell."

Curious, he walked up to two women, enjoying a joke. "Excuse me. What is this line for?"

One woman rolled her eyes. "Don't you know? Alexandra Ayers is here with her new book. It promises to be her best yet."

His eyes widened. His jaw dropped. Lexy? Was here? His heart raced. Surely, he misunderstood.

"The author herself is here?"

"Sure is. She's having a book signing."

How had he missed this?

"Come on, Emma. Let's go."

"You can't butt in." One lady stood in front of him, blocking him. "You have to go to the back of the line."

"Oh, I own this place. I'm in charge here, or at least I thought I was."

Hurrying up the stairs, Emma and Angel right behind him, he opened the door and was greeted by a smiling Wendy, holding an equally smiling Jacob.

"Well, hello there again." She rushed to shut the door. "Almost didn't recognize you without paint all over your face." She grinned. "I'll get right to the point. Alexandra's over there."

And she was. Arranging books on a table with another woman. A huge poster announcing who she was hung on the wall beside her.

Once again, how had all of this escaped him?

But he knew.

This had Meredith and his niece's hands all over it. Bet they were hiding any advertising that filtered through and, come to think of it, he hadn't checked the website in a while. That was his mother's domain, or so she said. Now he understood why.

Emma and Angel flew by him, and she wrapped her arms around Lexy. Their flushed faces of joy were touching to see. No wonder Emma wanted to come here.

"Asher is over there." Lexy pointed to a fenced-in area set up for the dogs. He was wagging his tail, seeing two of his best friends had arrived, Emma and Angel.

Chris' heart thundered as he stood there staring at her. Her red hair was back, longer, curlier, and she looked like that little kid he had once played with, now an adult he adored. The best sight ever. She lit up every space she was in, especially his heart, and just when had he gotten so flowery in his thoughts?

He had to admit. He was no longer just falling in love. He was one hundred percent in total love.

She looked over at him.

"You came." Not much of a leading line, but all the words he could get out.

"I did."

"And I noticed Wendy called you Alexandra."

"Yes, I'm back to my real self." She was beaming. "But you can still call me Alex, like you did when we were kids."

"It's good to see you."

"Good to see you, too. Oh, and this is Ingrid, my agent. Ingrid, this is Chris."

The tall woman turned around and held out her hand. "A pleasure to meet you."

"Likewise." He was startled to see Ingrid look him up and down, nodded what he hoped was approval, then turned to pull more books out of a box."

He picked one up. "This is your new one. *Unveiled*. Finished, cover and all."

"Yes. You once said we needed something to attract a large crowd, so at my request my agent moved my first book signing here. The money from each book sold goes to the center."

What?

"You're kidding. You don't have to do that."

"Yes, I do."

"Obviously my mother had something to do with this. And Emma."

"Of course. I wanted it to be a surprise." She moved closer, so close. "I'm sorry for misjudging you. I know you would never betray me."

"I never would."

She reached up and touched his hair, brushing it out of his eyes, just like she used to. It felt good.

Chris had often heard that saying – time stands still – but he had never experienced it. Right now, he did. For the very first time. Totally focused on her face, admittedly her lips, he tuned everything out, leaning down to kiss her.

Clapping pulled him into reality, and he could feel heat suffuse his face, especially when he realized Emma of all people stood there with the biggest grin on her face. He jumped back. "I'm so sorry I did that."

"Don't be." Alexandra's arms wrapped around him and her hand pulled his head back down.

More of time standing still.

"We're ready for the doors to open," Wendy yelled.

"Let them in," Ingrid yelled back. "Hey you two, stop canoodling. We have a reading and a signing to do."

Canoodling?

They jumped apart. Chris had completely lost control of his center and what was going on there.

And he wouldn't want it any other way.

Forty-three

"Good morning, everyone. I am Ingrid, Alexandra's agent and hopefully, good friend." She winked at Alexandra, who grinned and winked back. "I say hopefully because I'm the one who continually pushes her to get her chapters done fast. And I'm excited that her new book is finally out and ready for her fans. Alexandra will now do a reading from *Unveiled*, her latest creation."

Alexandra, getting used to being called by her real name and not Lexy, noted that Ingrid was beaming, thrilled to have this book wrapped up. This woman believed in her and she was glad she had come through on her promise to finish it.

"Thank you, Ingrid. You are definitely a good friend of mine." She hugged her agent and walked to the chair placed directly in front of the crowd of people sitting and standing before her. She could feel the heat on her face grow stronger, embarrassed by the loud clapping, enthusiasm, and obvious support. Looking around, she was touched by the many readers, both in town and those who had traveled to Willow to listen and purchase copies of *Unveiled*. All her new friends were there from the book club, pet store, bakery, and veterinarian clinic. Meredith had tipped them off and they had all approached her when they arrived, stunned to find Asher's mommy was the very author whose books they were reading. Even Dr. Dan was out there waving at her. Meredith sat in the front row. What? She was holding hands with Mayor Bill? Good for her. Chris and Emma sat beside them, as usual, a clump of his hair flopped over one eye. She felt like running over and pushing it back. Nope, she'd better not. She had work to do. A surge of peace suffused her and contentment washed through her. The first time she had felt like this in a long time. She was glad she was back.

Alexandra finally sat, pulling out a copy of her new book from her briefcase. "Thank you to everyone for coming out to greet me. Your support means a lot and I appreciate this, more than you'll ever know." She was sure she was gushing, too loud, and sounding over the top, but she didn't care. She really meant it. She opened her book and read until she was down to the last few sentences she wanted to share.

"Please leave." Sarah pointed to the door. "Now."

Lexy felt her voice quiver.

"But honey, I love you." Nick wrapped his arms around her. "And you know you love me, too. Come on, give me a kiss."

Alexandra shut the book and looked up. "And that's the end of an excerpt." She noticed one lady had her hand up. "Yes? You have a question?" Her eyes squinted. The woman was young, possibly in her twenties, with loose grey curls tumbling to her waist. She knew her. "Sandy, right?"

"Yes." Sandy beamed. "You remember me?"

"Of course. You've been to every one of my book signings."

Such a nice lady. She'd even written a beautiful review of her last book, asking readers to trust her and that the story would make sense in time.

"I have always supported you." Alexandra leaned in, curious about what Sandy had to say. "I'm sure *Fairy Tale Crushed* makes sense now. My guess is that first you showed us a toxic relationship. Basically, a hook-up to avoid. Then in the sequel it looks like Sarah is finally wising up, is going to leave that relationship with Nick, and hopefully find a better one. Not that everyone needs a romantic relationship in their life, but usually your books have lovely strong healthy ones."

Wow. Sandy got it. She should get her phone number and contact her the next time she struggled with a plot. She seemed to know her writing better than Alexandra did. It had taken almost a whole summer to figure out what was going on in her own head and heart.

Alexandra smiled. "Well, I can't give away the ending, so you'll have to read it to see, but thank you for your continual support. It means a lot to me." She was definitely giving her a free copy.

"Okay everyone," Ingrid announced. "Please line up so Alexandra can sign your copies."

Chris carried a table over and placed it in front of her. He leaned down. "Good job," he whispered. "And what a turnout."

"Sure is." Was she glowing? She felt so alive, sparkling, as if that indeed was a feeling. If not, she was making it so. She was thrilled she'd finally found her way out of her mess. She had gotten it right for a change and was so exhilarated, she wanted to jump up and perform handstands all around the room. Of course, if she did that, they would all think she'd really lost it. Besides, in truth, she'd be lucky to do even one handstand. Was she really giggling like a kid? Carefree? And just plain happy?

Yes, she was.

Life seemed full of promise again and she had also reconciled with what she chose to write about, thanks to Willow and all the incredible people she'd met who supported her.

Sarah, her main fictional character, did indeed marry sweet Brandon instead, so all was right in her book world. She knew her readers would be glad that she was back to who she was – a writer who created a happy world where things worked out. Sure, life wasn't often like that, and many critics made light of her fluffy writing – their term, not hers - but in her literary, creative world she offered an escape, a respite, a moment that shone. Definitely what she termed a calling, which was confirmed while listening to the participants in Meredith's book club. They showed her that many readers wanted to feel good after reading a book. They wanted a fun time, a break from often tough days, with characters rooting for each other, being kind, and falling in love. She was certain they would be thrilled with the new love story, especially Sarah walking away from toxicity.

Who was she trying to kid?

Sure, she was satisfied with her latest book, but most important, Chris had kissed her. Definitely well worth the wait. Not a fluke, either.

She glanced over at him and smiled. He smiled back. A mixture of bliss, wild excitement, and serenity all rolled into one, warmed her heart. She was in love – real love, this time. With someone who truly loved her back.

"I'm here to get my book signed and to collect Emma." Pulling out of her private love fest, Alexandra looked up to see Meredith. Beautiful, wonderful Meredith.

"Of course." She quickly wrote a glowing note and signed it.

"Is everything okay?" Meredith leaned over and motioned toward Chris.

"Yes. More than okay." She touched the older lady's hand. "Thank you."

"You don't need to thank me, dear. I knew you'd figure it out. Welcome home, Alexandra."

"Home. It has a nice ring to it."

Emma tugged at Meredith's hand.

"I know, I know. You're anxious to get to the carnival, candy floss, and the Ferris wheel. Let's go. Alexandra and Chris will join us later."

"Um. Unca Chris said I should call you Alex or Alexandra now. That's your real name?"

"Yes, it is."

"Well, okay then, Alex, can I leave Angel with Asher for a little while?" Emma looked so serious. "They're sleeping."

"Of course you can, sweetie." Alexandra looked over at the little pups, eyes closed, paws entwined. "They look quite content."

"Yay." Emma ran over and gently kissed the two of them. "I'll be back soon," she whispered, making sure they didn't wake up. She waved as she hurried out the door.

You're doing great. Really great. Good job.

Alexandra noticed the words echoing through her mind these days, once negative, were now positive. Definite progress and so good not to be thinking horrible thoughts about herself all the time.

One by one, she signed each book.

This was different from all her other book signings, mainly because she had changed and was much more positive and upbeat. Also, the money gathered was to go towards the center, which made her feel great to be helping a cause she believed in.

"One latte for you." Chris put it down on the table after her last reader left. "How are you doing?"

"Wonderful. Thanks for the coffee."

"You deserve it."

"Excuse me." A man walked up and stood beside Chris. "Please. May I get a photo and a few words, please?"

"You?" Alexandra jerked her head back. Oh, no. He was the same photographer she'd met on the beach. Long black hair scraped back into a ponytail, blue baseball cap. She'd never forgotten him. She started to get up.

"I figured you wouldn't be happy to see me." He squinted, eyebrows knitting together. "Please don't go. I never got a chance to explain."

"You're lucky I'm in a good mood today. I'll give you five minutes." Chris put his hand on her shoulder, signaling he was there for her. Or that was how she took it.

"Thanks. I'll talk fast. I'm Pete Willow, with the local paper. I was never going to sell your photos to anyone. I'm just trying to promote the town and local businesses, to help them thrive, and I figured advertising that a famous writer lived nearby would draw more people here. I should have knocked on your door first and talked to you, but Chris said he'd tell you and that you loved to be taken by surprise. I wouldn't do anything without your permission. And today I'd like to promote the center. You have advertised you'd be here, so not a secret. May I?"

"I'd like to see your credentials," Chris said.

Pete pulled out his card.

Chris stared. "Are you related to Matthew Willow?"

"Sure am. He was my grandfather. And you are?"

"Chris Leverton."

Pete took a step back, eyes widening.

"No, you're not. I met Chris." He looked at Alexandra. "Or at least we zoomed. As I told you before, he is the one who contacted me and for a fee, told me where you were. He encouraged me to sell my photos to the highest bidder. To make a big thing about you and where you're living. That I'd make a lot of money." He shook his head. "But I would never do that."

"And I have never met you before." Chris looked at Alexandra. "Seriously, I haven't."

And then it hit.

Alexandra scrolled through her phone and clicked on a photo. "Is this the guy you talked to?"

The reported looked. "Yes. That's him. That's Leverton."

She showed the photo to Chris. "Jake. I should have known." Rejected, he was still obviously out to destroy her. Alexandra shuddered to think she could have lost Chris because of another person's gossip and bad intentions. She was glad she had trusted her own gut feelings and trusted Chris, even before knowing the truth. One thing she had learned this summer was that love wins. Amid problems swirling around her, issues to face, challenges to overcome, their love grew, blossomed and was there to stay. She grabbed hold of Chris' hand and pulled him nearer.

"Smile for the camera, honey. Your center is the best cause ever."

He wrapped his arm around her.

"*Our* center."

Epilogue

One year later

A knock at the door. Asher barked his acknowledgement.

Alexandra looked out to see Emma and Angel on the porch and quickly let them in.

"I have something for you." Emma waved an envelope in the air while the two dogs romped around the living room. "Amazing. They're always so happy to see each other, even though they were together just this afternoon."

"Sure are, and thanks." Alexandra took the envelope and opened it.

"Meet me at the 'Always' place at eight o'clock. Love, Chris."

She thought it strange that Emma delivered it instead of Chris texting or phoning, but who knew? Maybe his phone wasn't working.

"Unca Chris is super busy, but I gotta go. Nana and I are baking something. See ya later." She called Angel and left fast. Like a whirlwind. Asher was looking out the window as if he'd lost his best friend.

"We'll see them soon." She tickled him under his chin.

She knew Chris had a meeting with the town council today about the possibility of building onto the center and she hoped he had good news. Yeah, that was probably why he wanted to meet at the Always place, to share something exciting. She glanced at her watch, realizing it was almost time. She'd better hurry.

Running a comb through her hair, super long and curlier, she decided she didn't have time to change out of her grubby, dirt-stained shorts and tee.

Oh, well. She'd been gardening all day and besides, Chris wouldn't care. They'd seen each other at their best and worse.

"Hey, Asher. We're going for a walk."

He grabbed his harness and trotted over.

"Good boy."

She put it on, hooking up his leash.

"We're going to the Always place." She said as Asher led her out the door and turned toward the woods. They went there so often he recognized the name and knew the route.

Arriving, she pulled across the branch and entered, surprised Chris wasn't there.

Wait.

Something was sitting on the rock.

Over the past year, they'd continued their habit of leaving little gifts to surprise each other and add excitement to their days. The presents were fun. Just a few days ago, he'd left her a hair scrunchy with little Havanese dogs on it, and a tie with the same pattern for Asher.

Today a little green box sat there.

While Asher did his whole sniffing thing, she picked it up, trying to guess what was inside. Hmm... probably a pretty stone, since he knew she had quite a collection of interesting ones she'd found along the lake over the years. He had added several of them.

Opening it up, she gasped.

Nestled on black velvet was a ring. Her heart picked up speed. An unusual one. She twisted it around, admiring the burst of color produced by tiny multicolored stones.

A rustling behind her, and she twisted to see Chris walk in. Asher ran over and he slung an arm around him. He then got down on one knee.

What?

"Alexandra Ayers, will you marry me?"

Stunned but thrilled, she screamed, "Yes, yes, yes." No hesitation at all. How fitting that he proposed at their Always place, considering he was her Always person.

He jumped up. "Ring, please."

She handed it over.

"Hand, please."

And he slid it on, cementing their engagement. Their hug could not have been any tighter. Their kiss, the stuff of dreams. Really, it was.

Sitting on the rock, Asher between them making sure he was included in this special occasion, basking in the moment, she kept staring at the ring.

"It's so beautiful, Chris. I've never seen anything like this."

"I hope not. I designed it to look like a sunrise with all the colors I know you love. The very ones your mom featured in her painting."

Chris being thoughtful, as always. Could eyes actually glow? Could her smile get any wider?

"I love it."

"Good." He glanced at his watch. "But now we have a few anxious people waiting down by the beach to celebrate with us."

"We do?" She glanced down at her clothes.

Chris picked up a bag she hadn't noticed beside the rock. "You know Emma, always setting a scene like her mother. Even insisting she deliver my note to make it special." He handed her a bag. "I was to give you this, just in case."

Alexandra took a peek. "A sundress. Yep, Emma thinks of everything. I should have clued in quicker."

"Glad you didn't."

They hurried to Yellow Rose Cottage, where Alexandra quickly changed, loving the sweet white dress Emma had chosen.

Led by Asher, they walked hand in hand to the beach. Alexandra was overcome by the small group of people gathered there. Amid twinkly multi-colored lights mimicking her ring, all her new friends from Willow were there, as well as her agent, Ingrid. Most surprising was Fred the doorman, with the hugest grin she'd ever seen. He winked. She winked back. Even Pete Willow, the reporter, was there, positioned with a camera on them, recording their arrival. They'd bought him a brand new one, considering he had lost money paying for Jake's so-called tip. Fortunately, her ex had completely left them alone.

She stopped for a second, taking it all in.

So much had happened in a year.

Alexandra had hired a team of workers who strengthened the foundation of her cottage, and it no longer tilted or looked on the verge of toppling over. She'd had it winterized and now called it home. Her last book, *Unveiled*, was a bestseller and she was almost finished with another one. Chris' center flourished and she helped as much as she could, enjoying giving back what she'd experienced there as a kid. Meredith had married the mayor after a happy whirlwind courtship. Asher and Angel were always a delight, and Emma, dear sweet Emma, had grown taller, happier, and stronger. They had grown so close, almost inseparable, and Lexy loved her so much.

And then there was Chris.

Her best buddy, the love of her life. He was an amazing person, always supporting her, encouraging her, building her up. And she did the same. Their teamwork was all she had dreamed of.

She looked up to the heavens.

Thanks Mom, Grandma and Grandpa. And thank you, Elizabeth.

"Are you ready to celebrate?" Chris whispered. And just like when he was ten, he slipped his baby finger into hers, signaling their long-ago pact.

"Yes." A brand-new beginning stretched out before her. "Always."

Meet Suzanne M. Hurley

Happiness to this author, is curling up with her laptop creating imaginary worlds that flow from her heart. Writing is her passion and dreaming up story lines is her love. Accompanied by Asher, her beloved Havanese, she tries out her new plots on the foxes, bunnies, possums, and all the animals she greets during her morning walks. Back at home, united with coffee, her fingers fly over her keyboard pouring out her thoughts, creating twists and turns, that somehow eventually become another tale to tell. Life is good.

Other Works From The Pen Of

Suzanne M. Hurley

Changeable Facades - A murder has been committed! No one believes it but a young boy and his high school counselor. Will they catch the killer before he or she strikes again?

Delusions - Narcotics are sweeping Milton High! A student is dead! Lies and deceit take over as high school counselor Samantha Barclay is immersed in yet another deadly drama.

Chances – FBI Agent Ryan Leam's son is missing. Psychologist Samantha Barclay risks her life to go undercover at Sacred Heart Academy, seeking truth. The results are shocking and unbelievable.

Shades of Envy – Dead bodies are stacking up! Teenagers want to be vampires! The sheriff is acting secretively! Psychologist Samantha Barclay sets out on a wild ride to uncover the truth. Her discoveries lead to confrontations of the deadly kind. Will she survive with her life, as well as her heart, intact?

Who did it? – Who killed the beloved principal of St. Michael's High School? Newly minted FBI agent Samantha Barclay's first case is to find the murderer. Only one problem. Everyone she meets has a reason to see him dead. Will she uncover who did it – before he or she strikes again?

Love? – Samantha Barclay discovers what people will do in the name of love, when a dead body is discovered in her basement and her beloved stepmother is arrested for murder.

Guilt – Who killed Doctor Ingrid Sayers? High school teacher David Harris says he did. Samantha Barclay disagrees and races against all odds to find the real murderer.

The Cookie Club – One by one, the residents of Landon, West Virginia, are dropping dead. FBI/school psychologist Samantha Barclay, sets out to find the killer before it becomes a ghost town.

Women's Fiction:

Nice Girls Can Win – Lawyer Jessie White is fired, evicted and jilted, all on the same day. Hitting rock bottom, she moves back home and immediately ends up in a sparring match with 'Red,' the hunky guy next door. She soon discovers that miracles really do happen and how love often finds you just when you're not looking.

Wings of the Past – Zoey Avery thinks she is happy until wedding thoughts infiltrate her marriage-phobic mind. Only one problem – the groom she is dreaming about is a man she hasn't seen in thirteen years.

The Dream Smasher – Best-selling author Tracy Hazel is devastated to discover she is the victim of identify theft when someone submits a horrid book claiming she wrote it.

The Christmas Rose – Sparks fly when Principal Olivia Lyons tries to uncover which student stole a million-dollar Christmas ornament. Her new guidance head thinks she did it. Will she end up in jail, love, or both?

Love Always – Jenna Evans has no idea she is in a coma. She believes she has somehow landed in a fantasy world where everyone is supportive and lives in peace. Will she return to her husband and children? It all comes down to love - real love. What will she choose?

Heart Gifts – Serena's Christmas pageant is the key to saving her mother's bakery. Will she be able to convince archenemy Matt to help before it's too late?

Words of Love – Journalist Ellie O'Brien wants to use her words for good. Is this attainable when often readers believe gossip is the truth? Time will tell.

You are Loved –Jake's life was changed forever by an anonymous gift. When he set out to uncover his benefactor, miraculously he was transformed for the second time.

Young Adult

The Teddy Bear Eye Club – Depressed fourteen-year-old Mayah Lewis hides from the worl, until she befriends new girl, beautiful bald-headed Celeste Daniels. Everything begins looking up, until one day, Celeste disappears.

Dear reader,

I hope you've enjoyed reading this story of disappointment,
recovery and love rediscovered.

Your opinion is valuable to other
readers like you,
who may be looking for books like mine.

Please consider taking a few minutes to post a review,
however brief,
on the site where you purchased this book
or on the Wings ePress web page.

You may also want to visit my author page
at the Wings' website where you can find the rest of the
books I've written.

Thank you!

Suzanne M. Hurley

Visit Our Website

*For The Full Inventory
Of Quality Books:*

Wings ePress, Inc

*Quality trade paperbacks and downloads
in multiple formats,
in genres ranging from light romantic comedy to general
fiction and horror.
Wings has something for every reader's taste.
Visit the website, then bookmark it.*
We add new titles each month!

*Wings ePress, Inc.
3000 N. Rock Road
Newton, KS 67114*

www.ingramcontent.com/pod-product-compliance
Lightning Source LLC
Chambersburg PA
CBHW071410300726
48976CB00006B/2047